What people

One Da

An extraordinary and moving story. *One Day In June* is a great piece of writing, full of dramatic twists, which I know will one day make an outstanding movie.
Eric Pleskow, Former President of United Artists Pictures and founder of Orion Pictures and a 14-times Academy Award winner in Best Film category

Sam Martin masterfully tells a powerful story in which the shadow of war brings the hero to self-knowledge and truth at the very highest price. This is the work of an excellent writer who has written an exciting and dramatic story.
Milan Cieslar, film director and producer

I was drawn immediately into Sam Martin's brilliantly-narrated, modern-day thriller. A story of an every-day man with a dark secret, who gets sucked into criminal and sinister events way beyond his control. *One Day In June* is a film that has to be made.
Rike Steyer, film producer; Skalar Film, Hamburg

One Day In June

One Day In June

Sam Martin

ROUNDFIRE
BOOKS

Winchester, UK
Washington, USA

JOHN HUNT PUBLISHING

First published by Roundfire Books, 2021
Roundfire Books is an imprint of John Hunt Publishing Ltd., No. 3 East St., Alresford,
Hampshire SO24 9EE, UK
office@jhpbooks.com
www.johnhuntpublishing.com
www.roundfire-books.com

For distributor details and how to order please visit the 'Ordering' section on our website.

Text copyright: Sam Martin 2020

ISBN: 978 1 78904 757 8
978 1 78904 758 5 (ebook)
Library of Congress Control Number: 2020948241

A CIP catalogue record for this book is available from the British Library.

Design: Stuart Davies

UK: Printed and bound by CPI Group (UK) Ltd, Croydon, CR0 4YY
Printed in North America by CPI GPS partners

We operate a distinctive and ethical publishing philosophy in
all areas of our business, from our global network of authors to
production and worldwide distribution.

Also by Sam Martin: *Pictures of Anna*.
Arrow Gate Publishing Ltd. 2019
ISBN 978-1-913142-06-3
EBOOK 978-1-913142-07-0

One Day In June is a fiction – but not all of it. It is based on a true story and series of historical events.

It is dedicated to two people who set off on the journey with me, but didn't make it through to the other end. Without them there would have been No Days in June. To my wife and my father, with all my love and my gratitude.

Yesterday was my fifth birthday and today I'm running across the field as if my life depends on it. I love running and I'm a good runner – I'm the best in my school – and I've never run so fast in my life. My heart is pounding... pounding like it has never done before. My lungs are bursting and I can't get my breath. But I have to keep on running. This is a race I know I have to win. Then I realise I can't go any further. It feels like blood is coming up into my mouth. Perhaps it is. Perhaps I've bitten my lip. I do that when I'm determined. Those trees up ahead. I'll stop there. No one will see me in there and know that I've stopped running. No one will ever find out. I'll get my breath back and then I'll carry on running. I can't lose this race. So I dive down into the tall grass at the edge of the small woodland. My head feels like it is exploding. I put my hands over my ears but still I hear a terrifying 'Boom, Boom, Boom' sound. It's probably my heart pounding. But at least it's still beating. I look up and the early morning sky above me looks like it is on fire. Then I look down and see that my knee is bleeding. I've torn my new dark blue socks which I got for my birthday. For some reason I feel proud of the fact that I'm now five. And I tell myself that one day when I'm even older I might understand all of this. I raise myself up and stare off through the long grass into the distance – off in the direction of where I've come from. I've run four hundred yards perhaps. Or maybe more. I don't know. And I don't know if I can run any further. Not at that speed. Everything hurts. I close my eyes to make it all go away. I've done that so many times before. If I can't see it then it can't be real. Then I open them again and ever so slowly I raise my head above the tall grass to look back into the distance once more, and tears begin to well up in my eyes. They begin to roll down my cheeks. But I have to carry on. I start to push myself up off the ground. But for some reason I can't. I have no idea why. Have I used up all my strength running? But then I realise. Something is pressing down hard into the middle of my back. It pins me to the ground. I can't move. I turn my head and I try to look up. But whatever it is only presses down harder and I go back down with it. I'm so afraid. I'm terrified that I'll lose this race. I try to convince myself that all of this isn't really happening and I try once more to twist around. But all I see as I look upwards out of the corner of my eye is the glow of the blood-red/orange sky above me.

And the heavy leather boot in my back presses down harder still, and harder still...

Part I

The Discovery

1

They say that the moment you know you're going to die pictures of your entire life flash by before your eyes (and then they add that all you can do is pray that it's been a life worth watching again). I have no idea whether that's how it really is, but it was different for Adrian Kramer. The only pictures that Adrian saw when it happened to him were a dinghy's red/orange-coloured sails straining against the wind, the smiling face of the boy who he used to sit next to all the way through junior school – the one who always made him laugh – and a long stretch of fine white sand reflecting the bright sunshine, so bright that it hurt his eyes to look at it. And he also caught a very quick glimpse of a fine castle perched high on the distant sand dunes towards the end of the sandy bay. He could have sworn that he heard his father's voice calling out softly to him, "Watch out, be careful Adrian." But he knew that couldn't be possible. He also saw the sheer shock on his girlfriend's face, followed by an image of his grandmother bending down right in front of the swing which he was playing on in the park, just as it came down and hit her and cracked her head open. That was the point that everything went black and when Adrian began to tumble into the abyss – the point when he decided just to let go.

At the time he remembered that he had no fear and that the only things which he felt were anger and betrayal as he began to fade away... to fade away into nothingness. Adrian would tell you later – he might even have said as much when he regained consciousness in a Hamburg hospital four hours after the assault – that being attacked wasn't the most significant thing that happened to him on that particular day. And it certainly wasn't the one which would cause him the most pain or leave the deepest scars. But he'd moved on a long way since then.

Three years later he was still angry, and he still felt betrayed, every bit as much as he had back then. Some days he even felt like he'd been born to suffer and to run. And he still carried around with him the secret which he could never tell and which he knew would haunt him forever. But he'd worked on himself, physically, emotionally and psychologically in the months which had followed the fateful day he "died", until he'd arrived at the point where he was finally becoming comfortable with himself once again, and he'd come to rest at a place where he knew he would never get hurt so badly again, cocooned off from the rest of the world in a self-imposed exile which he called his "isolated protectionism" – his own invention, to anyone who asked – and there had been a few who had asked over time. All he'd wanted was to lose himself, in the hope that one day, at the end of his journey, he would find a better, stronger, less cut-up and scarred "self". And what is more natural when you've been wounded badly than to put on armour plating? That was the shape of Adrian Kramer's soul back then.

It was the blood-red/orange sails which reminded Adrian of the moment that he'd "died", as he lay flat on his back on the floor of his small one-man dinghy and looked up at the lifeless sails above him. The early-morning sky above was the very same red-orange hue as the sails, which made it look like the entire world was on fire. Adrian knew he had seen it like that before when he'd been out in the boat so early in the morning, but he'd never seen it so beautiful and never that dramatic. And he thought to himself that a perfect day was about to begin. At least that's the way it looked to him right then.

That picture-perfect late-May Monday morning was the day after his twenty-ninth birthday. Adrian hadn't celebrated it. At least not like others might celebrate their birthday. His colleagues at the Hamburg language school where he worked had wanted to take him out. But Adrian told them that he'd made other plans and took off for his boat, moored at a lake an hour's drive away from the city, and stayed overnight at a small, timber-framed, bed and breakfast place at the lakeside. Adrian's dinghy was half-hidden in shallow green water among some tall reeds – far away from all the other early-morning sailors who were huddled together in the middle of the lake turning their continuous and monotonous circles. If he cut a solitary figure lying flat on his back gazing up at the cloudless sky – his dinghy just a tiny dot on the jade surface of the massive lake and a good half-kilometre from the nearest boat – that was exactly the way he wanted it. He felt invisible. Distant, but free and in full control of where he was heading. Alone but never lonely. Except that alone in the boat sometimes meant alone with his thoughts and when it was that way, he often ended up revisiting old battlegrounds, opening up old wounds, scratching at scars which had never really healed. And the old questions returned to try their best to haunt him: "Why am I always running away? What did I run away from?" Adrian knew the answers to those questions of course, and he had long since come to terms with them and had learned to live with the consequences. But what he didn't know that particular spring morning in May, two thousand and seventeen, was that a brand new question was about to be asked, one which would turn his whole world upside down and change his life forever. He ran his hands through his thick blond hair, swept back over his head, and squeezed tight. Then he looked at his watch. It was time to head back to the city.

* * *

They blew up Ahmed's Shisha Bar and Lounge in Hamburg just after midnight on the night of Adrian's birthday. Ahmed too went up with the blast. The bomb also took out the hairdressing salon to the left of the bar and a photographer's studio to its right. They didn't even think the shisha bar might be owned by a German, which indeed Ahmed was. Three people were killed in the attack and twelve badly injured by the nails which they'd added to the bomb as a bit of a bonus. Ahmed lived in the flat above the bar, but he was downstairs working when he lost his life, his wife lost both her legs, and one of their young sons lost an eye. Two weeks later Ahmed's wife died in a Hamburg hospital. She would have died of a broken heart anyway even if her injuries hadn't finished her, because she loved Ahmed and their only son even more than she loved life itself. The radio report the next day, and for the following few days too, said that the Hamburg police were desperately appealing for anyone who could help them with their enquiries to come forward – anyone at all with anything to tell them, even anonymously – which was another way of saying that they didn't have a clue.

Adrian didn't know about the shish bar bombing until he heard it on the car radio when he was driving back to Hamburg on the Monday morning. But as shocking and depressing as it was, he knew that the attack had no real or direct connection to him personally. That would soon change.

* * *

At seven o'clock that Monday morning, over seven hundred miles away on the east coast of England, a dark blue Opel Corsa with a German number plate drove off the P&O roll-on-roll-off ferry from Rotterdam and up the quayside at Hull. It had been a rough trip across the North Sea and the two men who were in the car had spent the entire twelve-hour journey trying to get some sleep in the cabin they'd shared, but the loud monotonous thud of the waves crashing against the ship's hull had put paid to that. So they didn't sleep much and they didn't speak to each other much either. They didn't even know each other very well if the truth be told, which in fact is the very point of this story: to tell the truth about what really happened. The Opel had been bought especially for the trip at a second-hand dealer back in

Hamburg the previous week. It was less than a year old – it only had just over three thousand kilometres on the clock when they picked it up – and it was fairly nondescript. But that was just how they wanted it – draw no attention, finish the business, and get straight back across the North Sea afterwards.

A tired Border Control official at Hull stifled a yawn and waved them straight through the customs check as if he was on auto-pilot, which he probably was that early in the morning after his ten-hour shift.

When the car pulled out onto the main highway the man in the passenger seat looked down at the scribbled note in his hand, tapped an address into the car's satellite navigator and they set off north for a town further up the east coast.

* * *

At the same time that the Opel was heading north up the A19 Adrian's red Mini Cooper was cruising along the inside lane of Hamburg's outer ring road with the soft top down. Even that early in the morning the north-German air was warm enough for that. Cars flew past him at break-neck speed in the outside lane. It seemed that the whole damned world was having to get somewhere fast. But in the red Mini Adrian remained cool and in control, a calm and cautious driver unconcerned by the intensity of the early-morning, rabid road-ragers who were hurtling by him.

He was living back then in a modest first-floor, two-room apartment just off the busy Borgfelder Strasse, not too far from the city centre and a brisk fifteen-minute walk into work. Inside, the flat wasn't exactly the home of an obsessive-compulsive, but it was nevertheless neat, ordered, where everything had its place and nothing seemed out of place. That was just how Adrian liked it; all under control. Around the living room walls were a handful of framed photographs and paintings – mostly sailing ships and coastal views, and one of an imposing castle set back amongst the sand dunes – the one that he had envisioned the moment he thought he was dying.

He didn't have his first lesson until ten-thirty that Monday morning, so he took his time getting changed for the day into a pair of grey jeans and a matching grey polo shirt. He slung his brown distressed-leather satchel over his shoulder and headed out of the door... and bumped straight into a solid, six-foot-eight-inch wall of pure Ukrainian muscle and beer gut. Andrej Oblenko was someone you really wouldn't want to mess with. He lived in the apartment directly above Adrian's – when he was at home that was. Most times you would find him propping up some dark and dingy St Pauli bar or other, which was where he had obviously just pitched in from that morning. He stank and he swayed – straight into Adrian's arms. Adrian steadied him, which wasn't easy, and set him off in the right direction – "On your way Andrej"– and Andrej staggered off robot-like along the landing towards the stairs, while Adrian carried on in the opposite direction, downstairs towards the front door. The sun was still up there in the sky where it always was, and still trying its best to brighten everyone's day when Adrian stepped out into the street.

* * *

In the north of England later that morning, in a city on the north-east coast, the sky was its usual slate grey and an icy cold wind, way too cold for the time of year, whipped straight in off the North Sea. A seventy-one-year-old woman stepped outside of her neat, semi-detached house in a quiet suburb close to the seaside promenade and locked the front door behind her. Through the dark tinted windows of the dark blue Opel Corsa parked about thirty yards away on the other side of the road the two occupants watched her turn up her coat collar against the freezing wind and make her way ever so slowly down the garden path with a shopping bag in one hand and a walking stick in the other. She moved gingerly, as if she was walking on the surface of an icy lake and was expecting to slip at any minute. Once maybe pretty and once maybe blonde, time and fate had played their hand and taken their toll a lot more on her than it had on others, and not kindly. She had red-ringed eyes which made her look as if she'd been crying forever and she looked a good ten years older than she actually was, and with each passing year the lines in her face had got deeper, the shoulders rounder, the stoop lower, the hair thinner and whiter, and the heart heavier. She'd even tell you herself that she carried a broken-heart around in a broken body, and that she was only staying alive for one thing. At the garden gate she stopped, turned around and shuffled back up the path to the front door. She checked again to make sure she had locked it properly, then she turned and repeated the exacting journey back to the garden gate once again, shutting it behind her and heading off in the direction of the bus stop just around the corner.

Once she was out of sight, the Opel's passenger-side door swung swiftly open and someone began to get out. But no one would ever know that it was the same blue Opel which made the trip across the channel from Hamburg earlier in the day because somewhere on the way up to the north-east it had pulled off the A19 onto a remote country road where its occupants had exchanged its German "HH" number plates for two old French "75" Paris plates which they had brought over from Germany with them, hidden under the car's rear seat.

* * *

Adrian sauntered down the busy Hamburg street in his usual carefree, unhurried manner. Up on the corner an old man with only a half-dozen cracked, brown teeth left in his mouth and a guitar which had two of its six strings missing sat on the pavement with his legs tucked under him and went through his whole repertoire of Leonard Cohen songs. On a good day he actually sounded remarkably like Leonard Cohen himself with his low growl of a voice, sometimes tender, sometimes mournful, but always with deep feeling, and he was remarkably good too. The old man was always there, no matter what the weather, and when he passed, Adrian always dropped a fifty cent coin into his tattered tartan cap which lay on the ground, at which point the old man would break into Torn Blue Raincoat, which Adrian once told him he liked best. It was, actually, the only Leonard Cohen song that Adrian knew other than Hallelujah.

There was no breeze that day to temper the mid-morning heat and Adrian had his sunglasses pulled down to keep out the sun and the world. At just under six feet tall, blond, lean and athletic and with a bit of a Nordic-look about him (many took him for Swedish) he certainly wasn't too hard on the eyes.

He decided that morning that he'd take the walk into work with someone.

2

Jermaine Worthington was that "someone". Jermaine was a short, wiry character, not too many muscles. His skin was smooth. And it was black. "Smooth" disturbed no one. "Black", however, could be a bit of a problem for some. And in the wrong place at the wrong time and among the wrong kinds of people it could be a problem for Jermaine. He was busy picking up clothes from a large pile on the bed and was dropping them into a large suitcase on the bedroom floor. Some items though he threw straight onto an old wooden desk chair which he'd pulled up right next to the bed. One of the items was a shirt with a gaudy African print on it – an old birthday present from his parents which he'd never worn and which he couldn't even remember that he had. He jumped when the door buzzer sounded. It had one tone when someone rang from down in the street – a friendly ding-dong bell sound – and another when someone called at his flat from inside the building – a louder, severe, buzzer noise. It was that second sound which made him jump. He went into the hallway and nervously approached the door.

"Who's there?"

"It's me. Adrian. The front door was already open."

Jermaine opened the door two inches – as far as the security chain which he had mounted on the door himself allowed him to. When he saw that it really was Adrian standing in the corridor outside, he slammed the door shut in Adrian's face. That was only so that he could release the security chain lock.

"Hey, Adrian," he said, but it certainly wasn't with his usual spark, and led Adrian along the hall and into the bedroom.

"What's happened to you, man?" Adrian said when he saw the two-inch scar on the side of Jermaine's head which had been sealed with four stitches. His right eye was very badly swollen and a front tooth had been chipped. And when he walked in front of Adrian, he could see that Jermaine was moving with a limp.

"I got jumped again, Ade," Jermaine said in his beautiful, soft voice with its beautifully refined accent.

"Where?"

"Everywhere I go it seems. On Saturday it was coming out of the Black Cat Club. But Saturday was my lucky day. You heard about the bombing?"

"On the radio."

"I was in Ahmed's just before the attack. We left just after ten-thirty to go to the club. A bruised and cut up face is better than no face at all, eh Ade?" He picked up a brown leather belt from the pile and looked at it like he'd never seen it before in his life. "Did you have a good birthday?"he asked while he dropped the belt into the case.

"It was how I wanted it," Adrian said and looked over at all the colourful, mostly wild-patterned clothes piled up on the bed and the open, half-full suitcase. A second suitcase, already packed and labelled, stood by the wall. Adrian knew immediately what that meant.

"You can't be serious?"

"I am. And I'm out. I've had enough."

Adrian shook his head. He hated the thought. He was having none of it. He'd worked with Jermaine for nearly three years – Jermaine had been the department head for the past eighteen months – and although they seldom hung out together or went places together, except for the few times that he'd managed to persuade Adrian to take him out on the boat to chill out or beat a hangover, Adrian had grown more than fond of Jermaine and a bond of sorts had developed between the two.

"You can't go, J. You can't let them force you out. You can't let them win."

Jermaine stopped his packing and just stood and looked at

Adrian for a silent moment out of his bloodshot, pumped-up eye. Without saying a word, he was shouting out to him. Look at me. Just look at this mess. Then he spoke. "I'm gone, Ade. I'm going home." Home was Winchester in England, where both of his parents were doctors. Then he turned back to his packing. "Anything there you fancy, just take it," he said and nodded over at the chair next to the bed with the pile of unwanted shirts and T-shirts, a couple of belts and the pair of jeans which he'd be leaving behind. "I don't think there's anything here that would fit you anyway," he said as an afterthought.

"You know what I'd like?"

Jermaine threw a baseball cap into the case. "Say it. Take it."

"I'd like you to stay."

Jermaine shook his head. Not a chance. His head had been sore on Saturday night, but it seemed to have become even worse over the next thirty-six or so hours. But it clearly wasn't for turning. "It's over for me here now. I've had enough."

"Hit back."

"Hit back... how?" he said and looked at Adrian as if he was out of his mind.

"We'll find out who did it. We'll get at them."

Jermaine shook his head once more. And once more it hurt. He picked up a second baseball cap – a New Yorker. He looked at it for a moment. Do I take it or do I throw it? he thought to himself and eventually tossed it onto the chair.

"I have a student, a journalist, claims she can find anything out about anyone anytime. She'll help," Adrian said.

"How about that?" Jermaine asked and nodded over at the large moose's head hanging high over the bed. When Jermaine had first arrived in Hamburg, he'd arrived with no money at all in his pocket and had rented an empty flat. So, his boss, who was Adrian's boss too, gave him the money to go out and buy himself some furniture. But Jermaine went out and bought himself the giant moose's head instead and spent the rest of the advance on a wild weekend on the Reeperbahn. Adrian loved him for that. He was different. He was life. He was colour. He was one of those people you felt better for knowing. And for some weeks the moose's head was all that Jermaine had in his flat except for an old worn, coffee-stained mattress which an ex-colleague had given him to sleep on, together with a tartan blanket. Adrian looked up at the moose, which had acquired three years of dust and always seemed to have a stupid grin on its face, like it was mocking whoever shot it – "no way will you hit me from there", and then he said sadly, "I think I'll give it a pass."

* * *

At the door to Inter-Lingua Sprachschule Adrian stopped and turned to go inside. The whole business about Jermaine had impacted on him immensely and it had been playing through his mind again and again the whole way into work, especially the part at the very end when Jermaine told him that his mother was dying of cancer and he felt that he should go back to the UK to help out at home anyway. "Oh man," was all Adrian could say to that before he hugged him.

Over the weekend some monkey had sprayed "Ausländer Raus" (foreigners out) on the language school wall in red paint and they'd even managed to spell it correctly – but they'd added a swastika sign underneath which they hadn't quite mastered and the hooked arms of the swastika were pointing in the wrong direction. A city council worker was busy trying to get the graffiti off when Adrian arrived for work. Adrian said, "Good morning," to him when he passed him to go into the building. A thirty-something in a business suit who was racing to get somewhere fast with his head down and speaking into his mobile phone shot out of the main entrance and barged straight into Adrian. It was clearly the "suit's" own fault, but he glowered at Adrian anyway as if Adrian was to blame. The twin arts of politeness and civility had clearly been lost on him somewhere along his journey to the top of wherever he'd arrived at. Adrian could have taken the guy out with a blink of an eye, but he just smiled at him and even apologised politely himself, in the way that the British always do – or used to do – and continued on into the building.

Up on the second floor, ten minutes later, he breezed into a classroom of eleven girls aged between eighteen and twenty-two, and one teenage boy. They were seated at desks which had been arranged in a U-shape around the room. This was the school's two-year foreign-correspondence diploma class and they were there to spend their rich daddy's money for him and hopefully learn enough English and French and Spanish along the way to get themselves a piece of paper which would get them a job which would get them off rich daddy's pay roll. Adrian nodded a good morning to the class and began to unpack his satchel. A couple of the girls at the back exchanged glances; the lesson coming up was quite possibly going to be the highlight in their school day.

Mario, the only boy in the class, sat two desks up from Adrian and took little notice of anything outside of what was going on inside his own head, which that day was buried in a magazine he had resting on his knee under the table. He had thick curly hair which he'd dyed shocking scarlet and his ear pods were pushed into his ears as far in as he could get them. Adrian moved up behind him, took one of the pods out, leaned right in close and whispered quietly into Mario's ear, "So what have you got that's more important than learning English?" and he flicked the magazine closed. It was that week's edition of *Computer World*. Mario turned and peered up at Adrian from under his shock of thick red curls with a blank expression, which might have said something like "did someone just say something to me?" Adrian gave him a knowing wink – he actually liked Mario – and moved back to his place at the front of the class.

* * *

Back on the north-east coast the seventy-one-year-old was back from her trip to the shops. She closed the rusted garden gate and made her way back up the path. The garden wall had started to crumble away, dandelions had started to grow out of the cracks in the concrete, and she always avoided looking across at her once-immaculately-kept front lawn, which was now overgrown and had almost as many weeds and dandelions as it had blades of grass. She put her key into the front door lock and was about to turn it when the door swung freely open for her. It hadn't been closed fully, which confused her. It alarmed her too. Is my mind starting to go now? she thought to herself. She stepped inside cautiously with her full shopping bag and stood for a moment in thought. She was sure that she had double checked the door when she went out earlier. Was old age finally creeping up on her way quicker than she would like? The body had begun to go long ago. Please God just leave me my sanity. You've taken everything else, please not that now too. The thought was still bothering her when she shuffled into the living room, the walls of which were dotted with paintings of old sailing ships. She looked over at one of them. It was a framed photograph of a middle-aged man and a young boy sailing together in an impressive yacht with yellow sails, and noticed that the door to the cabinet on which the photograph was standing had been left slightly open. And that the key was lying on the floor. Then she saw that a cupboard drawer hadn't been fully closed. She knew then that it wasn't her mind, and that it really had been visitors.

Up in her bedroom at the front of the house, which looked out over the quiet residential street, she found an open dressing-table drawer. Nothing had been taken from the drawer – she could see that – and there was no sign of the usual chaos and disorder that burglars leave behind them. But she knew for sure that someone had been in uninvited, and a thought began to form. It was a thought so horrific that her hands started to shake.

* * *

His lesson over, Adrian strolled along the corridor and into the teachers' room in his usual languid grace and went over to his locker at the far side of the room. A language school can be a curious, insular but colourful world all of its own, a world filled with character and characters. If it's any good, that is. The alternative would be a lifeless, stale, stiff and joyless establishment. Adrian's place thankfully wasn't like that. Except that particular day was an exception, and there was an odd, cold, pin-drop silence in the room when Adrian began to pack his books away in his locker. There wasn't even the usual heated Brexit discussion going on between the British teachers. Nor did anyone ask him how he'd spent his birthday. Eight colleagues were sitting around the large table in the centre of the room. Some twisted coffee cups around in their fingers. Others just looked straight ahead at nothing in particular. It was one of those mornings.

"Hey Adrian, have you heard about Jermaine? *Schrecklich, oder!*"

The person who broke the silence was a twenty-five-year-old from Bristol. He was prematurely half-bald, pale-skinned and had dead eyes which came to life only to talk about himself or what he was going to do with his precious life. We've all known someone like him. He was ambitious, he was intense, and his name was Jacob but never Jake and certainly never Jakey: it was Jacob and he took great pleasure in correcting you if you got it wrong. He was superior, pretentious and made a special effort to slip German words into his sentences whenever possible, even when the English language was more than adequately equipped to express what he wanted to say, and he had one of those mouths which made him look like he was permanently smirking. Jacob Price-Wallace was constantly plotting and stirring. His colleagues suspected that he was a "stoolie" – an informer for the school Director. He was the kind who'd say yes to his boss before he even knew what the damned question was. And the school Director suspected he was an agitator. Twice Jacob had tried to organise a teachers' strike at the school. And twice he contrived to get colleagues fired. In addition to his ambition, Jacob was also blessed with the wonderful quality of jealousy, and Adrian was often in his cross-hairs. He was testing Adrian at that very moment when he asked him about Jermaine.

Adrian turned. "What about him?"

"He got beaten up again. And…"

Another colleague chipped right in before Jacob could say more. "Very badly too, sweety." It came from Dixon, who was at the very opposite end of the table to Jacob, and that wasn't by chance. Sweety was Dixon's pet-name for Adrian. He usually followed up by blowing him a kiss, but today wasn't a day for that.

Often people go overseas to teach in order to escape or to run away from something –and sometimes even to run away from themselves. Others do it to find something which they didn't have before, believing it would add an extra layer to their persona, or a layer which they never had anyway. Then there are those for whom it is a modern-day "sailing before the mast" of sorts, an adventure but without the real danger of the gangplank or a cat-o'-nine-tails. But without exception they all come looking for love of some sort, and in Adrian's particular case it was an odd sort of love – one which came without having to pay a price for it – that price being emotional commitment. Adrian helped his students, and in exchange for his help he got back from them praise and a sense of worth. For Adrian, that was a fair return and a reasonable deal, and exactly what he needed back then.

The cast of characters in the teachers' room included the lonely, the lively and the loony, and Dixon was a wonderful cocktail mix of all three. His name was Peregrine Winterbottom, but he didn't like it and refused to call himself that. His father's name was Richard so he thought he'd call himself "Dick's son" and felt better about it. The Winterbottom part he left untouched. Dixon was gay, proud of it, and he would scream it into your face if you didn't know it already – but believe me, you would know it. Occasionally on a Friday he would dress up like the master of ceremonies in the musical *Cabaret* in a long black tailcoat and black bow tie with his hair all slicked back, and even some days with the thick pancake makeup. Only Dixon would be able to tell you why he did that. Each lesson was a performance, which satisfied the crowd-pleasing entertainer in him. The girls loved it too, and they loved Dixon, who they allowed to flirt with them lasciviously and menacingly, even predatory in a way which would be normally totally unacceptable by anyone else, and they were happy to let him get away with it. He also got away with it because he was an exceptionally good teacher. He was painfully slim but bigger than life – a mincing fag, a queer, a queen of the night and of the classroom – call him what you will and it's the tedious old cliché, I know, and I'm sorry for that, but it was exactly how it was and why hide it? Dixon himself would tell you as much. "I'm a ponce, darling" was his opening line to anyone new who he met.

There'd been a tear in Dixon's eye when he told Adrian about Jermaine's latest brush with Hamburg's hoodlums and that he wouldn't be coming back to work anymore and before Adrian could tell him that he'd already heard it all from Jermaine himself, or added the part about Jermaine's close brush with death earlier the same night at the shisha bar Dixon added, "And I think Whoopie wants to see you in his office about it."

Whoopie was the school director. He wasn't black, he wasn't female, he had no dreadlocks and he had never acted in his entire life, but he was called Whoopie by the teachers, although never to his face, because his surname was Goldberg. When Jacob Price-Wallace heard that the boss wanted to see Adrian the look on his face changed, because he knew what it meant. It was the "about it" part which he wasn't happy to hear – the part about Whoopie wanting to see Adrian "about it" – and the corners of Jacob's mouth suddenly turned downwards.

* * *

Back in England the seventy-one-year-old stood on the landing just outside of her bedroom and stared up at the small door which was the entrance to the loft. Her eyes suddenly filled up with fear. Then her distress quickly turned to something else. She began to breathe heavily. It quickly became a frantic, desperate gasp for air. She was fighting for breath and she was starting to lose the battle. Worse, she *knew* that she was losing the battle. Her hand shot up and clutched at her throat. Her face drained of colour. She began to tear frantically at the collar of her blouse, sending the buttons flying. A severe asthma attack was beginning to kick in. She struggled the few yards along the landing into the bathroom, steadying herself with her hand against the wall, barely able to breathe, her skin beginning to turn blue. She flung open the cabinet door on the wall above the bathroom sink and tried to grab at something. Bottles came tumbling down from the cabinet shelves. Glass shattered in the sink. She fell down onto her hands and knees and reached out desperately for the nebuliser which had fallen onto the tiled bathroom floor but it slipped from her grasp.

* * *

"I presume you've heard about Jermaine?" the school Director asked Adrian, who sat across the desk from him. Adrian nodded. What Adrian didn't know was whether his boss had also heard about Jermaine being only a couple of hours away from getting showered in TNT and nails, but he left his answer as a depressed nod. They were sitting in a bright, breezy office with brand new office furniture and plenty of glass with views out onto the busy pedestrian zone below. Whoopie certainly did alright from his business, even if most of the teachers struggled. "I received an email an hour ago. He's resigned. I'd like to offer you his position as Director of Studies?" Goldberg raised his thick, greying eyebrows in a "well, what do you think?" sort of way.

Adrian sat for a moment and let the thought run through his head.

"Give it to Dixon," he eventually said.

Goldberg shot him a "not a chance" look and said firmly, "I want you." He kept looking at Adrian for some reaction, with his eyebrows still slightly raised. Then, certain it would impress him, he followed his offer up with: "I'll give you a twenty-five per cent rise?" and raised his eyebrow even higher. The small Scottish Terrier which Goldberg always brought with him to work and which always lay at his feet under the desk got up and ambled slowly over to the window and slumped down there instead. What else could a poor dog do on such a hot and sultry late-May morning? For some reason that only Whoopie would be able to tell you, the dog always wore sunglasses in summer. The sunglasses had white plastic frames and if you didn't think it was mad enough that a school director had his dog at work with him under the desk, the sunglasses clinched it. A language school and its characters... and it often begins at the top.

Adrian remained impassive. He was naturally touched by the offer, but as ever, he was also equally naturally cautious in his response. "Thanks. Can I have a couple of days to think it over?"

The Terrier sat up and began to yap away at something down in the street. Goldberg waited until it was finished yapping then he said, "Of course. One thing though Adrian, it will mean giving up your private lessons. You understand that, don't you?"

Adrian thought about it. Finally, he nodded and got up out of the office chair.

* * *

The old woman sat on the side of the bath with her flowery blouse open at the front and soaked in perspiration. Her breathing was slightly easier but she was still very pale and drawn and there was worry etched deep into her gaunt, lined face. But she knew that for now she'd won her latest battle. She reached out for a face-cloth, ran it quickly under the cold water tap then wiped it across her brow.

"Oh Charlie, oh Charlie..." she whispered sadly to herself and shook her head.

3

She sat at the other side of a coffee table strewn with books and papers. Her name was Katharina Kozlowski and she was the private student who Adrian had told Jermaine about – the journalist who could find out anything about anyone, anywhere, anytime. What he didn't mention to Jermaine was that she was smart and had a smile which, when it came, you just knew it was full of mischief. She was a relatively new private student for Adrian – they'd only had four previous hours of tuition together – and she was good enough and certainly confident enough for Adrian to wonder just why she wanted the lessons. But as long as she paid and as long as she learned, that was fine with him. It also certainly didn't harm to look at her, even Adrian himself would admit that much.

"Did you learn the vocabulary list that I gave you?" he asked her as they were about to fold the lesson.

She looked at him over her coffee cup and in a subtle kind of way she gave him her provocative "try me" smile, almost but not fully sexy, but certainly cheeky.

"Test me," she challenged him.

"'Accidental' – the opposite?"

The exchange between them which followed was all rapid fire, and Katharina pinged back her answers as if nothing was ever easier for her. "Intentional."

"Give me another."

"Deliberate."

"Another."

"On purpose."

Adrian was impressed although he tried not to show it. "'Compulsory'... synonym."

"Mandatory."

"Or?"

"Obligatory."

"Reliable... synonym?"

"Trustworthy. Dependable. You want more?"

He ignored her and charged on.

"To embarrass... the noun?"

"Embarrassment."

"Spell it."

"I.T."

"Correct. To 'deteriorate' – the opposite?"

Silence. He finally had her! A satisfied smile broke out over his face. Katharina was smiling too. But for another reason. She was looking at her watch. "The lesson's over, 'Teacher'."

"I thought it was the teacher who usually says when it's over?"

It was all playful jockeying for position. They were both trying their best to believe they were in charge. And despite himself, Adrian was even enjoying their little game.

"Not in my lesson," Katharina told him. "And not when I'm paying." She reached over and pulled a one-hundred euro note out of her bag. "I've got nothing smaller."

While Adrian went over to a set of drawers on the opposite wall and took his wallet out of the top drawer, Katharina's gaze shifted to the room, casting a curious female eye over it, weighing it up, making her assumptions.

Adrian returned and handed her the change. "I might have to give up teaching you after the summer."

"Am I so bad?"

"I've been offered the Department Head's job at the school. It'll mean I have to give up my private lessons. It's a contractual thing."

"So, I'll come just for the coffee... you make fine coffee 'Mr Kramer'. And then there are all the fine pictures of ships of course. Well?" She swept a strand of stray, blonde hair out of her eyes.

Adrian stood and held her mischievous look for a charged moment while Katharina sat and wondered whether it meant she could allow herself to get her hopes up. Then he said, "Let's keep it professional."

* * *

Adrian was back on the lake again later that day. The business with Jermaine and the offer to take over his job as department head needed to be processed. So he took a drive back out to the boat to get a couple of hours sailing in and, against another spectacular backdrop of a red-orange sky – this time it was the early stages of a magnificent sunset – he spent a quiet, still, end-of-the-day moment to himself. Then just before dark he headed back to the shore, where he took out his mobile phone and speed-dialled a number.

* * *

In a north-east of England suburb, the ringing phone on the living room coffee table went unanswered. Lying on the floor next to the coffee table was a nebuliser, a bottle of medicine and an atomizer breathing apparatus. Across the other side of the room, on top of a glass-fronted cabinet set against the wall, there was a row of karate trophies and a framed photograph of a thirteen-year-old boy dressed in a karategi karate uniform, receiving one of the trophies. And next to that was another framed photograph, of an impressive thirty-foot yacht with pale yellow sails. A sixty-year-old man was looking on proudly and affectionately as his young son worked the main sail. It was a frozen image of an unbroken and unbreakable bond between father and son. The name of the yacht was Adrian. That photograph might have been the very last thing that Elizabeth Kramer ever saw. Because lying in front of the cabinet, face-down on the floor, was the lifeless body of the seventy-one-year-old. A weathered hand was reaching out for something it would never now reach. Her eyes were wide open. But she had stopped breathing, stopped living in fact, some time before.

* * *

The walls of Werner Retz's study were lined with leather-bound books. Hundreds and hundreds of them. In one corner of the room stood a magnificent eighteenth-century Coromandel and Ormolu antique standing-clock, all elaborately-carved wood and gold trimmings – an inheritance from an uncle – which was busy chiming out the hour. The rest of the furniture was all thick, dark oak. The chairs and sofa had deep leather padding. It was the safe, comfortable world of a classic, conservative intellectual. Werner Retz himself was in his early fifties. He had a thick, greying beard and round, tortoise-shell-rimmed glasses and he somehow matched the room perfectly, Adrian always thought when he was in there with him, which they were that evening, slumped in chairs either side of a large globe drinks cabinet. When Adrian first came to Germany, Werner had come to the school for English lessons. He was an historian and head archivist at the Museum of Modern German History in the city, and he often needed English for his contacts overseas. Then when Adrian hit the rocks some months later, Werner became a safe and comforting port in the eye of Adrian's personal storm – a dependable father-figure of sorts, who Adrian had come to trust and rely on – which didn't come easy for him back then. Werner was in fact, despite their age difference, the only person in Hamburg who Adrian would call a close friend.

The last of the clock's nine chimes was fading when Werner asked him in his soft, slight German accent, "So are you going to accept the offer?" He reached over and slid open the globe, took out a bottle of the finest Scottish whiskey, poured one glass for himself and was about to pour a second. Adrian stopped him.

"Water for me, Werner." Then he addressed Werner's question. "I don't know. Probably."

Werner smiled and nodded to himself – he liked the idea. He was happy for his friend. He poured out a glass of Evian and handed it to Adrian.

"What are we drinking to?" Adrian asked him.

"Financial ruin. And a farewell to all the finer things in life," Werner said and laughed out loud. And when Werner laughed the sky, the trees, the room, changed shape. He had one of those wonderful, endearing laughs which infects everyone in the room and you have to laugh with him even when you have no idea what you're laughing about. "My divorce came through today."

"And that's funny?"

"Not in a few weeks time it won't be," he said and reached over to touch glasses with Adrian. "To better times for both of us."

Adrian sat a moment and reflected on that thought while Werner fell in love with his first mouthful of whisky. Then Adrian too broke into the slightest of smiles – better times sounded just fine to him – and touched his glass against Werner's. The smile was still on his face as he dug into his pocket to answer his ringing mobile. But the smile didn't stay for long.

4

Adrian headed the long line of mourners as they followed the four black-suited pallbearers who were carrying his mother's coffin out of the low, narrow church doorway and up through the graveyard towards the waiting hearse. Another biting, north-east wind whipped through the floral tributes which covered the coffin. A seagull swooped low to see what was going on, and if there was anything interesting down there for it to scavenge. But there were only tears, and what can a seagull do with tears?

After the cremation came the party that no one ever wants to give and no one ever wants to go to. Adrian stood in a corner of the crowded living room and suffered the ritual respectfully, chatting to an aunt and an uncle, but constantly glancing around him as if he was on the look-out for someone. Because he knew that a particular "someone" was there.

"I'll help you sort everything out with the house," one of his aunts said to him as a way of reassurance.

"Thanks."

"So, how's Germany treating you these days?" his uncle said, trying to lighten the mood.

Before Adrian could say "good", a girl's hand tapped him on the shoulder and he turned to look straight into the pretty face and almond eyes of:

"Sarah," Adrian said, and there was nothing at all in his voice or in his expression when he said it. The word came out flat and dead. And when Sarah moved slightly towards him, Adrian maintained his distance with a deft step back, which was followed by an awkward, charged silence while they both stood and thought of what comes next. Adrian's aunt knew the history between them and dragged her husband away, leaving Adrian and Sarah alone.

Sarah was the first to break the icy stand-off. "I'm so sorry, Adrian."

All Adrian could respond with was a silent, gestured "thanks". No words, just a slight nod of the head. She waited for him to say something. But he didn't.

"Can we meet before you go back? Just to say a proper 'goodbye'?" she asked and added hopefully, "I'm here for another week."

Adrian didn't even need to think it over. It meant nothing to him. "We said our 'goodbye's' three years ago in Hamburg."

Before Sarah could react, Adrian had turned away and headed out of the room.

* * *

Once the party was over, the nightmare task began – clearing up and sorting out a loved-one's personal belongings; sifting like a voyeur through the leftovers of someone's private life. Adrian's aunt was at a set of drawers up in the bedroom, pulling clothes out and dropping them into a charity bag. Adrian wandered into what had once been the guest bedroom at the back of the house. The bed was no longer there – Adrian had thrown that out himself when he still lived there – but the same four deep holes were still in the ceiling, just as they'd been for some years. The wall close to the door had scratches running all the way along it and part of the wallpaper had been torn away and left hanging. A wheelchair had been folded up and pushed into the far corner of the room. And next to it stood a mobile toilet chair. For eleven long years the room had stayed just like that. Untouched, unvisited, unwanted. Adrian turned away and walked down the landing to what had once been his own bedroom. He stood at the door and looked around. That room too had been left untouched and exactly as it was the day that he'd moved out over three years before. Even the dark blue T-shirt which he slept in had been washed and carefully ironed and put back under the pillowcase where it always lay. He closed the door and was about to go out when he stopped and went over to his old bedside table. He opened the top drawer and looked inside. Yes, it was still there, the small notebook diary which he'd once kept. He closed the drawer, pushed the notebook into his back pocket and went down into the kitchen, where he grabbed a torch and a set of small aluminium step-ladders from a cupboard, and went back upstairs with them. He set the step-ladders directly under the door to the loft and climbed up to see what was left in the room under the eaves which needed to be shifted. Twenty years of dust and not much else greeted him up there, except for a strip of old rolled-up carpet which was close to the loft doorway and a large wooden packing trunk which had been pushed up against the far side of the brick dividing wall which separated the neighbouring houses. It was the sort of old, colonial chest which people used to take on romantic far-away sea journeys to exotic places, but might just as easily have been bought in Ikea for just a few pounds. Adrian flicked on his torch and cautiously walked along one of the thick, wood supporting beams towards the trunk. He opened the trunk's heavy lid and shone his torch inside. Dust particles danced around in the beam's light. An old, tattered, tartan blanket covered the trunk's contents. He pulled the blanket to one side, sending more dust flying everywhere. Several old, forgotten oil paintings of sailing ships were under the blanket and racked up against the side of the trunk. And that seemed to be all there was. He flicked quickly through the paintings, but saw nothing that he really wanted to keep. Then his torch lit up a small bag which was lying in a gap between two of the paintings. He picked up the bag and looked at it. It was made of crushed-velvet and appeared to be burgundy in colour, although the exact colour was difficult to make out in that light. In one corner of the bag a small round symbol, no bigger than a two-euro coin, had been embroidered onto it. The symbol consisted of gold lines, arranged like the spokes of a wheel into a strange abstract and somewhat mystical pattern. And around the outer edge of the symbol, in tiny gold braid, were four words in Old German. Adrian reached down into the bag and pulled out two pieces of old, silk ribbon which had been neatly folded together and unfurled them. They were the sort of ribbons which would be attached to a floral wreath and laid on a grave. One was a red/orange colour with a black swastika symbol at one end and the words, in faded gold print, *MEINEM UNVERGESSLICHEN FREUND UND KAMERADEN.* The other ribbon was in the red-white-green colours of the Italian flag with the words *IL DUCE* printed in gold at one end, but which had also faded over the years. Adrian stood on the thick wooden beams which spanned the loft floor and stared at the two ribbons with a mix of intrigue, surprise and loathing. Then, overwhelmed by curiosity, he turned and headed back towards the loft step-ladders.

He stood in his mother's bedroom holding the two silk ribbons. His aunt was looking at a framed photograph of Adrian's parents on their wedding day. Charlie Kramer and his pretty wife, Elizabeth, both stood outside the same church where Elizabeth's funeral had taken place the previous day with big smiles on their faces and Adrian thought to himself that it had been more than half his lifetime since he'd last seen his mother smile at all. "At least they'll be together again now," Adrian's aunt said, trying her best to sound comforting – perhaps trying to offer a sense of reassurance for Adrian – but there was deep sadness in her voice when she said it.

But Adrian had something else on his mind right then. "Have you ever seen these before?" he said and held out the ribbons for his aunt to see.

She looked at them and shook her head. "Where did you find them?"

"Up in the loft." He was staring down at the words

embroidered into the ribbons.

"What does it mean?" his aunt asked him.

"I think it says, 'My unforgettable friend and comrade'."
Then he nodded down to the other one. "'Il Duce'... that was
Mussolini."

As he stared down at the two bits of old silk in his hands,
mesmerised and mystified by them, Adrian's question was
more for himself than for his aunt when he asked, "Why the hell
would my father, a German, keep something like this?"

"I really don't know," she said and set the wedding
photograph back down on the bedside table.

But Adrian persisted, slowly realising that opening that
strange old velvet bag had opened something inside of him.
"You know, I know nothing about his past – before he came
to England. Apart from the fact that he was born in Hannover
and came here to study... I know nothing. Why did he never
speak about it? Why did he always block our questions when
we asked him?"

Adrian's aunt shook her head. She knew as little as he did.
"His family were all killed in the war," she reasoned. "A lot of
people deal with something like that by blocking it out of their
minds completely."

As his aunt left the room with her full charity bag of clothes,
Adrian sat down on the edge of his mother's bed in silence and
once more stared down at the two ribbons in his hand. He was
lost in a thousand thoughts.

* * *

The next morning another uncle shook his head and dismissed
Adrian's suppositions as if they were the most preposterous
ideas in the world. "Anyone who ever knew Charlie knew he
was no fascist," he said while Adrian watched him water his
tomatoes in his greenhouse. Adrian was holding the two silk

ribbons. "Charlie would do you good before he did you harm," his uncle told him. "You must remember that much, kiddo?" He always called Adrian kiddo – in fact he called everyone kiddo. "You more than anyone."

Adrian spent that evening going through his mother's address book, calling any and every relative that he knew, as well as all of his parents' friends who he knew well enough to ask, and probed them about what they knew about his father's past, meaning his time before he came to Britain. But all he heard was what he already knew anyway, which wasn't too much considering the closeness which he'd shared with his father in so many other ways, and the stories which Adrian heard were all consistent; that Charlie Kramer had come to England in the sixties and found a job as a naval architect in the planning department of a north-east shipyard, that he'd met Adrian's mother and settled there, and that he never spoke about his past in Germany. "It was probably all too painful for him" was the standard response that Adrian heard. "He lost his family in the war. He'd suffered. He didn't want to re-live what he'd experienced as a young boy in wartime Germany."

* * *

A long sweep of fine white sand stretching as far as you can walk, with soft deep dunes as a backdrop – Adrian had the image hanging on his living room wall back in Hamburg and now he was walking the empty beach alone. It was walking just to be walking. The heavy clouds were so low in the sky that it almost seemed like they were sitting on his shoulders.

He'd taken his uncle's car for the day and headed north up the coast to get some fresh air, to see something different, to revisit an old favourite place. It was a walk that he'd made a hundred times before in his life, maybe even a thousand – he'd spent all his school holidays there as a young boy, in a cottage which his family rented for the entire six-week summer break and he stayed on with his cousins even after his parents had left to go back down to the city to work. But that day it was different. It felt as if he was seeing and experiencing everything for the very first time. The waves seemed to be crashing onto the shore with an intensity and even a violence which he'd never seen before. The water seemed greyer, the sky looked angrier than it ever had in the past and the sand deeper and softer and he felt he was sinking right down into it and could hardly walk on it. The wind blew straight at him and he felt as if it was blowing him backwards. The sky, the waves, the sand, they had always been there of course, and often in exactly the same way that they were that day. But to Adrian they all seemed more extreme that day: Harder. Harsher. Heavier. It was as if their mystery was finally being revealed to him. He was close to the water's edge and just a few feet to his right the North Sea's waves were hitting the shore and crawling their way up the fine sand as far as his footsteps and even coming over his feet. But Adrian didn't care. He had something else on his mind.

The only other person on the entire two-mile stretch of sand was an old man walking his black Labrador. The dog ran up to Adrian, sniffed at his leg, wasn't too keen on what it smelled and trotted back over to its owner. The old man smiled, shouted something over to Adrian – maybe "he only wants to eat you" or whatever dog-owners say when their dog sniffs at strangers' crotches – but Adrian didn't even know the old man was there. He was lost in a thousand thoughts and fighting with questions which he'd often enough asked but which he had never been given answers to. And the question floating round first and foremost in his head then was "who was it really who died back then?" He'd thought about it often enough in the past, because he'd never really had it answered fully, but now, with his mother's death, it had come calling with a vengeance. "Why would my father keep fascist memorabilia? Why had he never

told me about those ribbons?" he asked himself, which led to
him wonderingif we ever really do get to know the people who
we think we know, and what those masks are which we so often
wear to present ourselves to the world, or which we wear to
protect ourselves. And was my father wearing one? The point
being that Adrian really didn't know what to think anymore.

He stopped walking and stood for a moment and watched
the waves coming in towards him and thought about how every
breaking wave appeared to be like any other when in fact they
are all unique. No other wave would ever break like the one
which he was looking at right at that moment, and no wave
was ever the last wave. There would always be a next one. And
a next one. It was like nature renewing itself, or rediscovering
itself anew every few seconds. That's how nature works, for
better or worse.And that's what he knew he now needed to do.
He took one last look out over the rough North Sea then turned
away and headed back in the direction that he had come from.
A decision had been made. For better, or for worse.

Part II

The Question

1

The Lufthansa plane which landed safely back at Hamburg airport two days later carried illegal cargo. Possession of Nazi memorabilia are illicit in Germany, and Adrian had pushed the burgundy velvet bag with its silk ribbons right at the bottom of his suitcase, buried under his clothes. Why the hell didn't I just post it to myself? he thought to himself while he was walking with a pounding heart past the customs officers who were standing close to the exit in the airport Arrivals. He took the ribbons out when he got back to his flat, along with his old diary and one of the photographs which he'd brought back with him: the framed image of himself and his father in their yacht with the yellow sails. He set the photograph down on the living room windowsill overlooking the street and stood for a moment and stared at it, somehow mesmerised by it. With the bag still in one hand, his eyes searched his father's face as if he was begging him to give him answers to questions which he'd never been given. Charlie Kramer had tried once, Adrian was sure of that, but by that time it was all way too late. Adrian himself had blocked out so much about his father and how it had all ended. It had been his very first experience of repression as his only way of survival – his first form of isolated protectionism, as he would later call it. "Who the hell were you?" Adrian asked his father's image, and he surprised himself by saying it out loud, because at that moment he seemed like a stranger to Adrian. When I used to look in the mirror it was always you who I thought I saw, Adrian thought. But now he wasn't sure anymore. What would you reveal of yourself now to me if I asked you? he begged the picture.

* * *

He walked into Hamburg's Museum of Modern History the next day after his morning lessons with his satchel slung over his shoulder. The walls of the museum's reception area were full of images of twentieth- and twenty-first-century German history, from the rise of the Third Reich to the fall of the Wall to the recent flood of refugees escaping war or persecution, with their high hopes of sanctuary and the promise of a better life. The museum's receptionist greeted him with a familiar smile – she knew him and who he was there to see. She picked up her phone, said a few words, then nodded to Adrian that he could proceed, and three minutes later he walked into Werner's office, passing another museum employee who had her hair pulled back in tight blonde pigtails and who used Adrian's arrival as a cue to leave. Adrian didn't know her, but they nodded their formal hellos as they passed. Werner moved out from behind his desk and greeted Adrian with an affectionate hug – a touching moment between two good friends.

"My deepest sympathies."

Adrian nodded a silent thanks.

"What exactly happened?" Werner asked him.

"She had a severe asthma attack. She..."

He stopped for a moment. And for the first time since his mother's death Adrian realised that he was becoming emotional. Forced to reflect, it was finally beginning to hit him. He cleared his throat. "She choked to death," he answered and then quickly refocused, because the truth was that he was there for something else entirely. "Do you have an hour for me? Right now?" Before Werner even had the chance to answer, Adrian pressed right on: "There's something I need..."

He stopped again and, a little nervously, reached down into his satchel. Werner watched curiously as Adrian's hand emerged with the two wreath ribbons. And the moment that he unfurled them his historian-friend's eyes positively lit up and the hairs on the back of his arm didn't so much stand up straight as jump right off his skin.

"I want to know what they are," Adrian said.

"Where did you get them?"

Adrian thought for a moment about how to say it. Then: "Let's say they're inherited."

"What? From your mother?"

"Something like that. Can you help?"

"May I?"

Werner took hold of the ribbons and examined them closely, clearly intrigued and deeply fascinated and sensing that he might be holding a piece of German history in his hands. While his mind worked, he fingered his thick beard.

"Anything interesting nested in there in the last two weeks?" Adrian quipped.

Werner was used to Adrian's little jokes and, happy that his humour was back, laughed it off and turned his attention back to the silk ribbons.

"Any ideas?" Adrian asked.

"Can you leave them with me till tonight?"

Adrian thought it over, nodded, and watched Werner walk back over to his desk and put the two silk ribbons into the top drawer and lock it.

* * *

It's an inherent talent which the Germans have in spades. They can construct something brand new and make it look as if it's a thousand years old. If they want to. They'd done that with all the old quarters in their cities after they were destroyed in 1944 and 1945 – made in the 1950s to look like the 1750s – and they'd done it too on a street corner close to where Adrian lived when they opened the new Cafe Miljöö. It was only eight weeks old but step inside and suddenly it was a place dripping with history. It was a slice of old Hamburg, with its walls lined with black and white pictures of the old Hamburg stock exchange, the old town hall, paintings of the old port, and of course, Hamburg buried under ash and rubble in 1945. It also had a new French cook who apparently made the very best Flammkuchen north of the Alsace – well, according to the menu which the new owners had stuck on the front door. Adrian knew the place before it was remade, remodelled and restyled and used to go in there regularly to find a quiet corner where he could sit and prepare his lessons, and he stayed loyal to the place – if Adrian was one thing it was loyal. He was even in the Miljöö once when some young woman, neatly dressed in a black waitress's uniform, came into the cafe and pretended to work there (she didn't), and asked everyone if she could cash up, after which she vanished completely with the money that she'd taken, never to be seen again.

Adrian had a lesson the next day with a student who was a stand-up comedian and who wanted to improve his English in order to "go international" as he put it. As if humour translated or travelled well. Or even travels at all. So Adrian went into the cosy corner bar-cafe, sat down at a table next to the window and away from all the couples who were sitting together but texting like crazy with somebody else. He ordered a cappuccino from the dark-haired waitress who could have been called Rita, Anita or even Conchita – it was hard to tell with the corner of her name badge chipped off – and took out his note pad and a pen and thought about the next day's lesson. That was the plan. But all he did was sit and twist his cappuccino cup around and around in his fingers – his imagination also turning circle after circle. And when he finally did put his pen to paper, that was all that came out, circle after circle after circle...

* * *

I'm a sixteen-year-old boy and my father has just sat me down and told me the truth. My poor mother is alongside him on the living room sofa but she doesn't say anything at all and leaves it to my dad to do all the talking. I should have expected something like this really. I mean, there has been a steady build up to it over the past few months which has gathered more speed over the past weeks.

I first noticed it last autumn when we were out sailing and he was having difficulty gripping the main sail's ropes and they kept sliding clean through his hand. That was the point when I realised that he was leaving it all to me to do. Then pretty soon the little finger on his right hand had "gone". By that I mean it just hung limp, like it had a life of its own and separate from the hand. He had no more control of it and it was unable to function properly. That, I know now, was the start. Very soon afterwards he couldn't grip a pen any more, which made it hard for him at work. Although he'd officially retired the year before, he still went in part-time, three afternoons a week. That soon stopped. And then he couldn't use a knife any more at the table. The rest then followed. The limp, lifeless finger became a rapidly thinning hand – the palm looked like it had been hollowed out with a carving knife – then a thinning arm as the muscles began to deteriorate and then vanish altogether – and soon his whole right upper body got weaker and weaker.

So they went to see the doctor. It was hard to pick up straight away and the doctor sent them for various tests. Once, a short while ago at the start of the school holidays, they were away for a whole week – in Oxford I think it was, although I didn't take too much notice at the time. It was the very first time that I'd been left on my own and I'd had the house to myself and when I didn't have my friends round, or Vanessa – my girlfriend at the time – I was out playing cricket or doing my karate or out on the sea with the boat.

"It's MND," my father tells me. I have absolutely no idea what that is or what it means or what M, N and damned D stand for or how it would come to define our lives and suck me in with it too and eat me up from the inside and eventually one day spit me out at the other end and my life would never, ever be the same again.

He explains it to me just like a doctor would explain it, clinical, detailed, precise, explicit; he is after all German. And he tells me how it will all end. Actually, as correct as he always is in everything, that's the bit he doesn't get quite right. He tells me that all his muscles will gradually but definitely decline and fade away to nothing, and that they have already started to. But I can see that for myself. And he tells me that there is nothing that anyone can do. "It's incurable, Adrian. And it's fatal," he says, and I know as soon as he says it and from the way that he says it, that is what will stay with me the rest of my life: those two words, incurable and fatal. And I know that if I live another two hundred years this conversation will stay in my head forever. "It's incurable and I'll die from it," he tells me, and no one has ever sounded so sad, so heartbroken, so defeated than he does right now. He tells me that eventually his lungs will cease to function and he will probably die from suffocation. What he doesn't tell me is the journey he will have to take to get there. Nor that it would take us all the way with him. That damned, vile, fucking nightmare journey into oblivion. I don't know it now, but I'll never be free of that journey. Because when Motor Neuron Disease takes a person down – and no one ever gets to win that game, no one has ever defeated it – it takes everyone around that person down with them.

But I'm a sixteen-year-old boy and I'm the lucky one. I'm everything that my poor father once was and everything he is now losing. And when I watched him just a few short months ago – a still-fit, handsome, healthy, strong, athletic man even when he semi-retired at sixty-five – my hero his whole life – and when I watch him now, gaunt and frail, struggling to put on his clothes, to cut up his food, to brush his teeth and comb his hair... actually, you try it. Go through twenty-four hours with one arm strapped to your side or tied behind you back – and with pain too... not easy, eh? But you know what? That's actually the easy bit. One day you'll look back on it and say: "They were the good times. They were the better days." Because soon you'll be in a dark place that you don't know and you've never been to before and you'll have to negotiate your way through it without a

1

torch and without a map, and with no guiding lights to show you the way.

You die a little bit every day and then you die some more... and then you die. That's how I'd describe it. I'd say it was like nothing else. Nothing else you can imagine. And in my father's case it would come with pain. God, did it come with pain. Intolerable, unending, unbearable, insufferable pain like nothing I've ever seen before or seen since.

So they tell me that there will be changes – changes to our home, to our perfect lives – and that my dad could no longer work – and that we will all get through it fine and with a smile. Just the way the Kramers always did. They tell me too that it might be hard for me. "Might?" "Might" doesn't even come close. I'm sixteen and I know nothing about illness. Illness hasn't touched my life yet – hasn't stolen and wrecked and distorted and dislocated and torn apart any part of me. I've breezed through life. My charmed life. Just as I said, I'm the lucky one.

"We're a strong family, Adrian. And we have love," my dad told me. "That's the most important thing–that we love each other very much." And I know as he's saying them that I'll remember his very words forever, like he's tattooing them onto my heart. "Because with love you can get through anything – but anything – that they throw at us." Then he looks me straight in the eye and says, "You're my strength, Adrian. You're what I'll live for. You and..." He can't go on and he begins to cry. He tries to control it, but he can't, and soon it's like watching a dam breaking and it becomes an uncontrollable sob from somewhere deep down inside of him. I have no idea how to react. I'm sixteen and I've never seen him cry before. Charlie Kramer doesn't cry. He's stoic, proud, invincible, tough, fearless, he's a survivor. He's my prince. With his princess next to him. Then she begins to cry too. These people on the sofa opposite me are my parents and it's all falling apart before my eyes.

I get up and go into the kitchen for a box of tissues and when I return, my mother is alone on the sofa. "Your dad has gone up to *bed," is all that she says through her own tears. "We'll get through this, Adrian – you and I..." And then she says it to me again as if she is trying to convince herself, and that saying it twice will do the trick more effectively than once... "We'll get through it together," – and she gets up and hugs me as if her very life depended on it.*

* * *

Circle after circle after circle... that's all Adrian drew on his blank notebook page, lost in his past and haunted by ghosts and spirits of the very worst kind. Until he gave up – "To hell with the pain," he told himself. In this life no one gets out unhurt. We all get broken somewhere along the way by something – and he packed his things back into his satchel and headed off to the school.

An hour later he sat and listened to his wannabe-stand-up comedian student gamely try out his latest stolen gags. Adrian's thoughts weren't really in the room, but that was okay because he was recording the session anyway to playback and go through with his student later.

"So, I am I going to ze doctors," Holger the student said. He was around forty and, most unusually for a German, he had badly-kept and yellowed teeth. "He said me 'I'd like that you lie on ze couch.' I said 'Vot for?' He said 'I'd like to sweep ze floor.'"

Adrian smiled and nodded for Holger to carry on. What else do you say to something like that? Where do you start?

Holger took a breath and continued. "I ask him why ze people always take an instant dislike to me. He said it save them time." Holger stopped and looked to Adrian for a response.

"Is that it?" Adrian said, wondering if the act was now over.

Holger shook his head. There was more. "Zis doctor vosn't no help so I vent to see another doctor. He stuck a finger up my ass and said you've got haemorrhoids... this is ze right word *ja*?

haemorrhoids?"

Again, Adrian nodded and Holger went on. "I said I vont a second opinion. So, he stuck up a second finger up."

"Okay," Adrian said and pressed the button on the recorder and rewound. "Let's go through it, shall we?" and go through it they did for the next forty-five minutes. Adrian had another three lessons that day before he was finished, but all he had on his mind the whole time was the trip to see Werner later in the day.

2

Werner had told him to be there at seven o'clock, and a minute to the hour Adrian rang Werner's front doorbell, although Werner was waiting and ready for him anyway and led him into his study, where a large television screen had been set up in the corner. He motioned to Adrian to take a seat, but Adrian remained standing and looked hopefully into Werner's face. His historian friend appeared excited, animated. He was clearly most impressed about something.

"So, could you find out anything?"

Could he? Werner was positively bursting to explain. "Do you know who Reinhard Heydrich was?"

"The name," Adrian replied vaguely. He could have added "but nothing else", but he didn't.

"Reinhard Heydrich was one of the very top Nazi leaders. He was probably the person who embodied better than anyone else the true Nazi ideology. The 'pure Aryan God' they called him. Sinister. Ruthless. In a regime of evil, he was the most evil of them all. Heydrich was a close personal friend of Hitler."

Werner was in his element. It was exactly this kind of moment that he lived for – the opportunity to throw light on our past – however dark. He hit a button on his remote and the screen in front of them lit up with images of the Aryan God himself, Reinhard Heydrich – the man who they said even on the sunniest day never cast a shadow, although as Werner told Adrian, that's exactly where Heydrich did his best work and where he operated in; right there in the darkness of the shadows. First up on screen was a black and white portrait picture. A lean face, bony you could call it, and even horsey if you are trying to be unkind, with blond hair and sharp eyes which seemed to be taking in everything all at once. A click of the remote button and next up was a photograph of Heydrich the athlete, posing with his rapier in hand and all ready to strike.

"Reinhard Heydrich was Head of the Nazi Secret Police and the architect in chief of the Final Solution – the plan to wipe out all Jews in Europe by systematic genocide," Werner continued in his best history professor mode. He was engrossed in his own narration. "Hitler made him Governor of the former Czechoslovakia. He sent him to Prague to stamp down hard on the Czechs... they were under Nazi occupation and were causing problems and Hitler saw Heydrich as the only one who could effectively stop the unrest and bring them into line. The Czechs feared him as much as they hated him. The 'Hangman' the Czechs called him. At the end of May 1942 Czech Partisans assassinated him in Prague."

Werner hit the button again and Adrian was suddenly staring at archive photographs of Heydrich's bombed-out, open-top Mercedes at the hairpin turn in Prague where the attack took place.

"The two assassins had been specially trained in Britain and parachuted in to carry out the killing. They didn't actually kill him in the attack... he died in hospital some days later from his injuries. Heydrich's death hit Hitler very hard. As revenge."

Werner hit the button again and old newsreel footage of the fate of Lidice came up.

"He ordered the Czech mining town of Lidice to be wiped off the map. Wiped off completely."

Adrian watched as a whole town went up in flames. The next day, the place would no longer exist. And nor would its people.

"The Nazis thought that the two assassins were hiding there. And they believed that a letter sent between two lovers in Lidice was a coded message about the attack. It was never proved. But the whole town was destroyed anyway. And all of its inhabitants... 'annihilated' do you say?"

Adrian nodded and watched as the screen filled with archive movie footage of Heydrich's funeral cortege – first through the centre of Prague, followed by the procession through the crowded streets of Berlin. Hundreds of thousands line the streets of both cities as Heydrich's coffin passes by.

"Heydrich's body was brought back to Berlin, where Hitler honoured him with a State funeral – the grandest funeral ever staged by the Third Reich."

On the screen then, stills of Hitler entering the church for the service and greeting one of Heydrich's young sons with a handshake and a pinch of the cheek. The young boy has a broad smile on his face. Another blond Heydrich boy greets the Fuhrer with a classic raised right-arm *Heil Hitler* salute. Then more stills as Hitler stands and gives his emotional speech to the congregation.

"After the service Heydrich's body was taken and was buried in... look!" Werner said and hit the pause button, and held on an image of Heydrich's grave. "There!" He got up, went over to the screen and pointed excitedly. Attached to two large wreaths which lay close to Heydrich's headstone were Adrian's ribbons. "Your mother had the ribbons from the wreaths laid on Heydrich's grave in the names of Adolf Hitler and Benito Mussolini."

It seemed to take an age for what he'd heard to finally sink in for Adrian. And even when it did, he simply looked numb.

"Do you know just what we have here?" Werner asked him, and in a way which sounded as if he'd just found the Holy Grail. "Where did your mother get them?"

"They weren't my mother's," Adrian said after a profound moment's silence and with no emotion or feeling whatsoever in his voice. "They belonged to my father. No one back home could tell me anything. Nobody knew about them. So yeah, now I know what we have. But I don't know 'why'."

Werner handed him back the ribbons and the two exchanged a look which said everything about their own secret suspicions.

Werner looked at Adrian sympathetically. "That's what I

can't answer for you. And what you'll probably never know now." He nodded down at the ribbons which were then back in Adrian's hands. "What are you going to do with them?"

Adrian just shrugged his shoulders and said, "I don't know. Wipe my backside with them?"

"You know, there are people who would pay a lot of money to have something like this," Werner said, and it came out as much a question as it was a statement.

But Adrian said nothing. Right then he was feeling nothing.

"Or..." Werner added hopefully, "we could use them at the museum?"

But Adrian just stared blankly at the paused screen and the image of the grave, the flowers, the wreaths, and the ribbons attached to two particular wreaths – the two ribbons which were now in his own hands.

"Whatever you do, just be very careful," Werner added. "Nazi memorabilia are illegal here in Germany."

They spoke for a few more minutes and Adrian told him as much as he knew about his father's past, which wasn't a lot. And when Werner was showing him out later at the front door he said to Adrian "Your father was born in Hannover you said? Let me make some enquiries for you. And if you have his birth certificate that will help?"

Adrian thanked Werner for the evening and for the information that he wished then he never had, they parted with a handshake, and he walked off down the flood-lit garden path in a complete daze.

* * *

Later that evening Adrian stood at the window which looked out over the Borgfelder Strasse below holding the two ribbons in one hand and the photograph of himself and his father on the yacht in the other. He looked from one to the other, then back again – his mind racing – trying to make some sense out of it all. And then suddenly he was an eighteen-year-old boy again. He remembered it because it was the day of his eighteenth birthday and he was alone with his father in his father's bedroom, which was actually the spare bedroom they had converted into a medical room in order to accommodate Charlie Kramer's specialised electric bed and all the other equipment that he needed. Adrian's father was trying desperately to tell him something, he was desperate to speak, but of course he couldn't anymore. That had stopped about six months earlier. He had a speech computer, but the time had sadly arrived when even that had become too much effort and he complained about headaches from all the eye work required to spell every single letter out on the computer's keyboard, and the whole business distressed him and exhausted him and on occasions he even began to cry, so great was his frustration that he could no longer communicate, that he could no longer speak the simplest and most basic of things to the world. But here he was now with something so urgent, so important on his mind. He called Adrian over to him. Adrian was able to read every gesture by that point and could usually, but not always, guess correctly what his father wanted. Often it would come down to Adrian asking him a series of questions to which his father could reply "yes" or "no" using his eyes, or using the computer, or even just a look... oh, *that* look. Charlie Kramer could speak a thousand words with just one look of the eye. If you ever see the film *The Theory of Everything* about Stephen Hawking's life, you'll see the actor Eddie Redmayne has that gesture down to heartrending perfection. He speaks chapters with just one look of his eye. Sometimes with just a millimetre raise of the eyebrow. It's a master-class in portraying how it is to be trapped in your body, to be trapped by your illness, and somehow still manage to speak to the world. Except on this occasion Adrian's father really couldn't communicate what he so desperately had to get out.

He raised one eyebrow just like Eddie Redmayne (he'd lost the ability to move the other eyebrow by then), while the pupils in both eyes shot up to the top of his head. And the heartbreaking guessing game started. "You want something? You want me to get you something? You're in pain? You want something to eat? The toilet... you want the toilet? You need more morphine? Shall I call the doctor?" With each attempt and every guess Adrian's father closed his eyes and started all over again. His eyes were pointing up, up, UP... But Adrian had absolutely no idea what he wanted or what he was trying to say.

But in Hamburg eleven years later it was clear to Adrian now. Up there in the loft. Go up there. Bring down the two damned silk ribbons which you'll find up there and I'll tell you my secret. Or something like that. And even if that wasn't true, Charlie Kramer always knew the journey he was on and knew where he would be getting off. How many times, when he was able to speak, had he said to Adrian and his mother, "You know that I'm not going to survive this, don't you?" (And how do you answer *that*, except with tears or a joke?) He knew the ribbons were up there and that one day someone would have to go up into the loft to clean up and clear out, and the "someone" would inevitably be his son. "Did he *want* me to find them?" Adrian asked himself. Was it his way of sending me off on my own journey to find out?

Looking down into the street outside his flat Adrian shook his head. He would never know the answers to his questions now. But what he was also asking himself back then was – how much did I really know about my father? And how much of himself did he conceal from others? Do we always give everything? Or is it sometimes nothing at all? Oh man, only questions and no damned answers.

He turned away from the window and settled down in front of the television screen. Better to numb his mind that night with some dumb, senseless eye candy.

3

It was a still, warm night and all you could hear in Adrian's flat was the tick, tick, tick of the clock on the kitchen wall and the constant whir of the fridge below it. The street outside too was just as quiet that night, as it usually was at three in the morning. A cat trotted slowly across the road as if it didn't have a care in the world. It was carrying a poor mouse in its mouth which still *did* have a care in the world, but for how long? – because it was fighting for its life and wriggled this way and then that to try and get itself free. The cat and its bounty disappeared into the thick bushes on the other side of the road, which was part of the narrow strip of park that ran the whole length of the Borgfelder Strasse. A streetlight flickered on, and off, then back on and back off – something had gone wrong with it earlier that evening and it would need a call to the city council the next morning for someone to come out and fix it. There was no traffic at all on the empty street that night until a car crawled slowly along and came to a stop at the kerbside directly outside of Adrian's building. The driver cut the headlights and the door swung open. Seconds later a torch's beam lit up the nameplate next to the main door and searched up and down, up and down, and eventually came to stop on the name "Kramer". Then the torch was clicked off, light footsteps padded back to the car, and the car engine started up again.

Just as the car turned the corner another cat crossed the street and it too disappeared into the thick bush at exactly the point where the one with the mouse had gone into. Perhaps there'd be some action in the old Oben Borgfelde park that night after all.

* * *

The next afternoon Katharina arrived ten minutes late for her lesson. She quickly unpacked her books and set them down next to the flask of coffee which Adrian had made earlier and had already set down on the table in front of her.

"Sorry I was late. I was in a meeting with my editor."

But Adrian, staring vacantly over her shoulder at the photograph on the windowsill, hadn't really heard her. In fact, he hadn't even been listening.

"Are you okay?" she asked, picking up on his mood.

Katharina Kozlowski had made a bit of a reputation for herself earlier in the year by exposing an ingenious drug-exporting ploy. Although she was working only part-time back then and was mostly covering mainstream cat-up-a-tree stories, she'd heard from someone who worked for the Hamburg harbourmaster about a rich Russian entrepreneur who had rented a large warehouse at the Hamburg docks. He had a fleet of container ships which were unloading there, and rumour had it that the ships were coming in with cargos of cocaine hidden among their freight – mostly fruit imported from the Middle East. The Russian businessman had also bought some old, disused vineyards in the Moselle valley which had been neglected for years and had become overgrown, but he had replanted red grape vines and had begun to produce wine there once again. What Katharina was able to find out was that the Russian was shipping the containers with their fruit and cocaine freight on from Hamburg to the winery at his Moselle vineyard, where the cocaine powder was poured into the red wine. The powder dissolved in the wine and was then bottled, held in chemical suspension, and exported overseas disguised as red wine, and then once at its destination it was being heated off, leaving the cocaine crystals. It was an ingenious way of getting cocaine across borders undetected and undetectable. Katharina was eventually forced to hand her story over to the paper's chief crime editor, once the Police had become involved, but not before she'd earned herself a bit of a name for breaking the case, and on the back of it, also negotiating herself a full-time, salaried job at the paper, although she always said that all she really wanted was to stick a pack on her back and walk coast to coast across the USA. That's where she said she would be happiest. "And to live in a world of harmony and fun and fairness, but with just enough mischief in it to keep things interesting," she always added.

Katharina also developed a reputation along the way for ruffling a feather or two, especially feathers that she thought deserved to be ruffled – she was certainly someone who "zigged" when the others "zagged" – and when something wasn't right, she had a good antenna for sensing it. She sensed something that day with Adrian as he looked straight past her, lost in the photograph.

"Adrian... are you okay?" she asked him again.

He snapped to attention. "Yeah," he told her.

But she could see that he wasn't. She looked at him with some compassion. "I lost both my parents too... two years ago. In a car crash in Italy. I know just what you're going through."

"So which little secret did your father take with him?"

"What do you mean?"

"I mean... my father..." He stopped himself. He knew then that his father had carried some sort of secret. But was it as big as the secret Adrian had to carry around with him?

Katharina's eyes were all over him, watching as he fought to say something, yet at the same time, fighting to hold it back.

"What about your father? What's wrong, Adrian?"

Adrian took a moment to think. Then he said: "When my father died eleven years ago someone said to me, 'until you've experienced your first death, you're still a virgin.' They had no idea. No idea what he went through... what we all had to go through. But they were wrong for another reason. It's only after the first *betrayal* that you lose that innocence. After a second..."

He looked at her, and wondered if he really should do it –

whether he really wanted to lay himself bare, and whether for the first time in three years he could allow himself to become emotionally naked. Those things no longer came easy for him. Then he got up, went into the bedroom, and returned with the ribbons. That day he really did need a friend.

"I found them at home. They're from Reinhard Heydrich's grave. You know who he was?"

"Yes, I know who Heydrich was."

Katharina looked at the ribbons with a cocktail-mix of amazement and revulsion. Then she looked back up and into Adrian's face, touched and privileged to have been taken so far into his confidence. She reached over for the coffee pot to fill his cup for him.

"I think this might need something stronger than coffee. It's a long story," he said to her.

She regarded him with a sympathetic smile. "We've got time. I've paid for it, remember?"

Still fighting some inner war with himself, Adrian began to tell her his story. And the story included parts of his father's forlorn fight in the war which he knew he would never win... but only certain parts of it. The whole sorry story, he knew he would never be able to tell anyone. And he opened up too about the heartbreaking impact it had on himself. "I saw things I will never un-see," he told her, still hurting badly. "I had to do things... they'll stay with me forever." And then he told her about finding the ribbons and what he'd found out from Werner.

But it came with a trade-off. Katharina too dug deep and told him what she'd told very few people in her life about her great-grandfather, who was a member of the SS and had worked at the Treblinka concentration camp in occupied east Poland, where over three-quarters-of-a-million Jews and gypsies were exterminated during the second world war – ironically Reinhard Heydrich's gift to the world in the shape of the Final Solution.

"Doesn't it haunt you?" Adrian asked at the end of her own

bombshell revelation.

"Why should it? It was nothing to do with me," she said matter-of-factly. "So, my great-grandfather was an asshole? I decided I'll spend my life trying to be something different."

They overshot Katharina's hour by two more, and the late afternoon had become evening by the time she collected her things together and held out her money for Adrian. He shook his head. It was him who had needed something that day, and it was Katharina who had supplied the shoulder.

* * *

The next day was overcast and breezy. It was a day in fact, just like so many over in the north-east of England. Except this was northern Germany and Adrian was out at the far end of the lake again, close to the reeds, alone and as far away as he always tried to be from the nearest boat. The breeze soon kicked up into a much stronger wind and he had to fight to keep control of the boat. Up above him, but not too far up because the sky seemed to be so low that day, some more dark clouds were gathering. But more ominously, the wind was beginning to intensify more and more by the second. A storm was coming Adrian's way. A family of grebes scuttled out of his way as he pulled away from the reeds and started back off up the lake in the direction of the distant harbour.

* * *

Outside of Katharina's bedroom window in Hamburg, some miles west of where Adrian was battling the storm which was then coming at him way too fast, lightening suddenly fractured the menacing sky and Katharina jumped. She was sitting at her computer screen in the corner of the room. She looked outside at the rain lashing hard against the window – great big bucketfuls of warm summer rain. She turned back to the screen, hit Enter on her keyboard, and the screen filled with a homepage of Nazi images; the usual horror show. She looked at it all with the same mixture of curiosity and hatred that she had when Adrian had shown her his ribbons, then she clicked onto an area which said *Kauf und Verkauf* (Buy and Sell) as another bolt of lightning lit up the darkening Hamburg sky outside. This time she didn't jump. What she did was begin to type.

* * *

Back on the lake the orange-red sails of Adrian's dinghy were straining against the rapidly rising wind as Adrian managed to guide his boat into the small lake-side harbour. He was one of the last boats in and by then he was soaked to the skin. He tied up the dinghy and sprinted the twenty or so yards across to the locked boat house for cover, where a half-dozen other sailors were huddled together in the doorway waiting for the chance to make it to their cars.

* * *

An hour away in the rain-lashed city, Katharina's curiosity quickly turned to something else, something between surprise and utter shock, when she saw an offer appear. And it had appeared so quickly too. It was for ten thousand euros. Then another, for fifteen thousand five hundred. She was about to log out when there was a third.

* * *

Adrian was forced to pull his Mini Cooper into an over-flooded lay-by on the autobahn, which had been steadily filling up with trucks trying to escape the worst of the fierce summer storm.

The Mini's wipers had no longer been able to handle the rain which was then pelting down onto the screen and had made driving impossible. While he sat waiting for a break in the storm his mobile phone rang. He didn't hear it the first time because of the heavy rain which was bouncing off the Mini's roof and sounded just like a snare drum. When he finally answered on the second call, it was Werner on the other end.

"I made some enquiries for you at work. Are you coming over?"

"When I can," Adrian told him and hung up. Then he settled down for what he knew could be a long wait by reading about Prague's "Hangman" on his Smartphone.

It wasn't good reading. He read about Heydrich's rise through the ranks of the dreaded SS to become head of the Nazi's even more feared *Sicherheitsdienst*, its counterintelligence service: "the man with the iron heart" as Hitler called him. He read about the terror, the intimidation and murder that Heydrich had been more than happy to deploy in the name of his twisted ideology. He read too that in addition to an iron heart, he also had a wandering heart which led to his philandering and whoring on the backstreets of Berlin and Munich, or anywhere that there was sex for sale, not that he paid for it anyway. And he read about the horrors of the Holocaust, which Heydrich himself had masterminded.

After twenty minutes he'd read enough and his thoughts turned to his poor mother, and he realised that he hadn't yet really mourned her death so much as he'd been obsessed about his father and his dumb wreath ribbons, and the thought began to tear him apart. His father certainly hadn't deserved his fate – but neither had his mother. It had all been more than she could bear, more than she could bear to watch, more than she could bare to cope with and be a direct part of, physically, mentally, emotionally, spiritually. She'd lost herself while she was losing her husband, bit-by-bit, day by day. And she lost her faith –

not in God, but in a good God, a kind God, a compassionate God, a fair God, a just God. What sort of twisted mind can put something like her wonderful, golden-hearted husband's illness into the world and not provide mankind with a cure for it? No priest or holy man would ever be able to explain that one to her. In many ways Adrian's mother had died when his father died. Adrian knew that. He was there to watch it. "You die a little bit every day and then you die some more... and then you die," was how Adrian had described it, and that was pretty much on the button. His mother finally had her own collapse a few months later, in the autumn, when she had to go away for a few weeks into a mental hospital of some sort – one of those institutions where they send broken people to get fixed. But she was never really fixed, not emotionally anyway, and just like Charlie Kramer, she had told her son that she would only stay alive for *him*, even when Adrian told her that he'd be moving to Germany.

He thought about all of that while he was sitting in his car in a north German motorway lay-by waiting for the storm to blow over, and about how his mother's death, and especially finding those two wreath ribbons, had dragged him back into the past and thrown everything back at him, including the part that he'd played in the whole thing, and he wondered how long it would be before he could rid himself of the nightmare pictures which he'd been carrying around in his head of those fateful final moments of his father's life, moments which he'd been trying to repress for eleven years. He could even have cried. But he didn't. He swore once that he would never give a single tear to Motor Neuron Disease and he was damned if he was going to break that promise now.

After fifteen more minutes the rain eased and he finally pulled back out onto the autobahn and headed back to the city.

Meanwhile, in Katharina's bedroom, the offers had come flooding in. She read a response in English from a group calling themselves WSA –White Supremacy America – who had offered thirty thousand US dollars, another in Italian with a bid of forty thousand euros, and a German offer of fifty thousand from someone called the Bayerische Nationale Front – the BNF. And there were others. She got up and moved away from the computer, either shocked or agitated or excited or disgusted – she wouldn't have been able to tell you herself which emotion was foremost – and began to pace the room. A ginger cat was lying on the bed in one of those half-asleep-half-awake states which cats are the absolute masters of. Eventually she stopped her pacing and went over to stroke it, a comfort of sorts. The cat couldn't have cared less.

4

Adrian followed Werner up the stairs and into his first-floor study. "There was no one called Kramer born in Hannover on your father's birth-date," Werner told him. "The only Karl Kramer born in the whole of Germany in 1937 for whom records exist died in the war. In Stuttgart." He picked up a piece of paper from his desk and read from the note that he'd made for himself earlier in the day. "The next was born in 1940. He is still alive, and he lives now in Friedrichshafen." And then he said, "I'm sorry, Adrian," because he knew what the news meant. And he was right, because it was yet another layer of mystery for Adrian, another level of incomprehension and disappointment which his face wasn't able to hide. He first looked up at nothing at all – how do you react to that? Then he turned away and gazed around the room. And it hit him. The room somehow seemed different. There was now an empty space where Werner's pride, his precious French antique clock, had once stood. And a whole bookshelf of old leather-bound books was no longer there. Adrian was about to mention it but Werner spoke first.

"Have you decided what to do with the ribbons?"

Before Adrian could answer, his mobile phone rang. He fished it out of his pocket and heard Katharina tell him to "Get here. Quick."

Moments later Werner stood at the window of his first-floor office and watched Adrian race over to his car parked in the drive below and speed off. Then he went over and emptied the last drops from his finest malt whisky into a glass tumbler and downed it in one. He looked sad. He was sad for his friend, but mostly he was sad for himself. And he did indeed at that moment look like a King who had lost his Queen, and with her, lost his Kingdom too.

* * *

The storm came back with a vengeance while Adrian was driving over to Katharina's place and at one point the heavy rain turned to hail stones the size of small golf balls and sounded to Adrian more like giant rocks when they were bouncing off his Mini's canvas roof. He sprinted the few yards from where he parked his car in the street but he was still soaked through when he arrived at Katharina's flat; he stood behind her and towelled his hair dry while he looked over her shoulder at the computer screen. She had placed her advert as "Kitty Kat" and used an Italian email address which she'd quickly set up in the name of "Eva Braun-Eyes." The offer from the BNF now stood at seventy-five thousand.

"You brought me all the way across the city in that storm to show me that filth?" He wasn't at all happy. It had also flung back hard into his face the reality of what the two wreath ribbons represented, and the dread every time he thought about why his father had them. "What the hell's this all about?"

The cat wandered in and rubbed itself up against Adrian's leg, marking its territory. He ignored it.

"I was curious. I'm a journalist, remember?"

"And what exactly were you going to do? Go out and interview each one of these arseholes for a 'think piece'?"

"You know, Hans Frank's son once paid hundreds of dollars to buy his father's leather overcoat, and now he uses it in his back garden, wrapped around a stick in the ground, as a scarecrow. Hans Frank's son hated him."

"Who was Hans Frank?"

"Hitler's man in Poland. A Jew killer. A Pole killer. What Heydrich did to the Czechs, Frank did to the Poles. Now his coat's a scarecrow."

"What does that have to do with me?" he said and turned away and took a seat on the edge of the bed. "Write back and tell them to go fuck themselves."

"Leave that out, Adrian. You don't mess with these kinds of people."

He shot her a look which screamed out "my words entirely", then he got up, left the towel on the bed and moved back to the computer. "If Kitty Kat won't do it Angry Adrian will have to."

He leaned over her and began to type.

* * *

Evening had become night, the storm had long ceased its nonsense, a candle had been lit in the middle of the coffee table, and the earlier tension between them had eased when Adrian and Katharina sat together in the living room. In the background, the cool mellow jazz of the man who they said could play the sound of a teardrop falling, Chet Baker, floated softly out of the speakers and drifted around the room like a comforting arm. A half-empty bottle of French Rosé sat on the table in front of them. The cat lay snuggled up on the floor next to Adrian, looking at peace with the world, even if Adrian wasn't.

Katharina took a sip of her wine and put her glass back on the table. "I'm sorry, Adrian," she said to him and looked like she genuinely meant it.

"Pretty girls just can't seem to stop saying that to me these days." He could see her mind working. "Go ahead and ask your question."

"Was she as bad as me?"

"Oh, you don't even come close. You couldn't."

"Thank you," she replied with pure sarcasm.

Adrian reached down and slowly stroked the cat's neck with an index finger. The cat slowly opened one eye – two would have been too much effort – then closed it again. It had already decided that Adrian was okay. Katharina watched them together. She liked that the cat liked him. And she liked too that he seemed to like it back. She smiled a secret smile to herself. Until Adrian said, "Because I wouldn't let you."

She might have been crushed but she tried her best not to show it. She waited for him to say more, until it became clear that she would have waited a lifetime.

"I always told myself 'he's a Hitchcock blonde'," she finally said to him. "You know what that is?"

Adrian shrugged his shoulders. "A blend of whiskey? An opening move in chess?"

She shook her head.

"Then it's a French cigarette," was his last wild guess. The truth was that he really didn't care either way.

"Ice-cold, polished and passionless on the outside... and on the inside a passionate, raging fire. Seems like I got that one wrong."

She got up and started to clear the table.

"Tell me, doesn't it ever get lonely being inside the big, safe Kramer castle? Because that's some wall you've built up around yourself."

Adrian just sat and looked at her.

"Don't you ever let anyone from the big, bad world outside in anymore?"

He leant forward and blew out the candle and then said, "Maybe one day... maybe someone might just slip under the radar."

He got up and moved towards the door which led to the hallway and out, while Katharina headed in the other direction towards the kitchen with her empty wine glasses and wine bottle. "Off to build those walls a little higher?" she called back to him over her shoulder, still playfully, but underneath hurting.

Adrian just smiled to himself as he walked out of the room and softly closed the door behind him.

4

Veins and muscles bulged, sinews tightened then strained, the sweat flowed down Adrian's face like a waterfall. The following day was the same as the previous one had ended – too wet and windy for the boat – so Adrian headed downtown to Cordino's gym and exorcised his demons out in the tight, dimly-lit fitness room which stank of cheap aftershave and reeked of perspiration – pushing himself to the limits, purging his soul. He stepped off the treadmill and started laying into an old leather punchbag.

What right does she have to gatecrash my world uninvited? What right has she got to threaten my independence and my splendid isolation? the voice inside his head screamed out. Who is she to question what I am and how I am? I'm safe this way. I'm happy like this. Adrian didn't even dare to consider that he might be kidding himself. He meant it. He really wasn't interested. The brightest, sharpest, most attractive girl in the whole of the city and he had no interest whatsoever. I don't need saving. Fuck her. Fuck them all!

WHACK – he hit the punchbag as hard as he could. If it hurt his hand, right at that moment Adrian didn't care one bit. He was thinking about what they had said the night before.

Before it had all become too uncomfortable, and for Adrian way too personal, Katharina had told him about her own relationships and about the boyfriend who she'd recently split from after two years. "Turned out we were both looking for completely different things and were completely different kinds of people. He was a block of ice too," she said and gave Adrian her most provocative, most cheeky smile. She was mocking him. "But *he* didn't have his reasons and *he* didn't have it all well thought out. It was just the way he was... the way he'd been brought up, in a family without love. No one showed him any, he'd never learned it. He was a victim of a generation here who blocked out every little thing from their past... no one asked questions... it was a culture of pragmatism, survival, denial... and they passed that all on. Turned out too that Max wanted *things*, you know?" She shrugged her shoulders. She meant possessions, symbols of success. "Stuff that you go out and buy and show to people,"was how she defined it to Adrian. "I just wanted *someone*."

"How come you two got together at all?"

"I was a hopeless romantic. And most romantic stories have a good-looking hero."

"So. he was the 'beauty' to your 'beast'?"

"What do you think?" She was testing him.

"I think what you think. Except for that nonsense earlier with the ribbons."

That had been the moment when she'd said to him "I'm sorry, Adrian", and the moment too that Adrian saw that she really was contrite. And that she cared. It was a point too when he wondered if he really was going in the right direction with his emotional and even physical seclusion? Jermaine had often tried to convince him that if he really did want to lose himself, lose his past, then the best way was in one of the whore houses on the Reeperbahn. There, Jermaine reasoned, you can lose yourself and still have fun – much more fun than the self-denial and isolation which Adrian practised like a holy man. "Isolate yourself with Mimi from Moscow," Jermaine joked with him. "Hell, I'll pay for it if that's your problem. You have one life Ade, you have to live it," his friend J had said to him many times, and he spoke the words like some divine guru. Did Jermaine have a point? Could Adrian become someone and something that he felt he wasn't? Was he only deceiving himself with all his distancing and discipline? Or was Katharina getting too close to the truth when she'd said to him "what you're doing is just a safe and comfortable refuge for someone who believes that they're not good enough to compete anymore"? Was that what it was, his acceptance that he was fighting out of his class?

What the hell does she know about my past and my pain?
Who is she to judge me?

WHACK!

What Katharina had also told him the previous night was
that her boyfriend didn't take her walking out on him at all
well and for a while he had stalked her, to the point where she
had to get a restraining order on him. But that had all been four
months earlier, before he'd moved away to Canada. Katharina
had left him one night when, after a fierce argument, Max
hit her – hit her hard enough to rupture an eardrum. "That's
where love finally ended up," she'd said. And that was when
she'd drawn her line. Deep, and definite, and from which there
was no turning back. She told Adrian too that the reason she'd
become a journalist at all was because one day someone had
hit someone else, and all because they couldn't get their own
way, because they'd been denied. And then that person did a lot
more to his victim afterwards. The victim had been Katharina's
cousin and she had been raped by a prominent politician in the
regional Government – he was the Minister of Family Affairs of
all things. He offered Katharina's cousin money for her silence
and the whole matter would be nicely covered up. But what
appalled Katharina was that her cousin actually took the money.

"What would I get from a court case?" her cousin reasoned.
"What would it bring back? I can't be un-raped. I know he's
guilty. Hearing it in some Court won't improve on that. You
want punishment? He paid me plenty. And he paid where it
hurt him the most."

"You don't get it. You just don't get it," was all Katharina
could say to her cousin. And she vowed there and then that
wherever she saw violation and injustice and an abuse of power
in any form and by anyone at all she would call it out.

So she told Adrian all about her turbulent, two-year roller-
coaster romance (if it could ever be called by that name), but
what she didn't tell him, and what Adrian couldn't know, was

that the more impenetrable the shield, the greater the challenge was for her – and the greater the challenge, the more attractive it became. And what she also didn't tell him was that she saw in Adrian someone very special, and she knew that buried deep down somewhere inside that apparently ice-cold shell beat a good heart, a kind heart, with a loving soul.

WHACK! Adrian belted into the bag again, and again, and again. There was an even greater intensity with every blow.

The final part of their conversation was playing over again in his head, the part about loyalty being the greatest virtue and how she hated cheating in all of its forms.

What did she want? What was she trying to do to me? Humiliate me? Insult me? Set me up? And for what? Just leave me alone, all of you...

WHACK!

5

When Katharina slept it was always with the shutters fully down so that the room was blacker than black. She was a very light sleeper and every little thing helped. Even the alarm on the bedside table next to her had a cover over the clock face to mask the light. Lying alongside the alarm was her mobile phone. It rang at just after three-thirty in the morning and Katharina reached over, still half asleep, to answer it. She didn't recognise the number.

"Kozlowski, Hallo?"

But all there was only silence on the other end.

"Hallo? Wer ist da bitte?"

Only more silence.

"Hallo?" she said, more urgently.

It was followed by the dialling tone.

Katharina switched off the phone and rolled back over to sleep. "Perverser Idiot," she said out loud and then it hit her: Max? Was he back from Canada? No sooner do you think about someone from your past than they appear in your present. Was he back in her life and back in her head again? We'll address that in the morning, she told herself. For now, sleep Katharina, get some sleep.

* * *

Adrian too was a light sleeper, although having too much light in the room didn't disturb him too much and his bedroom didn't have to be as dark as Katharina's. But Adrian's sleep too was broken that same night by a scratching and scraping noise coming from the front door. He listened for some seconds and when it didn't go away, he got up and crept slowly through the dark flat towards the door. He stood motionless for ten seconds in the hallway and listened to the sound of metal scraping on metal, as if someone was trying to find his lock with a key. Then he went up to the door, leant against it, and listened for a moment longer. Sure enough, someone was trying to put a key into his door lock. But they certainly weren't bothered about not letting anyone inside the flat know about it. Adrian picked up a porcelain vase from beside the door – it had been a Christmas present from one of his evening classes – and slowly he put his hand on the inside door handle. In a flash he twisted it and jerked the door open. It was followed by a loud "thud" as Andrej the Ukrainian piss-head from the upstairs apartment tumbled sideways and flopped down onto the floor. Man, you stink was all that Adrian thought as he stared down at the drunken heap on the ground and then shut the door on him. Andrej would have to find his own way up the stairs that night.

* * *

Adrian poured another cup of double Espresso from the machine for Katharina. She needed it. They were in her kitchen and she was holding in her hands a letter of sorts and it distressed her. It was on a sheet of yellow A4-sized paper and it was a collage of old cut-up German newspaper headlines. Or more precisely, it was single words cut out of old headlines. Although it was easy enough to understand, she nevertheless translated it for Adrian as she read: Sell. To. Us. We. Always. Get. What. We. Want. She looked scared and confused. "I made up the name and email address that I used. How could they find me?"

Adrian suspected he might know the answer to her question, and two hours later at school, at the end of the lesson as Mario was filing out of the room, head down and texting on two phones at the same time, Adrian once again surprised him by grabbing his arm and holding him back until the girls had all left the room.

Mario nodded and answered Adrian's question like nothing was ever simpler. "Any decent hacker could do it. It's like taking pennies off a dead man's eyes."

Oddly, it was the English and not Mario's answer which surprised Adrian the most. "Where did you learn that line?"

"From taking pennies off a dead man's eyes," Mario said, deadpan. "You want me to hack someone for you?" he asked with an excited tone in his voice.

Adrian shook his head and smiled to himself as Mario turned and trudged out of the room.

* * *

The following day, long after the morning's lessons were over and when he was sure that everyone had gone home and the school was empty, Adrian pushed his velvet bag with the wreath ribbons inside right to the back of his locker in the teachers' room and piled several text books up in front of it. Then he closed the door, made sure that it really was safely and securely locked, and turned to leave...

Only to look straight into the face of Renate the school secretary. How long had she been standing there behind me? What had she seen? How guilty do I look? She clearly thinks I'm a Nazi now and she's going to inform the Police.

"Your two o'clock lesson has just been cancelled, Adrian. You're free for the day." Then she smiled at him and headed back out of the room.

* * *

On his way home from work Adrian dropped a euro coin into the old Leonard Cohen singer's hat and he broke straight into "Torn Raincoat" again for him. Adrian took no notice. He had his mobile phone pressed to his ear and couldn't believe what he'd just been told. "How much?" He was incredulous.

"He calls himself 'Bernd O'," Katharina told him. "He's offering two hundred thousand euros!"

"I want nothing to do with it," Adrian barked into the phone. His mood was somewhere between cool and ice cold. "You handle it however you want."

He switched off his mobile and headed on down Borgfelder Strasse towards his flat. He entered the main door to the building deep in thought. Why does she have to mess with my life and complicate everything? What does she want from me? Sure, she's pretty. But so was Sarah and so probably was Delilah. And what did that bring me or bring old Samson? Next thing you know she'll have the god-damned scissors at my hair. He stopped at his mailbox and took out the two things which were in there – one was an advert for a new Indian restaurant which had opened in the neighbourhood. The other was a flyer from a political party asking him for their vote in the upcoming elections and setting out what an exemplary, upholding citizen their local candidate was, and it had a portrait picture of a middle-aged go-getter with a plastic smile fixed firmly in place, thinning grey hair and a matching greyish moustache which looked more like some big hairy caterpillar was crawling along his top lip. And it even explained how he was going to make the city the most wonderful place in all of Germany to live and how he'd never raped anyone nor tried to cover it up with a bribe afterwards. Actually, the flyer didn't say that last part, but that's what Adrian was thinking as he set off up the stairs, and he also thought to himself that the Indian restaurant's menu made much better and much more truthful reading than the propagandist crap from Honest Herbert and his populist party pals.

What Adrian didn't know as he took the stairs was that for the past ten minutes up in his apartment on the first floor, two skinheads dressed for the part in combat fatigues had been moving swiftly around his empty apartment, pulling things out here, looking there, desperate to find something.

Adrian tore the party-political nonsense in half as he walked up the stairs. As a foreign citizen, he wasn't even allowed a vote anyway.

Up in the living room the two skinheads continued to trash around the place. Every drawer in the room had been emptied, their contents tipped out onto the floor, the armchair and sofa cushions had been thrown into the middle of the room. The skinheads were about to head into the kitchen when they stopped dead in their tracks. They'd heard the sound of Adrian's key going into the lock. They clearly hadn't planned nor expected company. Neither of the intruders were what you might call physically intimidating, apart from their haircuts and clothing – skinhead attire always screams out "bother" – and of course the obligatory Doc Marten boots. One of the boneheads had a few kilos too many, the other a few too few and he was a good six inches shorter. It was the skinny one who picked up the same vase that Adrian had picked up himself the previous night to confront what turned out to be Andrej from the upstairs flat – the other skinhead picked up a brass candle-stick holder which had been tossed onto the floor – and they took up their positions either side of the door. When it opened and Adrian entered, almost in one movement, he was whacked over the head with the candle-stick holder and dragged straight into the living room.

He managed to break free of the shorter of the two skinheads and rolled the other off over his shoulder, smashing him against the wall. The candle-stick holder fell out of his grasp. They were straight back on him, but Adrian's strength and power were way too much for them. He fought like a demon as the three of them went tumbling and crashing through the room like something out of a Bond movie, with tables and chairs flying, and carried their death fight into the bedroom. Adrian had the upper hand. He was raining punches down on the smaller skinhead when, from behind him, the other one reached for the bedside table lamp which they'd knocked onto the floor in the struggle and crashed it down hard on the back of Adrian's head. For a moment he was stunned. And it was that moment that they dragged him half-conscious into the bathroom and shoved his head into the toilet and flushed it.

"*Wo sind die Kranzschleifen?*" the bigger skinhead screamed into his ear.

They pulled his head up out of the toilet just enough to get his answer.

"I... I don't know what..."

His head was pushed back down and kept there, staring down into the toilet bowl while the water still flowed.

A few yards away, in the hallway, Adrian's front door, which hadn't been fully shut when they'd dragged Adrian inside, swung slowly open and Andrej the upstairs drunk lurched in, in his usual bewildered, inebriated state with a half-empty beer bottle in his hand. He keeled over onto the hallway floor – the old dog hadn't yet learned a new trick – and the bottle smashed when he hit the deck.

In the bathroom, Adrian's head was once more pulled up out of the toilet bowl.

"The ribbons... WHERE ARE THEY?" the bigger skinhead screamed at Adrian, this time in English.

Before Adrian could splutter out his answer Andrej had staggered into the bathroom holding the jagged remains of his bottle. He stood and filled the entire door frame. To anyone who didn't know him, and to many who did, the giant Ukrainian wall of muscle certainly looked fierce and menacing. The skinheads looked over at him. In tandem with Adrian he was an extra problem that they really didn't fancy handling. One nodded to the other and they immediately released Adrian and made a break past the startled Andrej and straight out of the apartment.

Two minutes later Adrian stood and surveyed the wreckage of his ransacked apartment. It was a total mess. On the floor over by the window lay the photograph of Adrian and his father sailing together. The glass had been shattered and shards of broken glass covered the floor. His mind flashed back to the moment that his father told him he wouldn't be coming sailing with him anymore. There had been tears in his eyes when he said it because at that moment his world was shattered into pieces too.

Adrian turned and went back into the bathroom, got into the shower, turned the control fully to the right and let the jets of freezing cold water bounce off him.

6

From two hundred yards away on the other side of the street someone was watching the entrance to Katharina's flat through small binoculars. It was about four-thirty in the afternoon when they saw Adrian stride furiously up to the building. Gone was the old walk full of calm, languid grace. This was one which had at its heart seething anger. He held his finger on the bell until someone finally answered and stormed in when the door opened for him. He had a cut below his eye, a bruised chin, and he was raging inside.

Up on the second floor, when Katharina opened her apartment door, Adrian started in immediately. He was referring to how he looked. "Look what your curiosity has…"

Katharina stopped him in his tracks by dragging him off by the arm into the kitchen. Lying lifelessly on a bloody blanket in the middle of the kitchen floor was the cat. Its throat had been sliced open.

"Congratulations," she said to him. The tears she'd shed earlier in the day had by then been replaced by anger. "That's what your e-mail achieved. You and your *verdammter Nazischeiss—*"

Adrian's black mood became even blacker. "Woah. Whose Nazi crap? And whose letter? 'Cause I don't think it was me who kicked this whole *hardly legal* mess off."

"You came to me with it. You wanted me to help."

"What?"

"That's the truth and you know it."

"And how exactly was this helping?"

She shot him a defiant look. But it was the look of someone who knew she was in a nightmare of all her own making.

The look wasn't lost on Adrian. He moved towards her. "Listen, I'm sorry, Katharina, but…"

She surprised herself by pulling away from him.

Adrian studied her a moment. It all became tense, awkward, cold. There was suddenly a distance between them. Adrian realised she was either too proud or too stubborn to concede anything right then.

"Okay, okay." He turned away from her and headed towards the door. As he was opening it to leave he said to her, "Email them and say they've been sold... say anything. I don't care. Just make sure they know you don't have them. You call me when you want to."

And with that he was gone.

He returned to the mess of his ransacked apartment thirty minutes later and to the sound of a ringing phone in the hallway. He closed the flat door and picked up the receiver.

"Hello?"

"*Herr Kramer*?" The voice asked, and pronounced Kramer the German way, as in farmer.

"Kray-mer," Adrian corrected him.

"*Entschuldigung. Sprechen Sie lieber Deutsch oder Englisch?*" The voice asked in a Swiss accent.

"Preferably English. Who is this?"

"I'd like to purchase your wreath ribbons."

"I have no wreath ribbons."

"We don't believe you've sold them. Otherwise you'd have sold to the highest bidder. That was ours."

"Who is this?"

"We'll pay you two hundred thousand euros for them."

"How did you get this number? Who are you?"

"Or else name your price. My organisation will—"

"I have no idea what you're talking about."

Then the voice developed a more menacing tone to it. "What do they mean to you that two hundred thousand euros doesn't? You will sell to us or—"

"I don't have any ribbons. Leave me alone or I'll call the

Police."

"You won't call the—"

Adrian slammed down the phone and stared off across the hall at nothing at all. Just like Katharina, he knew then that he too was stuck in a nightmare all of his own making.

* * *

The next morning at work Adrian looked tired, he looked drawn, he looked as if he hadn't slept in a week, he had worry etched into his fine features and the scars and bruises on his face told a story of his troubles. He certainly looked far from the cool, in-control teacher that he'd always prided himself on being. He stood at the back of the class, looking vaguely out of the window down into the pedestrian zone below while the eleven girls and Mario wrote away in their exercise books. He didn't even hear the girl sitting close to the window when she asked him, "Should this be past simple or continuous?" Because Adrian's thoughts right then were a million miles away.

"Adrian?" the student said, this time a little louder.

It snapped him back to attention. "Erm... Just a minute," he said to her vacantly and walked straight out of the room, leaving behind him one very confused and surprised student.

He hurried into the teachers' room. It was empty. Then, hating, and now fearing what was at the back of his locker behind the pile of text books, he reached in and removed the velvet bag.

* * *

Later that day, while Adrian was heading out into the Hamburg suburbs, Jacob was sitting in the Director's office telling tales. He had been sniffing the air and what he smelled was opportunity. "I overheard one of his students," he told Goldberg. "She said he walked out in the middle of the lesson this morning. No explanation. He walked out just like that," Jacob said and snapped his fingers. "You can't do that. It's just not professional, it's not *verantwortlich*." And there it was, the obligatory German word slipped right in, which no sentence from Jacob was ever complete without. He looked hard into Goldberg's face for a reaction to what he'd just told him. While he was making his pitch for Jermaine's old job, he was also doing his worst on Dixon's behalf, telling the boss that he was "too sexual, too blatant with it, far too 'out'", as if who you choose to sleep with was a job qualification. "And I've heard that he's even used the 'F-word' in class. They're not comfortable with him," Jacob told Goldberg, which was a lie. The students all loved Dixon.

* * *

Werner was on his mobile phone when he opened the door to Adrian; he broke into a broad smile when he saw who was standing on the doorstep. Adrian pushed in past him, stone-faced, with his satchel slung over his shoulder. A fat white cat trotted in behind him. It had been Werner's wife's cat but she'd left it with Werner when she moved out, and over the past weeks it had got too fat and way too lazy to use the cat flap which they'd built for it in the kitchen. Adrian nearly stepped on it when he was striding up Werner's hallway. It felt like everywhere he looked that late-springtime there was a damned cat somewhere in his way. Werner closed the door and followed Adrian and the cat into the living room.

"That's right. With breakfast. Many thanks. Goodbye," Werner said in German into the phone then hung up. "I'm going on a two-day seminar. In Keilsbach," he explained to Adrian, except that Adrian didn't have the vaguest idea where Keilsbach was and Werner could see straight away that Adrian had other things on his mind. Before Werner could ask or say more, Adrian reached down into his satchel and pulled out the velvet bag, and from it the two wreath ribbons. He held them out for Werner to take.

"However you explain this at work, just leave me out of it, okay?"

Werner stood and stared disbelievingly down at the two pieces of old Nazi silk in his hands. It was as if he'd just been handed a million dollars.

"You're giving them to us?"

Adrian nodded. "You were right. They've been a lot more trouble than they're worth. And believe me, I know now just how much they're worth."

"What do you mean? You actually tried to sell them?"

"Not me. It's a long story. I'll tell you some other time."

"But you had offers?"

"A top bid of two hundred thousand."

"What! Who from?"

"Someone who was representing some organisation."

"What sort of organisation?"

"I don't know. 'Bernd O' he called himself. We spoke in English. But from the German he started with, I think he sounded Swiss. I hung up on him."

Werner looked down again at the two ribbons, unsure how to react to now having them. Then he pulled Adrian close and hugged him particularly tightly. "Let me take them upstairs," he said excitedly. Adrian handed him the burgundy velvet bag too and watched as Werner bounced out of the room like a birthday boy who had just been given his best ever present.

* * *

Later, back at his flat with a heavy weight now lifted, Adrian picked up the phone in his hallway and dialled a number.

Katharina was still at work at the newspaper offices in the

city at the time. She looked at her mobile and saw who was calling. She hesitated before answering, then she finally thought better of it and let it ring out.

On the other end of his non-call, Adrian hung up, disappointed. He was heading for the living room when the phone rang. He turned back and picked it up. "Hello?"

"Hi. You called?" It was Katharina's voice.

"Yeah. I-I was just wondering..." Suddenly, he had absolutely no idea what should come next.

Katharina came to his rescue and broke the ice. "How about Friday evening? I don't seem to know my future continuous from my future perfect anymore."

Friday sounded just fine to Adrian. He hung up and broke into a smile. Despite himself, and as much as he wanted to deny it and as much as he tried to resist it, he was growing fond of his private student. From the way she talked and the way she walked when she came into the room, from the way she looked over her cup when she drank his coffee and how she pulled the stray strand of hair out of her eyes when she did it. He even loved her curiosity and the questions that she kept firing at him. He loved the way her long slender fingers...

Stop it Adrian. Stop it. You know where this always leads.

7

Adrian breezed into the secretary's office at school the next morning smiling to himself, looking like he was once more beginning to feel good about life.

"Adrian, I have someone here who wants to join one of our 'Cambridge' classes," Renate the school secretary said to him. The Cambridge classes were for students who wanted to sit one of the Cambridge exams, which would give them a Certificate to prove they had attained a certain level of proficiency in the language, and all good language schools offer courses to study for the Cambridge Certificate as part of their standard programme.

Sitting across the desk from Renate was a man in his late seventies, perhaps early eighties. He was marked by a quiet dignity, and had a shy but kind and friendly face which you couldn't help but like. His hair, once dark, was now thin and greying. "Here is his placement test," Renate said to Adrian and handed him a form which the old man had already filled in, from which Adrian could see what standard his English was and whether he would fit into the class. "If you could test his spoken English?" Renate asked.

"Sure."

Adrian scanned quickly through the test as he led the old man into a small adjoining room, usually used for one-on-one lessons, where they sat down at each side of a small table.

"And you're one of the teachers... Adrian Kramer, I think she told me?"

"Kray-mer," Adrian corrected him.

"Sorry," said the old man. He held out his hand for Adrian to shake. "I'm Wolfgang Nord."

Adrian shook his hand, returned his friendly smile, and could see that the old man was a little nervous. "Don't worry.

This won't hurt. Your written test looks good."

"Thank you."

"Where are you from?"

"Berlin. And you?"

"The north-east of England."

"You have a German name."

"My father was German."

"Was?"

"He died eleven years ago."

"Oh. I'm sorry. May I ask how he died?"

"He had Motor Neuron Disease... I think it's called ALS here in Germany."

Wolfgang Nord's facial expression changed. He knew the illness. "Then your family went through a lot, I'm sure," he said and clearly appeared moved by Charlie Kramer's fate.

"We certainly did," Adrian told him.

"Do you have brothers or sisters?"

"No."

"Where was your father from?"

"Hannover," Adrian said, but it came out then with a little uncertainty and he even felt like adding "but I'm damned if I know if that's right anymore", but he thought better of it.

"And when did he move to England?"

"About nineteen sixty-two... maybe sixty-three."

"With his family?"

"No. Alone. His family were all killed in the war."

Wolfgang Nord took a packet of mints out of his pocket. His mouth had become dry. He offered one to Adrian. Adrian took it and said a quiet "thanks".

"So, you have no relations here in Germany?"

As the questions kept coming, Adrian became acutely aware once more of just how shallow his knowledge of his father and his background was. "No. None that I know of," he answered.

"What did..." He was unsure of the phrase so he said it

quietly to himself in German while his brain, or his memory, tried to play catch up. *"Was war er von Beruf?"* "What..."

"He was an engineer. In shipbuilding."

"He liked ships, and the sea?"

"He sailed. He loved the sea."

"The secretary told me you don't speak German."

"Not in the lesson. And not much out of the lesson either."

"Your father never taught you German?"

"No."

As Adrian looked back at Wolfgang for a studied moment, the old man realised he was making Adrian uneasy. "I'm sorry. I'm asking you too many questions."

"It's okay. Let's quickly go through the test, shall we?"

Wolfgang smiled, nodded, and offered Adrian another mint. It appeared that a bond was forming, and that Adrian might have acquired a new member for his own Monday evening Cambridge class.

* * *

The next day was a Thursday, and early in the afternoon when he arrived home after his morning classes, Adrian saw that Werner had left a message on his answering machine on the hallway landline and had asked him to call him back. And when Adrian did it wasn't good news. In fact, it was another bombshell that Werner dropped on him. "The birth certificate that you gave me," Werner told him, "your father's. It was a forgery. A very good one and hardly detectable, but still a forgery. But it was good enough it seems, to have convinced the British authorities."

It took a suspended moment for the news to sink in. But still Adrian couldn't believe what Werner had just told him. "That can't be true."

"Sadly, it is. I'm sorry, Adrian."

Adrian hung up. What do you do with that information? How do you process it? Adrian decided to get out of the flat and he went walking to clear his head, to think straight, or to try to. It overwhelmed him. And the questions kept coming. Who was my father really? Why did he have Reinhard Heydrich's wreath ribbons and what did it mean? What was he hiding from us and why? Why did he lie to us? They were questions which Adrian knew he'd never have the answers to, and the challenge now was to put it behind him. To move on. It is how it is he told himself, and he knew that could do nothing about it anymore, so let's put it all in a drawer and close the drawer and never take it out again was the conclusion he came to.

He made his way through the city streets and along its canals and waterways –that was the thing that Adrian loved about Hamburg, that it was a maritime city and you were never too far from water – it was a sailor's city. He walked on through St Pauli and its gaudy flashing neon, even in the bright light of daytime, and on past the cheap thirty-euro hookers and the other more exotic pretty things who turned their tricks in the seedy live-sex shops, and the clichéd pit-bull pimps who were never too far away from them, and the winos and the junkies and the groups of eastern Europeans with their flat brown caps who hung around the street corners smoking cheap cigarettes and drinking supermarket wine out of plastic bottles. He came to the cordoned off rubble and ashes which had once been Ahmed's Shisha Bar and Lounge, where two bulldozers had already begun the work of tearing it down. And he thought for a moment about Jermaine and how he'd nearly died there, but also how he'd once got his kicks in the streets of St Pauli and he wondered where Jermaine was now and what he was doing and whether his mother was okay, and he thought he really should try and get in touch with him once he'd cleared his head. And he felt sorry for Jermaine and Jermaine's mum, and sorry for all the two-bit whores who he passed and the tramps raking in the bins near Millerntorplatz. But mostly he felt sorry for himself, and he hated that more than he hated anything – self-pity for Adrian was the refuge of the pathetic.

Eventually he came to the Alsters – the two artificial lakes which lay at the heart of the city, where he often went running to clear his head. But now all he wanted to do was to jump right into the water, sink right down, and only come back up to the surface when he knew that everything which had happened to him hadn't really been true and it had all just been part of some mad surrealistic fantasy. A young punk wearing an old, dirty woollen hat, even in early June, stopped him and asked him for some money – an hour earlier he'd been stealing the post from people's letterboxes – but Adrian just shook his head – today wasn't the day. Besides, he had no money with him anyway. The punk turned away and Adrian saw his arse hanging out of the hole in the back of his jeans as he began to hook bottles out of a row of green, brown and white bottle banks and push them into his plastic Netto bag. There but for the grace of God… Adrian thought to himself before he headed off towards the emotional wasteland of home wondering just how bad a day can get.

He found out just how bad a day can get when he finally got back to Borgfelder Strasse and his heart sank further. Someone had taken a knife and sliced clean through the canvas soft top of his Mini's roof. They'd also dropped a small envelope through the gap that they'd opened up in the roof. In the envelope was a typed note which read: "You will sold at us." It had been written in the name of a proscribed Italian fascist group, the NNDI. Adrian crumpled the note up and tossed it and the envelope into the waste bin in the hallway on his way up to his flat.

8

The sounds of the city at night drifted in through the open living room window. Someone sounded a car horn, someone's baby cried, someone shouted to someone, and somewhere in the distance a police siren wailed. Faraway trains and planes were heading for faraway places – or maybe it was just a distant S-Bahn rattling off to another Hamburg suburb... that's the romance of it, you never know, you only guess or dream. The two local cats were probably out there somewhere too, getting up to their usual tomcat tomfoolery, but Adrian wasn't interested in any of that, nor was he in the mood for dreaming. He sat on the living room floor with his back propped up against the sofa, marking papers. It was a warm evening and a light wind moved the side curtains ever so slightly. Across the other side of the room the television was on but the sound was off and Adrian briefly looked up from his papers to see that the eight o'clock news was just starting. More stories about more refugees flooding into the country from across its open eastern borders, more pictures of rubber boats full of black men in orange safety jackets bobbing up and down in the Mediterranean Sea, more images of the regular Pegida anti-immigration-anti-Islam protest marches in the east German cities, more politicians playing politics – let them in, keep them out, welcome them, send them packing – with nothing ever really being achieved. That was how it was back then.

Dixon had stopped Adrian on his way out of school earlier that day to tell him that one of their students had super-glued Goldberg's office door shut because he'd failed her in an exam which she'd had to retake. He laughed when he told Adrian the story. He also pushed two complimentary tickets into Adrian's hand and invited him to go and watch him and his band later that evening at the Lampenputzer, a music club slap bang in the heart of St Pauli. Dressing up as Cabaret's Oscar-winning MC at the language school wasn't Dixon's grandest moment. He saved that for his Freddie Mercury role fronting a Queen tribute band. Galileo Figaro they called themselves, and they were good. Dixon would squeeze into his tight white leggings, stick a hairy wig onto his chest and a thick, downwards-pointing handlebar moustache onto his top lip which Adrian thought made him look more like the singer from the Village People than Queen's deceased frontman. "Don't come too late, sweety," Dixon had told him with his sauciest smile when he gave Adrian the tickets. But what Werner had told Adrian earlier in the day, as well as having his car roof sliced open and the offer from the Italian fascist group had hit him hard and he was in no real mood that night to "do the fandango" and he chose to stay home instead and catch up on some work.

But two things happened that evening which were significant. The first was that directly after the television reports about the Pegida marches the images of the two skinheads who had once raided Adrian's flat for the wreath ribbons filled the screen. Adrian reached for the remote to turn on the sound. He got up smartly off the ground and stood directly in front of the television and listened to a report about the skinheads being arrested for a petrol bomb attack on a local Turkish imbiss the previous weekend, which they had tried to disguise as an attack by Kurdish PKK militants. Two people had been killed in the attack – the Turkish owner and his eighteen-year-old cousin, who helped him out on a Saturday evening. The two skinheads were also being linked to another attack that same night only a few miles away in the town of Ahrensburg where a Syrian refugee had been doused in petrol and burned alive. But as hard as they tried, the Hamburg police hadn't been able to pin the recent bombing of Ahmed's Shisha Bar and Lounge on the two – CCTV evidence clearly showed them in a Bremen pool hall the whole night and until the early hours of that morning – and it would be some time before the shisha bar killers were finally brought to justice.

Adrian turned off the television and sat back down on the ground to carry on with his work. But he couldn't. He thought about what he'd just heard and he was sickened: man, it had been some day. It had been some "bad news" day. A gust of early summer wind lifted the top couple of papers off the pile on the floor next to him. Adrian got back up and closed the window. He picked up the stray papers and put them back in their place on the pile and went into the kitchen to make himself a coffee. He'd just got into the kitchen when the second big thing that evening happened and the phone in the hallway rang. He crossed back through the living room and into the hall to answer it. "Hello?"

The voice he heard was in English but with a strong German accent. It was a hard voice, a voice which he'd never heard before, and as he listened to it his ground began to shake.

"Herr Kramer, we have someone who needs to speak to you."

It was followed by a garbled, rustling sound, and then Katharina's distraught, desperate voice pleading with him "Adrian. Just do what they say!"

What Adrian didn't know was that she was speaking to him from a small, dark windowless room in a remote forest hut. Her legs and arms had been bound tightly to a chair with thick electrician's tape. Her head was covered by a thick black hood made of coarse canvas which had been raised only as high as her mouth in order to let her speak. "Do it. Or they'll—"

The hand which had been holding the stolen mobile phone to Katharina's mouth jerked it away from her as another man's hands forced a black cloth gag back into her mouth, fixed the gag in place, then pulled her hood back down and tied it around the neck with a length of cord. A set of headphones were then placed over her ears.

"—Or we'll kill her," the voice at the other end of the phone told Adrian. It was another voice he'd never heard before, not as hard as the first and with much less of an accent. But in its softer tone it sounded even more threatening.

The hut was a part of an old mill and the mill's giant waterwheel creaked and groaned as it turned its circles. Next to the stream which ran alongside the mill a black, top-of-the-range Mercedes with black-tinted windows had been parked.

"We want the two ribbons," the voice said.

Adrian stood in the hallway with the phone pressed to his ear and looked numb. It felt as if he was playing a role in someone else's movie. This wasn't his own life, surely. "I-I don't have the ribbons," he stammered out. "I honestly don't have them."

"Then get them. You have until nine o'clock. Not a minute longer. And no Police. Or we'll kill you both. One hour. And the clock is already ticking."

Then the line went dead. Adrian too. Everything was beginning to spiral right out of control. He was living the perfect storm. His mind was racing. But he was too confused to be in a real state of total panic just yet. He immediately hit some buttons on his phone.

In a hotel somewhere in the country an overnight bag lay on a single bed. A muffled ringing sound came from inside the bag. Then there was a click and Werner's recorded voice told his callers: "Werner Retz. Ich bin leider…"

Adrian hung up and quickly tapped out another number. "Be there… be there," he said out loud to himself.

All the shutters were down at Werner's house in the Hamburg suburbs and the street was its usual quiet self. But if you'd listened hard you just might have been able to make out the faint sounds of the phone ringing in Werner's hallway close to the front door. But no one was around that evening at Werner's place to take that call.

And no one answered the ringing phone in Werner's office either when Adrian tried his work number too. He let it ring for a good minute, until the answering machine message kicked in, and then he hung up.

Moments later Adrian's red Mini flew through the Hamburg streets, staying in the outside lane, hurtling carelessly past everything else and letting nothing at all go past it. The top of his convertible was up and it all suddenly felt claustrophobic, even though the material where the car roof had been sliced open flapped around and made a weird whistling noise inside the car. He'd tried to repair the cut earlier with some tape, which he hoped would suffice until he could get it into the garage, but at speed the tape had peeled away and had left a gaping hole where the wind now rushed in. He felt as if he was being pressed down into his seat by an overpowering and irresistible weight from somewhere up above him. He looked like he couldn't breathe. Barely on four wheels, he took a right turn and shot through a red light, just avoiding an oncoming motor bike. Inside of his own prison-cell of a car Adrian hammered down hard on his car horn and gestured for anything in his way to get the hell out of it. It was all becoming frantic. He was in deep shit now and he knew it.

The Mini finally screeched to a halt in Werner's driveway some minutes later. Adrian jumped out and stood with his finger pressing down hard on the front doorbell, while at the same time he banged on the door with his clenched fist. But no one really was at home that evening.

Minutes later, in the street outside of the museum, the Mini screeched to a halt right next to a "No Parking" sign with two of the Mini's wheels well over the pavement. As he sprinted up to the main entrance, he could see that there were several lights on inside the building. He looked up at Werner's office window – one of the rooms which were still lit up – so he knew that someone must be up there. He tried the building's main glass double-doors. But they were locked, just as they always were at that time in the evening. He pressed a bell next to the museum's

95

big brass nameplate and a buzzer sounded inside. But he could see through the glass anyway that there was no one at the unlit reception desk to answer it.

Then in the background one of the office cleaners appeared from around a corner. She was carrying a red bucket and a mop. Adrian banged like a madman on the glass door and got her attention. But she just looked at him, then looked away and wandered off down one of the corridors which led off the main museum entrance. She wasn't paid enough to deal with crazed callers at weird times of the night, nor save pretty journalists' lives. She'd just get on with her business of keeping things clean and tidy, thank you very much. Adrian started to bang again on the door even harder, ever more desperately – just as the cleaner returned with her bucket and mop. Alongside her was the museum's burly security night-watchman. He stood at the other side of the door and stared into Adrian's anxious face. The cleaner stood right behind the security guard and listened in. Curiosity or boredom, it didn't matter to her which. This might turn out to be a story which she could tell her husband later when she got back home, and you don't get too many of those when you go cleaning offices.

Adrian fought to stay as composed and as collected as he could. He shouted to the security guard through the door.

"I need to speak to someone. It's urgent," he called out in his weak and broken German.

"*Bitte?*" the night-watchman asked. He hadn't a clue what Adrian had just said to him.

"*Werner Retz. Ist er hier? Wichtig! Dringend!*"

The guard grabbed the thick bunch of keys which were dangling off his belt – there must have been twenty keys on it – and used one of them to unlock the main double-doors.

Adrian spat out in English. "There's still someone working up in Werner Retz's office. I have to speak to them. Please?" He was breathing hard by then and the sides of his temples were beginning to dampen.

He took the stairs four at a time and up in Werner's office a few short moments later he stood and watched as Werner's over-tired, overworked colleague – the one with the tight blonde braids who he had met only once before – rake through Werner's desk and cabinet. She turned and looked over at him and shook her head. "Sorry. No," she said to him and added "In any case, everything like that has to be officially registered." She nodded at the glowing computer screen. "There's no record of anything like that in the system."

"When's Werner coming back?" The sweat really was pouring out of Adrian now. His shirt was sticking to his back. His brow was a sea of perspiration.

"Tomorrow evening."

If it was possible, Adrian's heart sank even further and it's boom, boom, boom pounding got even louder. "What's the name of the hotel?"

"Is there a problem?" Werner's colleague asked him. She could see for herself Adrian's despair and his growing agitation.

"JUST GIVE ME THE NAME OF HIS HOTEL, DAMN IT!" he barked out at her.

"He's at the Kaiserhof," she told him, a little intimidated but also affronted by his attitude and his manners. "And if you—" she was about to admonish him but before she could say another word Adrian had turned and was heading for the stairs.

He hurried towards his car parked in the street outside the museum. What the hell do I do now? his inner voice was screaming out to him. But he stopped dead before he could think anymore. A Police car was parked directly in front of his Mini and a uniformed officer was peering through the Mini's side window. Adrian stood for a frozen moment. His mind was again racing. He was, at that moment, locked in his own personal hell, and directly ahead of him was someone who could offer him a possible way out. But at what cost? Someone's life? And what could he possibly tell them? What did he know about the people who held Katharina captive and where they were holding her anyway? And the clock really was ticking. He watched the Policeman walk around his car, glance up at the "No Parking" sign right next to it, and then down at the two wheels over the pavement. The cop then looked up and saw Adrian staring straight at him.

"Is this your car?" he asked in German.

"Yes, I—" Adrian replied, also in German.

Then he stopped. He was lost in one of those epic "should I, or shouldn't I?" moments. After a tense, agonising beat, a decision had been made. The only one that he knew made any sense. He took a step forward towards the officer. Stay cool Adrian. Stay calm. Tell him what you have to tell him and it will all be fine, he told himself.

"I'm sorry. I had to collect something urgently from the museum. I was only here a couple of minutes."

The Policeman took in Adrian's nervousness. "Is something wrong?"

"No, I... I'm really sorry."

The Policeman's mobile phone rang. From what he'd been told he said in to it, "Right. We're on the way." Then he turned back to Adrian. "Don't let me see you parked like that here again, okay?"

Adrian nodded and watched the Policeman head quickly back to his colleague behind the wheel of the squad car and jump in alongside him, and the squad car then pulled smartly away. Adrian looked down at his watch. It was ten minutes to nine. Ten minutes to Katharina's death. Maybe just ten minutes to his own death too. What the fuck do I do now? the voice inside his head screamed out at him again, but this time much louder, much more urgent, and now much more desperate. He jumped quickly into the car, a shaking hand shoved the key into the ignition, and the red Mini roared off into the Hamburg night.

9

All that Adrian could remember about his crazed chase back across the city that night was that with every single breath he cursed Reinhard Heydrich's two wreath ribbons and having ever set eyes on them. They'd taken away everything from him. They'd demolished the perfect vision that he'd had of his father. They'd torn down his own defences and destroyed everything that he had built up in order to protect himself. Now they were threatening to take the life of Katharina and probably even his own if he didn't get his hands on them. The ribbons had dragged him into a nightmare which he had no idea how to wake up from. He was angry. He was afraid. And he was alone with it all. There was no one to turn to, no one to offer a helping hand, no cavalry were going to charge over the hill to save him. But wasn't that how he wanted it? Wasn't that what he'd been planning for and working towards – his independence, his non-reliance, his self-determination? Hadn't he promised to himself that no matter what the challenge or how high they built the wall in front of him he'd rise above it and rise up over it? And that he'd do it alone. But this here, this was no challenge. This was nothing at all except pure hell. This was life and death and it hadn't been in the plan at all. But hadn't he faced that before, this question of "do I help someone to live or help them to die?" Hadn't he once lived with that for months on end, and then for the eleven years after? I'm just a normal, regular guy damn it, trying to do normal, regular things, his inner voice screamed out. What the hell did I do to deserve all this? He brought his palm down hard on the steering wheel and stamped down even harder on the accelerator. The lampposts and the advertising hoardings went whizzing past. The world outside the windscreen was all just a blur. A huge roadside billboard showed a crunched-up car and the image of a teary, mourning wife and her small daughter and the stern warning in big bold letters that "Speed Kills. Slow Down", which was no option at all for Adrian. He was in a mad race to *save* someone's life – and possibly even his own, not a race to end it. He looked at the clock on the Mini's dashboard. It was two minutes to nine.

Three minutes later, although it might have even been a whole lifetime for all Adrian knew, his car screeched to a halt in Borgfelder Strasse directly outside of his flat. He leapt out almost before it had come to a stop. He shot up the stairs like a demented idiot and let himself into the apartment. When he got inside, the hall telephone was already ringing. He snatched it off the cradle.

"The *Stuhlmannbrunnen*, the fountain in Altona," the voice said to him in English. It was the softer of the two voices which had spoken to him earlier. "Go there and wait for—"

"I don't have them. I need more time."

"*WOLLEN SIE UNS VERARSCHEN*?" the caller howled down the phone. It was suddenly a different animal that Adrian was dealing with. He knew what the German phrase meant: "Are you trying to take the piss?"

"You'll get them," Adrian said. There was sheer desperation and a tremor in his voice now. He'd never been that afraid in his life before. "I- I promise you. Just give me—"

Right then, in the background, he heard Katharina's frantic, piercing screams, muffled by the gag in her mouth, and over it the voice told him "You have until midnight."

"I need longer. I—"

The caller lowered his voice back to little more than a whisper, which only made it sound even more ominous and threatening. "Midnight. Or you are both dead."

Then there was just a dialling tone as the line too went dead.

Adrian stood for a moment. What in God's name do I do now?

What he actually did was again take the stairs four at a time and jump back into his car. He gunned it off up the Borgfelder Strasse and in the direction of the autobahn, which would take him out of the city. Once calm, cool and cautious, he was now a crazed, outside-lane driver flying like a madman past the few other cars which were also heading east out of the city.

He took out his mobile phone from his pocket and hit speed dial. "Come on, Werner... ANSWER!"

But no one was listening.

"Call me back, call me back immediately if you hear this, Werner," he shouted into the phone then tossed it onto the passenger seat and looked down at his watch. "He has to be there," he said to no one but himself and once more out loud, then he looked down yet again at his watch. A full seven seconds had passed since the last time he'd looked. Fucking ribbons! Fucking Heydrich! Fucking—

He stamped down hard on his brake. The light had by then begun to fade and Adrian hadn't seen the old lady who had stepped out into the zebra crossing without looking. The Mini screeched and swerved to a stop only millimetres short of hitting her. There were black skid marks left on the road behind it. The old lady just stood there in the middle of the road in shock and looked in through the windscreen at Adrian. His car was almost touching her leg. But all Adrian did was reverse a couple of yards, drive around her, and shoot off up the road. She was alive. Someone else soon wouldn't be if he couldn't get his hands on the ribbons. The damned ribbons!

* * *

The Kaiserhofv was about five miles out of Keilsbach and was a picture of old-world charm. It was a fine, timber-framed, four-star hotel set back from the main road and hidden by lines of tall conifers and poplar trees. It was the kind of hidden gem of a place where a person could disappear and nobody would ever know.

Adrian's car roared up the gravel driveway and came to a stop right behind a police car which was parked directly outside of the main entrance. He raced up to the reception, asked for Werner Retz, and could hardly believe what the Thai receptionist behind the old oak desk who was working the evening shift had just told him.

"WHAT!"

"If you'll wait a moment, I'll get the manager. He'll explain it to you," the receptionist told him in her cute Thai accent and two minutes later Adrian sat in the manager's office and heard it for himself. The manager was short and round and was probably in some sort of decent shape once, but that would have been twenty years earlier, about the same time that his dark blue suit might have fitted him, but only "might have". He loosened his tie and unbuttoned the top button on his shirt and his chubby hand resting on the desk in front of him shook a little when he spoke to Adrian. He looked like he could really have done without that particular problem on that particular day when all he wanted was to be home with his wife or his mistress – anywhere in fact and with anyone, but not right there right then.

"The Police said that Herr Retz's car crashed through the barrier at the approach to the Keilsbach bridge," he told Adrian. "I'm terribly sorry Herr...?"

"And Werner?" Adrian asked, ignoring the question.

"I don't think they have recovered the body yet."

What he went on to tell Adrian was that earlier that evening, or possibly late in the afternoon – although he couldn't tell Adrian at what time exactly – a crane had pulled Werner's car out of the river at Keilsbach bridge, about three kilometres further down the road from the hotel. The car had skidded off the road – the Police still hadn't established how Werner had lost control – and it smashed clean through the metal barrier at one end of Keilsbach bridge and rolled down the embankment into the river.

"The car caught fire before it hit the water," the hotel manager told him. "The detective who I spoke to said that it was very unlikely that anyone could have survived."

The detective also told Adrian that police frogmen had been searching the river, but so far without success. The hotel manager knew for himself that the river Keil was fast-flowing and fairly full at that time of the year and that's what he told Adrian.

"If you'll wait a moment, I'll get Detective Geissinger to tell you more," he said to Adrian, seeing that he was distressed at the news, although he could have had no idea what the distress really meant.

Adrian watched the portly hotel manager struggle up out of his seat and waddle across his office towards the door. He was about to close it behind him when the receptionist appeared and Adrian heard her tell him in her sweet Thai accent that "Frau Eckert from the 'Nordwestdeutscher' is back again." (The Nordwestdeutscher was the regional daily newspaper.) "What should I tell her?"

The hotel manager puffed out his flabby cheeks and then slowly let out a long, exasperated breath of air. "Okay. I'll see her. Has she spoken to Geissinger yet?"

"No."

The manager poked his head back around the door. "I'm sorry, this won't take too long," he said to Adrian, which really meant "I'm sorry, but this might take some time" and he shuffled off with the Thai receptionist.

What Adrian had just heard about his friend Werner had been the very last and the very worst news that he could ever have expected to hear. While the hotel manager was off somewhere in the building trying his best to tell Frau Eckert from the local rag absolutely nothing at all – which hotel needed that kind of publicity? – Adrian got up out of his seat and began to pace around the room like a caged tiger. He was now all out of nerves, running fast out of time, all out of options, and worst of all, now all out of hope. He went to the office door, exited the room, and walked back into the reception, where no one was around. The whole reception area smelled strongly of lavender, although he hadn't noticed it when he'd first come in. At the desk he looked left and then right, and then sure that no one was coming, he spun the computer screen around and read that a "Retz W" was staying in room 213. He knew that this was now his only chance. He grabbed the ornate brass room key with the number 213 engraved on it, and moved off quickly towards the broad oak staircase.

Room 213 was like any other room 213 in any other hotel in any other country in Europe. Clean, tidy, functional, a television, a fridge, a Bible, a desk, a landscape painting of the pretty local countryside... the usual. Except the furnishings in that room were all old oak and antique, the landscape paintings on the walls were set in beautiful, elaborate frames, it smelled here too of lavender and the bed linen was of the finest, which possibly put it a cut above most of the other 213s and why the Kaiserhof could charge top rates to its guests. Adrian began to rake frantically through all of the room's oak drawers and oak wardrobe, and through Werner's overnight bag lying on the bed, but Werner had left nothing behind him to find anyway. Adrian opened the door to go out... and stood face-to-face with the hotel manager (he never did find out the guy's name). But worse, alongside him was the wily old Detective Geissinger, Keilsbach's finest, Keilsbach's cleverest, Keisbach's canniest – the man who his colleagues on the force had even nicknamed "The Ice Pick" because he was so damned cool and so damned sharp.

"What are you doing in here?" the hotel manager said to Adrian abruptly. He wasn't at all pleased that someone had been snooping around his establishment uninvited.

"I... the key was in the door. Werner has something belonging to me," Adrian managed to stammer out. He was trying to think on his feet. "I'm getting married tomorrow. He has the ring."

The hotel manager looked at Geissinger to see if that made any sense to him, because it sure as hell made none to the hotel manager.

"I think we'd better go down to the office," Detective Geissinger told Adrian and they led him back down the oak staircase.

"Why didn't you ask the manager if you could look in the room?" Geissinger asked while his eyes scanned every bit of Adrian suspiciously. The two of them were alone then in the manager's office. Adrian thought Geissinger looked just like a barn owl with his flat pale face and his hooked nose and big round eyes. All that was missing were a couple of wings and a neck which could rotate a full three hundred and sixty degrees.

"I-I don't know. When he told me about Werner... I couldn't think straight."

He began to fidget in his seat, trying to keep it together. He was agitated, he was nervous. And Geissinger could see it. While the detective's keen mind worked, his fingers worked too, twisting a paper clip cleverly between them.

"And Werner Retz was your..?"

Adrian snapped out the word which Geissinger clearly didn't know and was fishing for. "Best Man. Yes. He was my Best Man. Can I go now?"

Geissinger, more than a little vexed at Adrian's curtness, held Adrian's uneasy look for a tense moment. Then he said "The hotel won't press charges... although they'd be within their right to do so."

Adrian got up out of the office chair, more than desperate to get away. "So, I'm free to go?"

The Detective looked hard at him for a long, intense beat. There was something about Adrian's agitated state which he clearly didn't like and that he wasn't prepared to let go. He motioned him to sit back down. Then he stood up himself, picked up Adrian's ID card from the desk, and headed for the door. "Not till I've run a check on you," he told Adrian and went out.

Left alone in the room, Adrian immediately got back up and once more began to pace the small, cluttered office. He looked at this watch. A fly which had been circling his head the whole time he'd been in the office landed on the manager's desk. Adrian picked up a note pad and slammed it down on the fly. At least it had a quick and painless death Adrian thought, unlike someone he'd once watched die, or the slow drip, drip, drip of what he and Katharina were then going through. He was suffocating. The walls now seemed to be closing in on him, the ceiling was pressing down on him. The muscles in his lower cheek and lip began to twitch. He'd seen the same thing happen to his father when his facial muscles began to die. He slapped himself hard across the face. Get control Adrian. Get a hold of yourself. Truly at the very end of his nerves at that point, he walked over to the door, exited the office, and headed back into reception where Geissinger was standing impatiently at the reception desk alongside a tall uniformed police officer who was so thin you could call him skinny and who looked young enough to have just joined the force fresh out of kindergarten.

"Can I go?" Adrian asked Geissinger and it came out exactly like the desperate plea it was.

Geissinger was still shaking his head when his cell phone rang. Like a shot it was out of his jacket pocket and up against his ear. He listened for a short moment to news which was clearly as disappointing to him as it was surprising. Because he would have just loved to have some reason to detain a guy who looked for all the world like he was guilty of something.

"Well?" Adrian pressed him.

With the phone still pushed up against his ear, Geissinger left

Adrian's question hanging in the air a little longer and eyed him with a dark, disapproving look. The silence was excruciating for Adrian. "Only after we've had you fingerprinted," Geissinger told him and nodded to his colleague to go into action. It was possibly just out of spite, or maybe out of devilment – just so long as it inconvenienced Adrian. It might even have been outside of the laws of the land – Adrian didn't know – but right at that moment he had other things on his mind. He rolled his eyes and muttered a silent "shit" to himself and twisted a full circle on the spot.

It took Geissinger's colleague another thirty-five minutes to fingerprint Adrian. He could have done the job in five but Geissinger didn't like nor trust Adrian one bit and anything that he could do to hold him back from wherever Adrian was so desperate to get to after the Kaiserhof was fine with Geissinger. So "Take your time" was what he told the officer. "Take as long as you want."

While Adrian was waiting they took him back into the manager's office, locked the door from the outside, and left him in there alone. He once more began to pace the room back and forth and his mind turned endless circles, thinking about everything at once in a collision of crazed thoughts, and also nothing at all, in the way that a mind always works in those situations and only chaos seems to survive. It can be a picture of a place, or even just the sound of a word, or the sound of your own voice telling yourself over and over again to do something, and it gets locked in and repeated and repeated in an endless loop of nonsense until you think you're going out of your mind. That's the way it felt for Adrian. The picture which he had in his head right then was of the unlit autobahn flying towards him as seen from the inside of his Mini; the sounds he heard were Katharina's manic screams and her captors' "Or else we'll kill her"; and his vision was the dumb, single word RIBBONS in big bold capital letters and set against a red-orange background. He was going crazy. His head was one big ball of ugly confusion. Most of all he wanted to stop the clock. Or even better, he wanted to turn back its hands. Would fifteen years be okay? Fifteen years and he'd travel back to the days when his life was so easy, so innocent, back to the time when no one had died and no one had been killed – not yet. Even fifteen hours would have been fine. But he knew he was locked into the here-and-now and the evil, out-of-control, downward spiral deep into his own personal hell. He continued to pace the room demented... until the door opened and Geissinger's tall, skinny colleague came back in with his fingerprinting equipment and a laptop. He set it all down on the office desk and went back out again. Tick, tick, tick went the clock and boom, boom, boom went Adrian's heart.

10

The actual fingerprinting itself didn't take longer than three minutes using a digital scanner and the cop's laptop. And when they were finished, he and Geissinger hung around for another five before they finally let Adrian go and even accompanied him to the hotel door and watched him walk over to his car like a man going to his own funeral. More precious time and probably his last chance had now gone. He got into the car, drove to the end of the long driveway where he knew he would be out of sight, stopped and leaned forward against the wheel and buried his head in his hands. Then with a cocktail mix of every possible emotion in his voice he let out a pained "God... Werner!" And for a moment he thought about his good friend and how the end of his life came to him in a ball of flames.

Then he sat back in his seat. "Go back, Adrian" the voice in his head was now telling him. Turn around and go back and tell Geissinger the truth. Why don't I? Because it will take much more time than I have for the Police to trace the calls that the kidnappers made to me and too long to locate the callers – time that we just don't have – because by then Katharina would be dead. I believe those guys. I really do believe them. They'll kill to get their stinking hands on what they want. So think, Adrian, think. But he couldn't. He fired up the engine and raced back towards Hamburg, fighting hard to control the sheer panic which had kicked back in. Then right out of the blue, when he was just four miles out of Keilsbach and speeding down a dark, country road, a thought hit him. It was his one, very last hope to save himself.

* * *

It was already well after eleven o'clock when Adrian parked up in the street outside of Werner's place and jumped the garden gate which for some reason Werner had locked behind him when he'd set off for his seminar at Keilsbach. Just like his own mother's garden on the north-east English coast, Werner's had seen its better days, in this case ever since the day that Werner's wife had run out on him, because the garden and its rose garden was her little domain and death to anyone who dared to interfere with it. The nighttime street was as quiet and as tranquil as it always was. Even in the daytime, where Werner lived it was never more than silent perfection. Adrian began to walk the few yards up the driveway towards the house. It triggered off bright floodlights which immediately bathed the entire garden and driveway in an intense white light. Adrian stood where he'd stopped and waited until the lights had died, then he crept around to the back of the house just like a cat-burglar. He was carrying the small pocket torch which he always kept in the boot of his car, but no swag bag for the jewels. It was pitch black at the back of the house and there was a total, still, eerie silence. He could see that all of the windows had their shutters lowered, and he knew too that Werner had security locks fitted on them from the inside anyway. He moved back to the front of the house with his hand over the front of the torch to mask its bright beam slightly and to avoid drawing attention – not that anyone ever ventured out in Werner's street after eight at night anyway. He shone it onto the front of the garage, which had been built onto the side of the house. The garage door was made of long, wooden lattice panels. Adrian shone his torch up and down one of the wood panels which had, over the years, begun to detach itself from the panel next to it. He pushed three fingers into the gap. Then he used his force to snap the wooden panel free. As it broke away from the door frame there was a loud crack which Adrian thought would have been heard all the way to Berlin and a splinter from the door panel ripped flesh from the side of his hand. He winced in pain. His hand felt numb. He shook it wildly up and down and clenched and unclenched his fist. It hurt like hell. Blood began to flow from the wound. But he had to get in... he simply had to get in. The ribbons were in there and he had to get his hands on them. With one wood panel free he removed more. A second, a third, then a fourth all came free. Soon there was enough for him to be able to squeeze through the narrow gap which he had created and step through it into Werner's garage.

The garage itself was connected to the house by a locked inner door. Adrian removed his hand from the front of the torch and shone it freely around the inside of the garage. In the far corner, among a pile of the usual garage tools, was something which he knew he could use, a large monkey wrench. He went over and got it and in three blows he smashed the lock on the inner garage door which led into the house. He pushed the door open, went through into the house and made his way up to the first floor and into Werner's study. So far, so very, very good.

A near-empty bottle of scotch was still on the ledge of the globe drinks cabinet and next to it was an empty whisky tumbler. Adrian shone his torch around the rest of the room. Its beam of light fell on the crushed-velvet bag, right in the middle of Werner's desk and next to his black Acer laptop. Thank you, God. Salvation at last! He started to move towards it... but stopped dead. From somewhere downstairs he'd heard a loud crashing noise. Then another, and the sound of something breaking. A vase maybe, or crockery? He turned off his torch and stood frozen to the spot. The sound of his own heartbeat was again almost deafening as he waited a few moments, until there was nothing left to hear anymore, and then he switched his torch back on and crept out onto the landing. He looked down over the banister rail at the top of the stairs. Werner's fat white cat trotted silently along the hall.

Adrian finally dared to breathe once again.

He returned to the study and picked up the velvet bag from

the desk. It felt way too light and way too full of nothing. He opened it. But he knew even before he did that it was empty. He searched frantically through Werner's desk, and then all the other drawers and cabinets in the room. But there was nothing there to find. It was the same in all of the other rooms in the house. He looked in all the obvious places and in all of the non-obvious places. But Werner's house was a wreath-ribbon-free zone. He went back into Werner's office and powered up the laptop. Maybe there was a clue there. But his access to it was blocked by a password. He closed it down, pushed it into the laptop case which he found in one of the cabinets and slipped his velvet bag into one of the case's side-pockets.

Now he had to get the hell out and away from there. And fast.

* * *

The red Mini pulled up outside his apartment. His pulse was racing, he was fighting panic, his guts were set on full spin cycle, he was utterly exhausted. He looked down at his watch and saw that it was two minutes short of midnight. He could have sworn that he heard Werner's wonderful laugh booming out loudly and echoing around the quiet street, but now it seemed to be laughing at him and not with him. He looked around him in every direction to make certain that no one was around. Then he picked up Werner's laptop case from the passenger seat next to him, got out of the car and headed towards the main entrance to his building. He took out his key and let himself into the main door and was about to close it behind him. Except that it wouldn't close. A thick leather boot had come between it and the door frame and stopped it. Then the door flew fully open and two men in black balaclavas with baseball caps on top of the balaclavas grabbed him and shoved him up against the hallway wall. Both of the men, if they were in fact men, were wearing sunglasses. A gun with a silencer attached was pushed into Adrian's face. Werner's laptop fell out of his hand and hit the ground with a thump.

"Where are they?" one of the masked men shouted at him in German through the round mouth-hole which he'd cut out of his balaclava.

Adrian was shaking. He was unable to utter a word.

"In there?" the masked man nodded towards Werner's laptop lying on the ground. He kept his gun pushed hard into Adrian's cheek while his accomplice bent down and unzipped the case and looked inside.

"YOU DON'T HAVE THEM, DO YOU?" the guy with the gun shoved into Adrian's cheek screamed at him. He had moved to within a millimetre of Adrian's face and when he shouted, he splattered Adrian with spittle which came spraying out of the cut-out mouth-hole.

"I'll get them. I-I said—"

The masked man's finger tightened around the trigger. Then he squeezed and the gun went off. Pffuff was the noise that the silenced gun barrel made and the small glass panel in the main door to the building shattered.

He got right back into Adrian's face. "It's past midnight. You're as dead as your girlfriend."

Adrian sank down onto his knees like a condemned man at an execution.

"Shoot the bastard," the second intruder told the first in German.

He pressed his gun hard against Adrian's forehead. Adrian closed his eyes. He wasn't even afraid, only resigned. A finger began to squeeze the trigger once again... just as a black Mercedes with darkened windows pulled up at the kerbside directly in front of the building; its rear door swung open.

The two masked men turned directly around and watched as Katharina, with her hands still bound together and the hood still over her head, was pushed out of the back of the car. She landed with a thump on the pavement. The two masked men turned away from Adrian immediately and left him kneeling there, his head bowed like a man at the guillotine awaiting his decapitation. The two jumped smartly into the back of the Mercedes as it roared off into the night. Adrian got up off his knees. He stood at the door and watched the Mercedes disappear around the corner like it had been part of some strange, surreal nightmare. Then he dashed over to Katharina, who was lying on the ground, and untied the hood and pulled it from her head. She was shaking. Tears were streaming down her face.

"Are you hurt?" he asked her.

All she could do was shake her head.

"Let's get inside," he said and pulled her up off the ground.

Inside the building's main door, with its shattered glass panel, Adrian began to rip the tape off Katharina's wrists. A neighbour from the downstairs flat had come out to see what all the commotion was about. She was standing at her door as Adrian, with his arm around a distressed and shaking Katharina, led her towards the stairs.

"It's okay," Adrian said to the neighbour. "Everything's okay. Just part of a game, that's all. I'll explain in the morning."

He had absolutely no intention.

* * *

Ten minutes later they were up in Adrian's living room. Katharina was sitting on the sofa with her legs drawn right up to her chest and her hands clamped tight around them. Her skin was the colour of cold cement and she was still shaking. Adrian came in from the kitchen with two cups of sweet tea – his mother's recipe for anything out of the ordinary. He had no idea why, or if it worked, but it was the only thing he could think of at that moment. He set the cups down on the table and began to clean the vicious cut on the side of his hand – the one he'd suffered breaking into Werner's garage. He applied some antiseptic lotion to the wound and cut a large piece of plaster and covered the cut with it. "I didn't give them the ribbons. I couldn't get them," he told Katharina.

Katharina set her legs back down and reached a shaking hand out for her cup of tea. She looked up at him incredulous.

"What?"

"Werner still had them somewhere. He's dead."

"Dead? How?" This was getting all too much for her to take in.

"His car skidded off a bridge, into a river."

She sat for a moment in stunned silence and they both gazed into their reflections in the empty television screen, which seemed like the most neutral place to look. Then a thought hit her. "How do you know he wasn't killed?"

Amid all the chaos, it was a possibility that Adrian hadn't yet considered. He let it run through his mind for a moment. He shook his head. "I was there. I went to the hotel where Werner was staying. The Police aren't treating it as suspicious. Besides, nobody else knew Werner had the ribbons."

"So why did they release me?"

Adrian could only shake his head. He was as confused as she was.

"What did you tell them?" he asked her.

"Nothing. I couldn't. What could I tell them anyway? They injected me with something when they took me." She closed her eyes and tried to think hard. "The only thing I remember is when they woke me up... when I spoke to you... I could hear water. And one of them was Swiss. The one who told me they'll kill us if we go to the Police."

Adrian sat down on the sofa next to her. After a worried moment he asked her, "So what do we do now?"

"What do you mean, 'what do we do now'? I'm alive. I want

to stay that way."

"Do we go to the Police? What do we do?"

She turned and looked at him as if he'd lost his mind. "We're dead just as soon as the Police start poking around," she told him. She was clearly petrified.

Adrian got back up off the sofa. "You're just going to sit there and do nothing?"

From her look he could see that was exactly what Katharina had in mind. He threw her own words back at her. "Where's the 'I'm a journalist' disappeared to?"

She stared at him. She hated him for that. He had no idea what she'd just been through, no idea of the ruthlessness or the seriousness of her captors. "You don't get it" – the very words that she'd once said to her cousin – was all she said to him.

He countered. "I've just been through the worst four hours of my entire life. To try and get you free. And I'm—"

She jumped straight in and cut him off. "They'll kill us. Get that into your thick, dumb head, will you? I believe them. They'll kill us. Besides, you have nothing. You know nothing."

"You have his emails."

"Whose emails?"

"Bernd O. The Swiss guy."

"I deleted everything. Besides..."

The look she shot him right at that moment told Adrian everything about how she felt. He met it with one of defiance. Somehow, for the first time in a long time, a calming breeze seemed to be blowing through him. "When I opened that bag up in my father's attic, I wanted to know. I owed it to myself. You understood that. Now a very good friend – the one I gave those ribbons to – drowns in a river. If you're right, and Werner did get caught up in something – then I owe it to him." He looked directly into her eyes when he delivered his next line: "I want to know."

But she was afraid. She was at her wits' end. Her ordeal had left scars. She was now deeply disappointed in him and she had simply stopped listening.

"I want to know what all this is about, Katharina. No one pushes me this far and gets a free ride."

And she could see it crystal-clearly in his face: this far and not an inch further. But she didn't care anymore. His determination didn't impress her. It wasn't her fight. But it was her life. She shook her head. For her the journey was over.

"Did they offer you money for your silence or what?" he baited her. He said it because at that moment he felt that he still needed her.

His words stung her. They stung her like never before. "Call a taxi for me," she said to him in German and got up off the sofa.

As she was heading for the door, and staying in German, she called out to him "Now I know what you meant by betrayal."

That cut like a knife through Adrian's heart.

And with that she was gone.

Adrian stood for a moment and stared at the closed door. What was that she'd just said to him? It had been so unfair. But had it also got close to the truth? Adrian knew even less then than he'd known before.

11

He went into school at eight the next morning looking like he hadn't slept for a year. His hair was uncombed. He was wearing the same clothes that he'd worn the day before, which was something that Adrian never did. Blood had seeped through the plaster which covered the cut on his hand. He looked a mess. He *was* a mess. Up on the first floor, the classroom he was teaching in seemed half its normal size. Everything appeared tight and claustrophobic to him and as if it was about to fall in on him at any moment. He stood in front of the class with a vacant, glazed look in his tired eyes. He had no idea where he was or what he was supposed to be doing. Some papers slipped out of his unsteady hand and floated down onto the floor in front of him, but he made no attempt to pick them up. He probably hadn't even noticed them fall. He looked dreadful, he looked like he was in no condition to teach. The girls in front of him exchanged confused looks. This wasn't the Adrian they knew. As for Mario, he just sat with his head buried in his magazine.

* * *

That evening, back in his flat, Adrian picked up the hallway phone and made a call. It was a call he had to make, a call he wanted to make. But before he could even say a word to her Katharina had already started. "It's no good, Adrian. If you're going on with this madness... just leave me alone."

He tried to say something to it but she just ploughed straight on. "There was a time when I didn't know what I was afraid of most, seeing you again or never seeing you again. Now I'm sure about it."

And that's all she said. She'd come to her own conclusion. Adrian had previously been "pretty packaging, damaged goods" and that had been okay with her. Now, however, there was "dangerous" stamped on the outside of the package in big red capital letters and that was a label too far for her. The "great challenge" which once was Adrian had lost its appeal for her.

Adrian put down the receiver. He felt sad. He didn't feel guilty or responsible. Why should he? He just felt sad, which was something he thought he'd never feel about a girl again. He was about to turn away from the phone and go back into the living room when it rang. Like lightening, he picked it up. It will be her. I'm okay with her. It's all cool again. She understands.

"Hi," he said, and the way he said it carried a tone of hope within it.

"We want-a you ribbons. We are-a interest in—" some Italian screwball said.

"Fuck you and I'm calling the Police," was the response they got and Adrian slammed down the phone.

He didn't call the Police. He didn't call anyone. He took a shower, sat for an hour and just stared into space, and then he went off to bed and stared up all through the night at nothing at all. He was still staring at nothing when his alarm rang at six-thirty the next morning.

* * *

Goldberg looked straight into Adrian's eyes. They once more looked tired. They looked troubled. They looked like they belonged to a man who had been to hell and back and still feared that there was more of the same on the way, even though he knew that particular chapter in his life was now over.

"We've had complaints now from three classes," Goldberg told him. "And your Cambridge class has asked for a change of teacher. What's wrong, Adrian?" The school Director looked as unhappy as he was confused at having to break the news to him and simply couldn't understand how it had come to this.

"What's wrong?" he repeated.

But Adrian just sat across the desk from his boss and looked right through him.

Goldberg sat for a moment waiting for an answer, his eyes continued to search Adrian's face for a clue, or even for some sign of life. But nothing came. Goldberg took that as an answer of sorts. He cleared his throat and shifted the weight in his seat. "I'm afraid, Adrian, that I'm forced to withdraw my offer."

Without a word Adrian got up, stepped over the dozing Terrier which had taken up its position on the floor next to his feet, and headed straight out the door.

* * *

That weekend Adrian spent alone on the boat, as far away from anyone else as it was possible to get, mostly just slumped down on the floor of the dinghy staring up at nothing again – so lost, so very alone, just drifting. It was a good weekend for that anyway – windless and still, cloudless and sunny. He thought back to Werner's particularly affectionate hug the day that he'd given him the ribbons. And he thought that he'd never get to hear that booming, addictive laugh of his ever again. He thought too about their evenings and afternoons together talking about this or about that or about nothing at all in particular – sometimes it was just talking for talking's sake – and how it had always been so comforting for him to confide in Werner, and how he'd been the *only* comforting figure for him at times over the past three years.

Werner was still very much on Adrian's mind when he got back to the flat and sat and stared at his laptop case, still exactly where he'd left it three nights earlier on the living room table. He went over to it and opened it. He unzipped the inside pocket and removed the crushed-velvet bag. He sat down on the sofa and stared at it, and then over at the cracked photograph image of his proud, smiling father – there were now even more unanswered questions whirling around in his head. Then, injected with a new resolve, he put the velvet bag down onto the sofa next to him, got up and picked up the laptop case, and walked with some purpose over to the door. He needed to know.

He got Mario's home address from Renate the office secretary and paid him a visit on the Monday afternoon after his last lesson. Mario lived alone in the Sternschanze district, in a flat which his father paid the rent and picked up all the bills for. He answered the door to Adrian in a sleeveless Sex Pistols T-shirt – not that Mario would have known who the Sex Pistols were or what they'd once represented, but they looked angry and they looked manic and they appeared alternative enough to him, so why not? He also came to the door with a thick joint stuck between his teeth and led Adrian along the hallway and into his weird and wacky world, which was his small computer room at the back of the building. Adrian didn't know what to expect from Mario's place except he was sure it would certainly be as odd as Mario himself – which it certainly was, and more. The computer room resembled the inside of a futuristic ghost train and it stank of weed, and Adrian was sure that he would get high just by being in there. Mario even kept a full-size skeleton in the corner of the room which he used as a clothes horse, and had several layers of jackets and shirts draped over and around it. The shutters on the windows were all down to keep out any signs of the day outside and stray beams of sunlight were thrown off at obscure angles by the sun streaking in through the gaps. The place was, in fact, exactly how Adrian might have imagined it would be with papers strewn everywhere across the desk and a five-high pile of cardboard boxes, one on top of the other and packed to bursting with old computer magazines. Adrian took Werner's laptop out of its case and handed it over to Mario. Mario connected it to one of several consoles in the room. There was an old Star Wars pinball machine on the wall beside the skeleton. "Amuse yourself," Mario said to Adrian and nodded over to the machine, and while Adrian flipped and tilted, Mario worked like a magician with his bright red fingernails typing away at lightning fast speed, and in no time at all...

"There's your password," he told Adrian.

Adrian turned away from the pinball machine and pulled a twenty euro note out of his pocket. He held it out for Mario to take, but Mario made no move towards it.

"How about 'one' in the next exam instead?"

"You'll get a one if you earn a one," Adrian said and took a second twenty out of his wallet and added it to the first.

Mario pocketed the money with a shrug of the shoulders. "You can't blame me for trying," he said and broke into a sly smile.

* * *

Back in his flat and armed with his passwords Adrian fired up the email package on Werner's computer and opened up Werner's very last email. It was written on the afternoon that he died. It was the most recent in a series of letters which Werner had exchanged over the previous few days with someone called Friedrich Hildersheim. Adrian began to read, starting with the very last email, and then quickly jumped to the very first, which had been written a week earlier. And what he read set the alarm bells ringing.

Each email had the title KS.

Sent by Werner, Adrian read: "They're authentic."

Friedrich Hildersheim's reply: "Are you sure?"

From Werner: "Yes I'm sure. And I have them."

Friedrich Hildersheim responded: "Good. Very good. Keep me informed."

From Werner: "I'll call you tomorrow."

From Friedrich Hildersheim: "Call after six-thirty."

Then two days later Friedrich Hildersheim wrote again: "He is who I thought he is. Meet me on Tuesday at 12.00. Quo Vadis, at Teufelsbrück near Jenischpark."

Finally, from Werner: "I'll be there."

Adrian looked hard again at Friedrich Hildersheim's line "He is who I thought he is" then he panned over to the window and stared once more at the photograph of himself and his father sailing, almost losing himself in the image, looking at it now with very, very different eyes. The question had now become not just "who was my father?" but "who the fuck am I?"

And "who the hell is this Friedrich Hildersheim?"

Part III

The Devil's Bridge

1

With his mobile phone on the seat next to him as a Satellite Navigator, Adrian headed west out of the city and out into the suburbs, passing through St Pauli and Altona on the river road. He had no idea what he would find when he got to Teufelsbrück (has a place ever been more perfectly named: the Devil's Bridge?), but as he got nearer he sensed that he was leaving something of his old life behind him and that in seeking answers to the questions which he now felt compelled to ask, a new chapter of his life might just be about to begin. But he was unsure whether to embrace it or to fear it. Without doubt he'd been scarred and badly hurt so much by his "old" life; he had spent the past eleven years sinking deep into himself in an effort to exorcise the demons which had been eating away at him, so in that way a new start was something he could welcome. But this wasn't the same as a snake shedding its old skin. This was a different beast. And it had come with a price. This mad, personal odyssey which he'd now been thrown into had come to him via the most evil of Nazi monsters. It had come to him with violence and it had arrived screaming murder. He'd just lost a very close friend in Werner, and he'd now lost Katharina. It had twisted and turned everything which he'd ever known inside out. It had started a war which was raging on the inside just as much as on the outside.

As he skirted the Elbe river on the Elbchaussee and got ever closer to Jenischpark, the same questions kept coming back at him over and over: What will I find here? And who the hell is this Friedrich Hildersheim? Naturally he'd tried to Google him, but all he'd been able to find under that name was a blind Jehovah's Witness elder who lived in Halle, and an Austrian ski instructor who had been killed in an avalanche four years previously. And he could find no Hildersheim in the local telephone book either.

The bigger question though was "who was Charlie Kramer?" And that had now been joined by its brand-new ugly sister, "who am I?" Adrian knew instantly that once he knew the answers he wouldn't be the same anymore. It was threatening to rewrite a past and render it ever more painful for him. "He is who I thought he is" Friedrich Hildersheim had written to Werner – what did that mean? What was behind that statement, other than nothing was what it appeared to be? And how did Werner become involved? Adrian was afraid of what he would find out, and he knew that there was nothing which he could possibly hear or see which would make good what was bad about the past. But he knew he had to go there. He was slap bang in that most poignant of moments, the moment when his greatest fear had crashed head-on with his greatest compulsion.

He pulled up in the Quo Vadis' car park early, at fifteen minutes to twelve. His mobile phone lying next to him on the passenger seat made a shrill screeching sound. The battery indicator showed only five per cent of the phone's power remained. Adrian slipped the Smartphone into his pocket and headed into the restaurant.

The Quo Vadis was close to the ferry point on the banks of the Elbe and inside, the place let you know exactly where you were. It was all dark timber frames and around its walls hung sailing ships' wooden steering wheels, some old nautical maps of the Hamburg area, a handful of model sailing ships, full rig galleons and several mermaid figureheads. On another day Adrian would have felt right at home in the Quo Vadis. But this wasn't home. This was the Devil's Bridge and he felt a million miles away from home and on enemy territory.

The place was empty when he went in, except for two tables close to the door which were both occupied by young couples deep in conversation. They didn't know Adrian, didn't care that he was there, didn't want to know him and wouldn't have blinked an eye if he'd dropped down dead on the floor right there in front of them. He took a seat at a table on the far side of the room facing the door. Right next to him on the floor was a brass deep-sea-diver's helmet. As soon as he sat down a waiter approached him. Given the old-world, sea-faring charm of the place, Adrian half-expected him to hobble over with a crutch and a wooden leg wearing a patch over one eye and a parrot on his shoulder. But all the twenty-something had was yellowy eyes, a ponytail which he'd tied back with a navy-blue bow, and a side tooth missing which showed when he took Adrian's order with a smile. Adrian ordered coffee and a croissant and checked his watch – it was seven minutes to twelve. Two women in their sixties came in dressed in hiking gear, but they didn't really look like they collected Nazi wreath ribbons. They took the table right next to Adrian and began a conversation about their one-and-a-half-hour walk along the river from the Blankensee Lighthouse. Then a minute later a tall, slim man in a grey summer business suit entered the cafe. He stood at the door for a moment and looked around the room. That's him, Adrian knew the moment that he saw him. That's Friedrich Hildersheim. The man walked directly towards Adrian's table. Adrian tightened as he watched him approaching. But the man moved past him and joined the two lady hikers on the next table. One of them turned out to be his mother, the other was her sister. He kissed both women lightly on the cheek, took a seat and signalled to old ponytail to get himself over to their table. As he was settling into the two women's conversation the door opened and another man walked in. It was a face which Adrian knew. It was Wolfgang Nord, the old man whose English he had tested the previous week. But that wasn't the only surprise. Wolfgang was wearing a white, vicar's collar under his black jacket.

The man who had called himself Wolfgang Nord stood inside the door and scanned around the faces in the room, looking hard to pick out Werner Retz. He froze when his gaze fell on Adrian sitting at the table on the far side of the room. They both stared at each other for a tense moment – like in one of those young kids' staring competitions, the first to look away loses. Until finally Wolfgang walked slowly over to Adrian's table. Adrian knew immediately from Wolfgang Nord's nervousness that this was indeed the man from Werner's emails. That he was Friedrich Hildersheim. Before Hildersheim could even ask "what are you doing here?" Adrian had already started.

"So, who do you think I am?"

His words shook the old man. He cleared his throat and scratched at something at the side of his chin which didn't itch. "Can't we go outside?" he asked Adrian.

Adrian didn't like the idea at all. Off his reluctance, Friedrich Hildersheim said: "Please? I'll explain there."

Adrian sat motionless for a moment and just said the old man's name out loud. "Friedrich Hildersheim." Then he added "Who the fuck are we really?"

If his choice of words had shocked the old man of the church, then all the better.

2

Friedrich Hildersheim, or whatever he was really called, walked slowly along the riverside walkway. A few miles away upstream was the distant skyline of tall cranes and ships masts which made up Hamburg's busy harbour-side. Walking alongside Friedrich Hildersheim, but not too close to him, was Adrian. They were two men suspicious of each other, and of the events which had brought them together.

"Let me be honest with you, Adrian. Because I don't think anyone has ever been fully honest with you before," Friedrich Hildersheim said. He was eager to win Adrian's trust. "Even me," he admitted, and pointed up to his white collar. His conscience was weighing heavily on him and just like at the language school he'd become nervous and his mouth had become dry again. He dug into his pocket for his packet of mints and invited Adrian to take one. Adrian shook his head. "My name is Wolfgang von Dornbach," the old man went on. "Have you ever heard the name before? Von Dornbach?"

"No."

"I thought not. Your father, Karl von Dornbach, was my brother."

Adrian stopped dead in his tracks. Even time stopped dead in its tracks. He shot the old man alongside him a look full of doubt and suspicion.

"Why should I believe you?"

"Indeed, why should you believe me?" Then Wolfgang von Dornbach had an idea. "Come with me... please?"

Adrian just stood and stared at him, and for the moment he probably even forgot to breathe.

"Please?"

* * *

Some minutes later, in a darkened room with its shutters pulled right down and the lights turned off, Adrian sat and watched in disbelief, and there was even an inner denial, at the images which were flickering on the bare white wall in front of him. It was the only wall in the room which wasn't covered in books. From behind him an old cine projector click, click, clicked away. The images Adrian was watching had been taken somewhere on the north German coast in the spring of 1944. While Europe was only weeks away from the allied invasion, the von Dornbachs had taken time out to relax by the sea. Wolfgang couldn't remember where exactly, but he told Adrian he thought it was somewhere near Heiligenhafen. Adrian sat transfixed, but not in a good way, at the jerky, hand-held shots taken from the beach of a small sailing dinghy about twenty-five yards off the sandy shore. In the small boat with its yellow sails, a proud father was showing his handsome, blond seven-year-old son how to sail. "That's your father. And your grandfather," Wolfgang von Dornbach told Adrian.

What the camera couldn't show, because it couldn't get in close enough, was that young Karl von Dornbach had piercing blue eyes, a perfect face and a young athlete's figure – in fact he looked remarkably like Adrian once had at the same age.

At the very bottom of the frame, sitting all alone at the water's edge, was another young boy, the dark-haired Wolfgang, a solitary soul throwing stones into the water. He looked up and waved and shouted frantically to try and attract the cameraman's attention. But in vain. The shots remained fully focused on the small boat and its two smiling occupants. The name of the boat was Karl – Adrian's father's name.

"Karl was always his favourite son. His perfect, young 'Aryan God'," Wolfgang said with sadness. "I was the... the 'black sheep' you say?" In the darkness Adrian nodded his head. Whether Wolfgang could see him or not wasn't important right then. "I was the unwanted..."

Then he stopped speaking. He got up and began to fiddle awkwardly with the projector. Even after all that time it still hurt him just as much as it had back then and there was great sorrow in his eyes.

Then the images on the wall changed and Adrian watched the final, flickering seconds of the two brothers, Karl and Wolfgang, both in Hitler Youth uniform. Karl stood proudly, chin up and his chest puffed out. Wolfgang stood next to him, miserable and ashamed. They were positioned either side of their uniformed, SD General father. He had his arm affectionately around Karl's shoulder – and only *Karl's* shoulder. The pictures on the wall all seemed to slow down then, and it was as if Adrian was watching the film in extra-slow motion. It wasn't slow motion of course, but that's how Adrian saw it – until it all suddenly stood still for him. The images on the screen continued to move and flicker, but in Adrian's head they were frozen. He was seeing his own past through very different eyes now. His world had been turned upside down. His notion of where he came from had changed, and he knew it was forever. His father was part of what Adrian despised. Of what the world despised. Whatever the opposite of an epiphany is, Adrian was experiencing it. The enlightenment horrified him.

Then the picture suddenly vanished, as if it had all been part of some bizarre mirage. Wolfgang had switched off the projector and moved over to pull up the blinds and let daylight spill into the room.

The place smelled of cough medicine and herbal tea. There were several carved wooden religious figures dotted around the room and a pot of tea and two cups on a small table. The cup in front of Adrian was chipped slightly. He noticed it, but he said nothing. He couldn't have cared less.

"Who was my grandfather?"

"General Manfred von Dornbach. A General in the SD. He and Heydrich were very close friends."

Adrian shook his head. He'd done that a lot over the past few minutes. He hated the very thought. Wolfgang turned over an old black and white photograph which had been lying on the table and held it out for Adrian to take. It had curled slightly over time and the very bottom corner of the photograph had been torn off. It was a picture of young Karl posing for the camera in his Hitler Youth uniform, with his right arm raised in the Nazi salute.

"It's the only photograph that I have of him."

Adrian stared at it, just as he'd done so often back in his flat with the photograph of his father and himself – the one which he'd brought back from England with him. His nightmare suspicions had now become reality. He felt nauseous. He felt light-headed, as if he could faint any minute. But the strangest feeling of all was that he felt himself somehow implicated and a sense of guilt began to weigh heavily on him, as if he himself had been complicit in it all. I wish I didn't know now what I didn't know then, was all he thought to himself.

"Keep it," Wolfgang told Adrian, meaning the photograph.

When Adrian made no move whatsoever to take it, Wolfgang placed it back down on the table right in front of him. Then, reading Adrian's thoughts as he continued to stare down at his father's image Wolfgang added, "Your father was a victim, Adrian. He had no choice. I was lucky. I was rejected. I had a choice. If you remember him as a good, loving father, then that's what he was to you. Nothing less. I'll not take that away from him. Or from you." Then he said with deep regret and with much envy, "He gave you something that I never had."

Wolfgang closed his eyes for a moment. He was travelling back to somewhere painful. Just as it was for Adrian, Wolfgang's dark past was being dragged out into the light and it was blinding him.

"Your grandfather was a very cruel man, Adrian. He was cruel in his profession and he was brutal at home. But only with me. He beat me up badly and regularly. For anything, and often for nothing at all. It didn't matter to him. If he was angry or frustrated or unhappy with anything around him, he took it all out on me. He made me choose which of his belts he would beat me with. I always chose the thinnest, the shortest one... so he picked up the thickest and longest. But at least when he was hitting me, I knew I was getting his attention. That's what he did to me. That was how he made me feel. And I have to thank him for what I became. He beat the goodness into me," Wolfgang said with a slight self-reflective smile. "If he hadn't hit me so hard and hit me so often... if I hadn't bled so much... then I wouldn't have turned to God in my life. I wouldn't have reached out for goodness. Can you understand that? I should really be grateful to him – he beat the godliness into me."

What Wolfgang told Adrian was only a part of the truth. Adrian's grandfather would force the young boy to strip naked, bend him over the arm of a chair, and order Karl to watch while he unleashed his considerable anger and brought the end of his belt with its enormous metal buckle down hard on Wolfgang's bare backside. It was ferocious; twenty times, thirty times, or as many times as it took until the tears began to flow – which could take some time because Wolfgang vowed to himself every time he was punished that he wouldn't cry. He was determined that his monstrous father wouldn't break him, nor steal his pride away from him. But the pain for a five- or six- or seven-year-old boy was too much to withstand and inevitably the tears would begin to roll down little Wolfgang's face. Which only made it worse. "Shut it!" the good old General von Dornbach would yell at him at the top of his voice. "As long as you cry, you'll continue to be punished," he taunted him. "A man never cries," he would shout out and then he would turn to look at Karl. "Does he, Karl? A real man never cries. He never shows weakness," and then the next heavy blow would inevitably rain down on Wolfgang. "Tell him, Karl. Tell him," and Adrian's father would repeat the mantra to his suffering brother, "a real man never cries." And when Manfred von Dornbach tired of hitting his son relentlessly he'd hand the belt (or sometimes it was a long branch from one of the birch trees in the garden) to Karl and Karl would be forced to take over where his father had left off. There were occasions too when von Dornbach beat him so hard that Wolfgang even lost consciousness and was left lying naked on the ground for his mother to tend to later.

It was the ultimate, even the *perfect* vicious circle. And an unbreakable vicious circle. Wolfgang's father would beat him until he cried and wouldn't stop beating him until he'd stopped crying. And it was a truism that von Dornbach would take with him out onto the battlefield where his brutality, even with his own men, became legendary.

As a young officer in the First World War he would personally shoot any of his comrades in his own battalion who threatened to show weakness or desert their positions, even under the heaviest of fire or facing certain defeat or death. Just the slightest show of any feebleness or vulnerability was for von Dornbach enough to render them poison to the cause and therefore dispensable. They became the enemy, or even worse than the enemy, because the enemy could command respect. It was his own sick twisted form of death or glory and the rumour at the time was that he had personally executed twenty-three German soldiers who had refused to follow orders or shown weakness in the heat of battle. How did he ever come to terms with the German defeat in 1918? The answer was that he didn't. For von Dornbach, the war went on. He was someone who would always need a war to fight and would always seek out the battle. And he brought it home with him. It was like someone had opened the flaming door to hell and the devil himself had come racing out. And boy was he angry, and boy was he vicious.

So poor Wolfgang with his soft, loving, caring, compassionate personality was never worthy of his father's respect – or whatever twisted kind of respect it was which the General had in him. That was the privilege which Karl and only Karl would have bestowed upon him. Even von Dornbach's own wife was at his side only to obey and serve and support. It was almost as if Manfred von Dornbach wished that his only biological son, Wolfgang, was in fact Jewish so that he could dispose of him once and for all.

But as Wolfgang himself said, he had the goodness beaten into him and the evil beaten out, and for that he could be thankful. He reached for the teapot and gestured whether Adrian wanted more.

Adrian, in a total daze, shook his head. "I need some air."

Wolfgang put down the teapot. He had an idea.

3

Adrian and Wolfgang walked slowly side by side along a tree-lined avenue in a plush Hamburg suburb, the most exclusive suburb in the city. This was where old money, new money, in fact any kind of money at all came to live and call home. And the homes were the very finest. On each side of the street were grand, late nineteenth-century mansion-style houses. Big houses. Big money. Big expensive cars in the big expensive driveways. Wolfgang stopped at the very grandest house in the street – a four-storey, white-stucco villa with ceiling-to-floor French windows which looked out onto an immaculate front lawn, flanked on each side by a rose garden,it had ornate second-floor balconies on all four sides. Chandeliers which must have once each cost the entire budget of a third-world country hung from the carved wooden ceilings in every room. A white marble staircase led up from the front lawn and rose garden up to the main door on the first floor. From somewhere inside the house a dog began to bark, the kind of deep and loud bark which only a dog the size of a small horse would make, and only when it was angry or hungry or wanted to take a chunk out of a trespasser's leg.

"That's our old family house," Wolfgang told him. "I was born here. I think I also died many times here too," he added while he stood and looked in at the old von Dornbach home like some grimy voyeur, except that it wasn't affluence and someone else's privileged life that he was seeing at that moment, it was his own past with all its pain, its torment and abuse. Suddenly it all felt so real again to him, so present again – the insults, the humiliation, the brutality, the blows and the blood oozing out of the open wounds on his raw backside. He could see his father's twisted, sadistic face taunting him, hating him, while he was trying his best to destroy him. And with the images, many of the feelings returned – the feelings of morbid fear and terror, of panic and inadequacy and yes, jealousy too, of his favoured brother. If Wolfgang had believed that seeing number twelve Planstrasse after all that time would no longer hurt him, he was wrong.

Adrian stood alongside him at the giant, ornate iron double gates and peered in. He looked at that moment too like a peeping tom – a pauper drooling at the rich man's table.

"We had to sell it eventually, to pay off debts. I haven't been here in over forty years," Wolfgang said and took one final look at the grand old house like a captain taking one very last look at his sinking ship. Then he turned away and began to walk off further up the street. Adrian was still in a daze. Just then there was a loud click sound and the villa's automatic gates began to slowly swing open. Adrian moved back and turned his head to see a red top-of-the-range Jaguar sports car begin to swing into the driveway. Inside the Jag was a blonde – it could have been a man but it could also have been a woman – it was one of those frozen faces – and it had recently had a ton of Botox shoved into its duck's lips and billiard ball smooth forehead. Adrian turned away and caught up with Wolfgang as he trudged on up the road.

"My father... your grandfather... was captured on the Eastern front in nineteen forty-five. He spent eight years in a Russian prison..." Wolfgang stopped talking and swallowed hard. The shame still haunted him. "As a convicted war criminal. When he returned, it was very difficult for everyone. He was a broken man. Not because of the Russians but because there was no more war for him to fight. He had no purpose in his life. Even his relationship with Karl suffered. We were sixteen when he came home."

"You were *both* sixteen?" Adrian asked, not fully getting it, but knowing with absolute certainty that he wasn't looking into the twin-image face of his father.

"Karl was adopted. Didn't I tell you that? He came to us when he was five."

It was yet another layer of surprise, another wrapping of mystery for Adrian. "That can't be true," was all Adrian said.

"It is."

Adrian tried hard to take it all in. After a thoughtful moment he asked, "Do you know who his real parents were?"

"No. When he came to us, he never spoke a word for months. And when he finally did, it was never with me. We never spoke. It was like we lived in two different worlds. He—" Wolfgang stopped once more for an emotional moment. This all clearly still pained him very much. "The photograph I gave you, it was taken on Karl's seventh birthday. I remember that much."

"The ninth of June. It would have been his birthday in two days' time," Adrian said and Wolfgang nodded.

"Eventually even Karl went away to escape the persecution and stigma which haunted the von Dornbachs. No one told me where he was. I didn't care anyway. But I can tell you this, Adrian – without our father's presence... when he was away... Karl saw and learned different things. He had better teachers. I can't tell you if he hated his father in the end, but he came to hate what our father had represented. He was proof that a man can change. In the same way that the country in which he'd been brought up finally emerged like a phoenix out of the smoke and ashes of war and fascism to become the open, tolerant, liberal and responsible society that it is today. The challenge for us all now is to prevent it falling back."

"It will never fall back."

"But we must be on our guard. We have to keep the world safe from fools."

"Why did my father have Reinhard Heydrich's wreath ribbons?"

"When your grandfather knew that he was dying, he passed them on to the only person who he saw as the rightful heir to the Heydrich's legacy. I can't tell you how he did it. I don't know that. It was only when Werner Retz contacted me that I realised — "

Adrian jumped in. "How do you know Werner Retz?" It felt as if Werner had become just a forgotten bit-part in the whole story.

"He knew the name von Dornbach – from history. And because I... well, let's say I've spent my life actively opposing the fascists and their Nazi ideology. Werner Retz once helped us some time ago with some research."

Adrian, his head spinning, fought hard to make some sense of it all. "And you wanted the ribbons?"

"Yes."

"I don't get it. Why?"

"Simply, to destroy them. To prevent certain... certain evil people from getting their hands on them. That's what Werner and I discussed together. The fewer there are of those reminders of National Socialism in the world, the better the world will be."

"Why did you use the name Hildersheim?"

"Friedrich Hildersheim was once my partner. We worked together in the fight against fascism and against the rise of the neo-Nazis. Friedrich died last year. He was my partner in the fight..." Wolfgang turned and looked directly into Adrian's eyes. "And he was my partner."

He let the statement sink in for a poignant moment. He had just revealed everything to Adrian without saying it out aloud. It was a confession of sorts, an "outing" to his nephew.

"I'm sorry," Adrian said. And he was indeed sincerely sorry. "I tried, but I couldn't find anything out about him," he added.

"No. No, you won't. That's not how you work when you choose to work in this area... in this *thematic*."

Wolfgang surprised himself that he hadn't asked his next question before. It came to him almost like an afterthought.

"Where is Werner Retz anyway?"

"Werner's dead."

"What!" It was Wolfgang's turn to be stunned.

"He was killed in a car accident."

For a silent second, Wolfgang stood motionless and tried to take in what he'd just been told. Then the penny began to drop. "Who knew Werner Retz had the ribbons?"

"I don't know. No one."

"Who knew *you* had them?"

"You don't want to know that story."

"But someone knew?"

"Yes, someone knew."

"Who?" Wolfgang was getting animated now. Adrian's news had disturbed him.

"I had one offer of two hundred thousand euros. And another of someone's life if I didn't hand them over."

"Who from?" Wolfgang asked, alarmed.

"Some organisation. A guy called Bernd O seemed to be the front man."

"Bernd O? Is he Swiss?"

"Yeah." Adrian looked at him and thought to himself how the hell does he know that? He began to sense that it was all leading somewhere. He also sensed that the somewhere would be somewhere dark.

"So, they have them!" Wolfgang said. There was alarm in his voice.

"Who?"

"The Brotherhood. The very people who I wanted to keep the ribbons away from."

"Who are the Brotherhood?"

"People for whom Reinhard Heydrich's ribbons have a meaning far beyond what you or I could ever imagine. People who would give a fortune for something like that. Bernd O is almost certainly Erich Messmer, the Head of Globo-Com, the international electronic and telecommunication corporation here in Hamburg. Messmer is said to be the leader of the secretive Brotherhood – rich, powerful, protectors of the Nazi ideology and its ancient occult rituals. If you ever wonder where all these right-wing groups are getting their money from..." His voice now had obvious fear in it. "I wanted the ribbons. But I never wanted to go up against them."

They had arrived back at Wolfgang's car by then, an old Opel, which had three deep scratch marks running right along the passenger side door and a cracked wing mirror. It was parked in an adjoining street. "You know the German saying *Der Fisch stinkt vom Kopf her*? A fish rots from the head down? The fish that is fascism stinks all over and in every direction," Wolfgang said to Adrian. "It rots at the bottom, and it stinks worst at the top with people like Messmer."

"Why don't you go to the Police with what you know?" Adrian asked while he was getting into the car and strapping himself in.

"They are killers. And what actually do I know? These men are clever. They leave no proof. We know... but we don't know anything, if you understand what I mean? Messmer and his colleagues are powerful. You think you have proof... but the proof—" He made a gesture with his hands demonstrating that it all just vanishes into the air.

He turned on the engine and pulled away.

"Does this Messmer know who I am?"

Silence. Adrian's question unsettled Wolfgang. It was one of those moments when what is *not* said becomes much more powerful than what *is* said. Wolfgang felt awkward, and he *looked* awkward. He took one hand from the steering wheel and began to tug at his collar as if it was a size too tight for him. He was clearly reluctant and unwilling to say more.

"He does, doesn't he? And he knows who my father was."

After another agonising silence, as if he was purging himself of all sense of guilt, Wolfgang pulled over to the side of the road and killed the engine. He turned in his seat to Adrian. "The Brotherhood helped to reintegrate your grandfather when he returned from Russia. They were a sort of Odessa-like organisation. Messmer's father ran it from Switzerland. They also traded back then in stolen Nazi art."

For the first time, Adrian began to see light at the end of his pitch black tunnel. Wolfgang noticed and became anxious for him.

"Leave it, Adrian. Those people... they're very dangerous. You've found out what you wanted to know, now —"

"No. I want to know who my father was. Not what he was turned into. If Messmer knows —"

"Stay away from them," Wolfgang cut him off, and his interruption came out as a form of order. He was worried for Adrian. He started up the engine and pulled away.

On the drive back across the city to Wolfgang's place Adrian told Wolfgang all about his father's illness and about the heartbreak and suffering that it caused and how his mother never really recovered from it. Because of what he'd heard earlier that day, it came even harder for Adrian to talk about it all and several times he came very close to breaking down. And Wolfgang too became emotional when he heard Adrian's story.

* * *

At the same time, a few miles away in Borgfelder Strasse, two men walked up to Adrian's flat and pressed the front doorbell next to the name Kramer. They were both handsome men, well dressed, well groomed in the way that Italian men usually are. They waited. No one was home to answer. They pressed the doorbell again, waited a little longer, and then they turned and walked away. One of them said to the other in Italian, "We'll try again tomorrow."

And they did.

* * *

Wolfgang's car pulled up in his driveway. Sitting alongside him, Adrian looked like someone who either had ten thousand questions still racing around in his head. Or nothing at all. He looked numb and empty, and filled to bursting all at the same time. Wolfgang took an old creased calling card out of his inside jacket pocket and handed it to Adrian. "I'm happy for Karl that he became a father late in life," he said, and he did indeed look genuinely happy for him.

"He was fifty-one when I was born."

"And your mother?"

"Nine years younger. She was seventy-one when she died last month."

"What did she know about Karl's past?"

Adrian shook his head. He didn't know – in fact no one would ever know the answer to that question now. "None of the family knew much at all," he said. "I don't think she knew anything."

They got out of the car and stood facing each other. Neither was really sure what came next. Wolfgang spoke first. "There are no more von Dornbachs left, Adrian. You and I are all we have. I'm glad we met. Hopefully, it won't be the last time."

"I'm not a von Dornbach," Adrian said.

"Neither am I," Wolfgang added with irony and they both broke into a smile. "But we *are* family all the same."

Adrian held out his hand for Wolfgang to shake. He'd come to like the old man. Wolfgang ignored Adrian's outstretched hand and instead pulled him towards him and hugged him tight.

"Remember what I told you. Leave it alone," he told him as a deadly serious final word.

* * *

One day in June, the Bank of Austria's chauffeur dropped Gerhard Pfeifenberger off at his home in the affluent Hietzing district of Vienna just after eight-thirty in the evening, which was two hours later than he usually arrived home from work, give or take ten minutes or so depending on the Viennese traffic, but about normal for the last Tuesday in each month when he chaired the regular live telephone conference between the Bank's other Directors in their New York, Chicago, London and Frankfurt headquarters. He was agitated when he arrived home that particular evening because things hadn't gone to plan and he'd been told earlier about some financial irregularities in the Bank's New York offices which had led to the resignation of two of their leading investment bankers.

Home for Gerhard Pfeifenberger was a four-and-a-half million-euro luxury villa with a heart-shaped swimming pool in the back garden which no one used anymore and enough bedrooms to house a small army. He'd helped to design the house himself and had it built for his family in 1992. But his wife had been killed in a skiing accident in the Italian Alps twelve years later, and his three daughters were now all grown up, had married and had moved away. So every time that Gerhard Pfeifenberger came home from the Bank where he was Director, it was to an empty house. Once in a while he would pick up the phone and order himself in one of Vienna's finest escorts just like you would order in a pizza or a number twenty-two from the local Chinese takeaway. But really, Gerhard Pfeifenberger's interests lay elsewhere. He was an ideologue, and a passionate one at that, as well as being a stinking rich Austrian bank director.

That particular early-June evening when Gerhard Pfeifenberger arrived home though, he had company. It wasn't a fishnet-stockinged, olive-skinned escort-service beauty but two men dressed up in blue zipped-up overalls wearing black ski masks, blue plastic gloves and plastic blue over-shoes. Whatever turns you on, I guess. But they had indeed been ordered in by phone. They'd been sent there by a man called Renzli. They'd disabled the house alarm system and were waiting for Pfeifenberger in his spacious living room – his "white room" he called it, because everything in there was white, even the carpet. One of the men pushed a Czech-made CZ 82 pistol into Pfeifenberger's face and told them why they were there and what they wanted. Gerhard Pfeifenberger limped off (the heavy limp was the reason he was no longer able to drive) and led them down into the cellar at gunpoint, unlocked the door to a separate small box-room at the very back of the cellar where he twiddled the dial of his safe this way and then that and then back again, until the safe door swung open for him.

When Wolfgang had said to Adrian "If you ever wonder where all these right-wing groups are getting their money from" it was almost certainly the sort of place like this plush Vienna suburb which he had been referring to.

4

Imagine everything you've ever known or you've ever grown up believing was wrong. Your left was really your right, your inside was your outside, your up was down... your father was a Nazi. And *his* father was one of the very worst. When Adrian got back home early that evening, he tried to settle down. But how do you settle down after that? It felt like the two wreath ribbons had opened a door and the rest of Adrian's life was on the other side of it. And where was the trusted shoulder to cry on now? Werner was dead. And for Katharina, he was now dead himself too. He tried to go for a walk but the streets meant nothing to him, the wild thoughts were no good to him, the city air was suffocating. He didn't want to think, to reflect, or to consider. A big part of that was because he knew that whatever had happened and whatever he had experienced or discovered he had been responsible for. Where did I think it was going to lead me anyway? he asked himself. Seriously, what did I expect, poking into things which had fascism and terror written all over them in big gold letters with a dirty big black swastika alongside as a bonus? Did I think it would all have a happy ending? No, you asked for this Adrian. You invited it all in, all of it. Those thoughts didn't make him feel any better.

He passed a hotel where a pretty bride and her handsome groom were standing on the entrance steps for their wedding photographs. Poses. Smiles – real smiles and not plastic ones either. Look up. Look left. Look straight at me. Now look deep into each other's eyes. Adrian walked on by – he had no time nor space in his heart for any happy-ever-afters. On a day which for someone was about union and love-everlasting, for Adrian it was a day of dislocation, distance, disillusionment.

What he did conclude while he was out there was that he would try never to hate his father for what he had been. Charlie

Kramer had been the perfect father for him and had taught him well. If Adrian had got damaged along the way well, that was the result of other things – things which his father had nothing to do with or had no control over. All he'd shown Adrian was love and a sense of fairness and compassion and an ethic of "work hard and your rewards will come". And fun and laughter and adventure – it had all been in there. As Wolfgang had told him, when Karl finally had the opportunity to make his own decision, he had chosen the right path for himself. He'd broken free and had chosen the path of goodness. And if he'd chosen to keep his secret to himself... well, who was Adrian to judge or condemn? Don't we all carry secrets which we can never tell?

And yet... and yet... the dark thoughts still kept pushing their way back into his mind and he couldn't shake loose the fact that what he'd discovered about his family was a true horror show. He saw his grandfather out drinking and whoring with Heydrich, he saw his own father dressed as a Nazi with his arm raised high, he saw emaciated Jewish bodies, just skin and bone piled up high and ready to be dumped somewhere, he smelled death and he somehow imagined that he stank of death himself. Crazy, you're crazy Adrian. And you're wrong and unfair.

Walking the streets was no good so he made his way back to the flat. Fill your mind with something else Adrian, he implored himself. Occupy the empty space in there where the crazy thoughts are crashing in. So he tried to read, but couldn't. It was the same line, the same line, the same line... over and over and over again. We've all done it. He took out the mini-chess computer which he'd once been given as a birthday present but he couldn't concentrate on that either and got no further than the first three moves. He turned on the television. So many channels and nothing on. Nothing for a young man who had just had his world blown apart. So he just sat and watched meaningless images fill a meaningless screen. What else was there to do? He'd seen all the moving images he needed to see that day already. And while he sat there, he decided that he wouldn't tell anyone what he'd discovered earlier that day from an uncle who he never knew he had. His father hadn't told anyone, so why should he? And he could never blame his father. Wolfgang had got it right too when he said that Karl had also been a victim. He'd come to the von Dornbachs from somewhere else as the son of someone else. But who? Adrian looked over at his photograph standing on the windowsill. *I know now who you once were but who were you before that?* the voice inside his head was asking. *Where did—*

The front doorbell rang and broke the spell. But Adrian was in no mood to see anyone or speak to anyone. He had to be alone with himself and his thoughts. The bell rang again. *You can stand there and ring all night*, Adrian thought. *I'm home to no one.*

So, the two Italians turned and once again walked off down the street to where they'd parked their car.

Adrian got up out of his chair – not to look out of the window and down into the street to see who had called – he had less than zero interest in that. He went into his bedroom and took out the diary which he'd brought back from England with him and sat on the bed and began to read it.

One Day in May
I haven't written in this for a while, not since the end of March, but that's probably for the best because the past few weeks have been the very worst. It's almost three months now since I was last at school, but that's okay, I'm needed here more. Mam really can't cope any longer and I'm worried about her too now. The doctor was right when he told us at the very beginning that this illness can take the carer down quicker than it takes down the patient. She can't sleep, she doesn't eat, her hand has started to shake, her body is breaking down from all the lifting and carrying, although I'm doing all that now – that and everything else. The worst is that I hate myself. I should be doing this

with love but I hate every single minute of it, and I hate myself for feeling that way. I'm at war with myself. But who wouldn't be? Who could love doing what we have to do? The carers who come in every morning to help get Dad ready for the day? No. They get their day off. They get their holiday. They pack up at the end of the day and go back to their families. They can turn off. They can go out in the evening. They can even walk away if they want to walk away. They chose to do this. I didn't. And I can't walk away. I'm "on" twenty-four hours of every day and every night, every day and night of the week, every week of the month. I do it because that's what you do. That's what you do when you love someone. When you know that they would do it for you. When you know that they would lay down their life for you if they had to. So you cook and you clean and you feed and you shave and you wipe the shit off someone's dirty backside. Yesterday was the very worst moment yet. Why the fuck do they call it, "pass a motion"? He hadn't "passed a damned motion" for over three weeks because all the muscles that you need to take a crap had long since packed up, so they went inside and hooked the shit out of him. The carer rolled him onto his side and I held his body and my mother supported his head. My father would have been screaming in pain (every part of his body now is in incredible pain and any movement is pure hell for him, even the very slightest of movements) – except that he can't scream any more. He can't do anything anymore. He just has to lie there helplessly and take whatever comes his way. So the carer went in with something – a finger? An instrument? I don't know, I couldn't look. And that, right there right then, was the very worst moment of my entire life, having to stand and watch it all – I couldn't, I just supported his head and held him while he was on his side. How dehumanising is that? I felt so sorry for him while she was doing it and I thought then what differentiates him now from an animal? What is left of him which is human? Where is the dignity lying on your side, trapped in your pain, trapped in your body, trapped in your illness, trapped in the psychological torture and the knowledge that you know where you are heading and this here, this now is the journey there – and someone is raking the shit out of your backside? You're now without hope. You can't speak, you can't eat, you can't move, and if something hurts, how do you tell someone? You are still in the world but you're not, the world has long ago left you. What life is that? What are you alive for? And all of that, all that I've just written, my dad says himself.

You have a machine to feed you, a machine to breathe for you, a machine to speak for you, a machine to lift you up and one to put you down. Except that my father's body is so wracked with pain, even to the touch, that we can't use them and I have to carefully lift and place him wherever he wants to be: the bed, the toilet, the wheelchair. Actually, that IS his world now. His bed. The toilet. The wheelchair. And the wheelchair is only to get him between the two. There's a machine to put him in the bath. But he can't use that either because he can't stand water on him now. How far gone are you when you can't even stand the touch of water? We have a machine to get him up the stairs and down the stairs, but he's long given up going downstairs anymore. But the machine which can heal you? That one doesn't exist.

All those machines to keep you alive when all you want and pray for is one which will kill you and put you out of your misery and show you mercy. Where is the machine for that? Where the fuck is the one which shows mercy? Where is the mercy in the technology that you're strapped to and wired up to? What compassion does it show you? You're bunged up with pipes in your stomach and tubes in your throat and an oxygen mask over your face and pills to get you to sleep and pills to dull the pain. When all you want is the right to die, or to live with dignity. But that's not in the deal. "Dignity" isn't part of the package. And "hope" – the thing which keeps us going – the thing which keeps all humans going through the bleakest of times... that's stolen from you. And the one thing you might want to stay alive for – your family – you get the pleasure of watching them go down with you. You witness up close their heartbreak, their back-break, and you know that you are the reason for their ruin. You're taking them down with you.

And yet all that my father has is gratitude. When he was able to nod his head and when he could still half-smile, that was all he did every time we helped him – nod his head "thank you", and give me a twisted, "almost-smile" which could still light up an entire continent. What I would give now to see that smile again? What I would give now to turn back the clock? To be out on the water with him on the boat. To watch him happy and healthy and full of joy. That was my dad. Joy and love and an unbreakable bond.

Three days ago, using his eyes as the mouse to scroll across his computer screen to pick out the letters which the machine then read out aloud for him, he spelled out "I can imagine a life without this" (by "this" he meant the Motor Neuron Disease). "But I can't imagine a life without your mother or without you."

I had to turn away from him because all I wanted to do was cry. And he knew it. But I didn't want him to see me like that.

I miss the life outside. I miss my friends. I'm losing my friends. Life is passing me by. A while back, Dad even said we should sell the boat to pay for the alterations that we need to make to the house. I don't know...

Okay, that's enough. One day I might understand all of this. One day it might all make some sense, and the twenty-eight-year-old Adrian or the eighty-eight-year-old Adrian might be able to look back and tell the eighteen-year-old Adrian what it was all about. But right now, I don't know. All it means now to me is death and misery and loss and pain and hopelessness and helplessness and fear and a long journey into the darkness.

It isn't fair. That's what I do know. It just isn't fair.

5

When Adrian wrote that entry into his diary, he had just turned eighteen and he was alone at home. His mother had already had her first breakdown – physical and emotional, although a bigger and much more serious one would come later – and she had gone into a clinic for three weeks to recover. So Adrian did it all. He *became* his father. Whatever he wished for or needed or had to have, Adrian had to provide. Scratch this, clean that, cook that, mash it into pulp and shove it into the bottle so that you can get it into my stomach through the PEG tube which is poking out of me... now arm to the left an inch... too far... back half-an-inch... too far again... tears from the pain... prop the head up... no, back down again... I want to tell you something... AAARGH! I CAN'T! I'M TRAPPED. I'M TRAPPED FOREVER. I LOVE YOU and I'm trapped. I'm thirsty and I can't tell you. My speech computer isn't lined up correctly and I'M CUT OFF FROM THE WORLD! You can see me but you don't know me anymore. You don't know what I want. How can you? Inside I'm still Charlie Kramer but you CANNOT BEGIN TO IMAGINE what he's going through. I'm afraid. I'm dying and I know it and I know it will come soon – I hope it will come soon – and THIS IS HELL and I can't tell anyone anything. Prop my head up... no, no my head... MY HEAD! Look into my eyes... can't you see what I mean? My neck is killing me and you have to do something about it. My neck... no, not there, MY NECK! MY NECK! LOOK INTO MY EYES! LOOK INTO MY DAMNED EYES and please God try and understand me. MY FUCKING NECK IS BREAKING and I CAN'T TELL YOU.

So I scream, "What do you want, Dad? I want to help you but I don't know what the fuck you want. He's panicking and I'm panicking and we're both out of control and we're coming at each other from opposite sides of the sky. I want to ease your pain but I don't know

*what you want from me. Fuck, this is madness. Is it this you want?
No? Then this? This? This?..." And so it goes on. And on. And on...
You think I'm making this all up? I wish I was.*

Now I'm aching all over. The pain, the PAIN! And the constant
twitching in my arms, twitching in my legs, my stomach, my
throat, my face... everywhere, as bit-by-bit I die off. MAKE IT
GO AWAY! SOMEONE HELP ME <u>PLEASE</u>! My muscles are
killing me – literally they are killing me! I'm hurting all over.
Pain all day and always somewhere different. Nerve wrecking.
And my ears are driving me mad. I can hear my own breathing
from the inside. My whole body is breaking down. But more
than that... MY HEART IS BREAKING. It's aching. It hurts me
so much. I'm going to leave you – I love you – you're all I ever
lived for – and it will be over soon. I'll never ever see you again.
I'M SORRY. God, God, God... I'M SO SORRY ADRIAN. I didn't
deserve this. <u>YOU</u> didn't deserve this and I LOVE YOU! This is
what love finally is. This is what it came to. You wipe my bottom
and I cause you pain. You feed me and I make you cry. I want
to tell you something... I *have to* tell you something... but how
can I? WHY CAN'T YOU UNDERSTAND ME ADRIAN? It's...
it's– Now I can't breathe... I CAN'T BREATHE PROPERLY
ADRIAN... I'M GOING INTO THE DARK... I'm slipping into
darkness... I'm.... Kill me, Adrian. Just kill me and make it all
go away...

A local authority male carer went in every morning at eight-
thirty for an hour, but by then Adrian's father was no longer
a one-man job and Adrian had to help with all the lifting and
positioning him onto his toilet stool and then putting him either
back into the specialist medical bed which they'd installed
for him in the bedroom, or else into his wheelchair. But even
the wheelchair had become too uncomfortable for him as his
muscles had dwindled away to nothing at all and he was more
or less bed-bound. Not that he cared anymore. All he wanted
was to die. And to do it with dignity. Some hope!

"Please help me. I don't want to go further than this. My life was too beautiful than to end it bedridden, only kept alive by machines and the kindness of others, cut off from the world, denied my language and only waiting for the next pneumonia to finish me. I want a humane exit. I hope we can find one." They were Charlie Kramer's exact words in a letter that he wrote to his doctor. He asked Adrian to print it and give it to the doctor on one of his visits. But all the doctor could do was to offer him sympathy and a promise to help him as much as he possibly could, but never to kill him.

"I can't play God," the doctor told Adrian when they were alone later in the living room. Why not, Adrian thought to himself? The original one hasn't made much of a job of it. How much more can you fuck it up? But he kept his thoughts to himself.

They even looked into going to a specialist euthanasia clinic in Switzerland. But his father decided that he wanted to die in the home he loved. So he was permanently attached to his oxygen mask and his drips and his tubes which fed him and his speech computer which was suspended over his bed in direct line with his eyesight. And he was stuck too with his intolerable bed sores which were impossible to heal and caused the sleepless nights – not only for him but for Adrian and his mother who constantly had to get up and turn him and re-position him and put more healing lotion on the open sores.

"It's like watching an ice cube melt" is how Charlie Kramer's neurologist once described witnessing a Motor Neuron Disease patient's hellish and inevitable journey into oblivion, which Adrian thought was a pretty apt description.

I've met some wonderful people, he would also write in his book. *Some truly lovely, caring people – nurses, doctors, carers, neurologists, social service personnel, the physiotherapists who come in three times a week to try and keep his limbs moving and the speech therapist who came twice a week before his voice went completely – who all, without exception, at the very mention of MND, understand immediately the battle that Dad is in. The hopeless, helpless, unforgiving LOSING battle. And many of them have become almost like friends. The carer who we get at the weekend is also a sailor, just like us. He even keeps his dinghy in the same part of the harbour as our yacht and said when we get time, we can even go out together. "When we get time"... you know what that means. But wonderful as they all are, I wish I'd never met a single one of them,* Adrian added, because he'd only got to know them because of his father's cruel, fatal illness. *Wonderful human beings, every single one of them, but why God did our paths have to cross in this way?*

After his father left the world, Adrian fell into a deep hole. Not as deep as the one his mother had fallen into, nor did he need the kind of professional help that she needed in order to get back on track again, but he suffered from depression of sorts. Mostly he suffered from sadness and a broken heart and the inability to understand death and he just wasn't able to get his mind around why he would never again be able to see his father. There was also the question of his conscience, and the feeling that he hadn't been a good enough carer. That was what haunted him the most; the fact that he felt he'd let someone down and that he'd disappointed them. But isn't that something which haunts us all? That we simply weren't good enough for someone? We give them everything but feel we've come up short? Or are they the fools for expecting something better? Adrian never really did work that one out.

But he made a pact with himself that he couldn't afford to let that feeling of inferiority, of inadequacy, become an issue. He'd done his best. He'd done as much as he could. The rest was fate. He rejected the idea that he had been the hero, just as he rejected the idea that he had been a victim. "My father was those things, not me," he would say. A chunk of his youth, a crucial slice of his formative years, had been ripped away from him by Motor Neuron Disease. He learned what a bad day really was, and no one who he had ever known up to then had come even close to experiencing what his father had to go through. You think you've had a bad day? Think again my friend. Be next to someone with MND (though I wouldn't recommend it) and we'll speak again.

It was then that Adrian began to withdraw from the world – although he reckoned the world wouldn't miss him too much while he was gone. What he'd had to go through had left him full of uncertainty – it had left him with the belief that nothing in the world was sure anymore, nothing was safe, nothing was forever – and its legacy was mistrust. And worse, a morbid fear. He'd looked at death right up close and he was left with the feeling of "there but for the grace of God..." He also felt abandoned. He felt bitter–how could someone inflict this pure crap of a destiny on his father, his perfect father – and he felt emotionally scarred. Who wouldn't? Who has ever been through such an experience as he had to go through and hasn't felt as if they would be scarred forever? His self-hate also increased. Why didn't I do *this* better, why did I have to do *that* with a scowl? Why couldn't I have been more patient when he was taking an age to spell out his sentences on his damned computer? Why was I so often angry at having to do the things that I had to? (Although Adrian would also tell you that anger got him through a lot. Worked wrongly, anger can tear you up from the inside and allow in uncontrollable forces from the outside, and as sure as night follows day it will destroy you. But channelled right, used right, anger can take you a long way, it can even bring out the best in you, and it did that for Adrian. It carried him through some of the very toughest moments.) He hated himself because too often he'd thought about what the illness had done to *him* and how *he* had suffered. Surely that was selfishness, stone-cold heartlessness, callousness of the very worst kind? How can you possibly put yourself and your own needs first at times like that? He hated himself too because he was a perfectionist, even as a teenager, and looking back he realised that he'd been anything but perfect. Well, that was Adrian's version. Ask his father and all he would have told you was that he was so proud of his teenage son. His son had done it all for him. And "all" meant the very worst, the very dirtiest, the most humiliating, the most demeaning things imaginable for him. His son had done more than anyone could ever expect anyone to do. His son had stood in for his mother when it all got too tough for her. His son was a greater man at sixteen and seventeen than someone who had lived three times his age. His father would, just as Adrian had described him, have only been grateful.

People around Adrian told him that he should go to a psychologist, and that therapy might help him. But Adrian's answer was always the same. "I'm not sick. And unless they can tell me two things: one, that they have a cure for the illness and two, that they've invented a time machine so that we can travel back in time with the cure, I'm sorry but they have nothing for me. What do they tell you anyway? 'Don't worry it will all work out right in the end?' Yeah, like fuck it did. Or else they promise you 'it's all your parents' fault'. Or *you're* not to blame'. Well thanks for that. Then they come at you with 'Think about all the good times you had together'. Isn't that the standard sell, to 'cherish the good and forget the bad', as if the illness had never really happened? As if we'd imagined it all, and now we can just imagine it away? Don't they understand that's what makes a loss even greater? The richer the memories and the greater the love, the higher the bill you get to pick up at the end of it. Believe me, you get to pay big for all your perfect pictures. Besides, what do people expect of me? I'm incredibly sad. I'm hurting. I'm not ill in the fucking head. I've just lost the most precious thing in my life in the most awful of circumstances and I'm heartbroken. What do they want? Someone to persuade me that I shouldn't be sad? A god-damned stand-up comedy routine? I'm okay. I can function. I've always been able to function."

And in that, Adrian was right. He had, all throughout the hellish journey which his father had lived through, and then afterwards, he had always functioned, reacted, responded, organised, stayed strong, carried on. I'm okay. I'm sad. I'm angry. I'm scarred. But you know what? I'm the lucky one. I'm alive. I'm fit. I'm healthy. I can eat, I can walk, I can scratch my head if I need to and dance if I want to. I can scream and I can whisper. I'm fine. I'm still in the game. And unless someone has lived through what I lived through – unless they've seen it close up and felt it – hated it – suffered it – understood it – they have nothing for me. If all they've done is read a text book or ten... then they really don't know.

Harsh, but that's how he felt at the time.

It took Adrian a good couple of years to get over the traumatic and painful previous three. It was love measured in pain. He spent a lot of time alone on the boat. They didn't have to sell it in the end because his father's death came before they'd needed to. When his father's muscles and his body were at war, he had been prescribed Dronabinol – cannabis in other words – to help him to relax and to get to sleep. It came in the form of drops and he took it with sugar, until the point that he was unable to swallow. Adrian kept the bottle and took it out on the boat with him, lay on his back, tapped ten drops onto a spoon, added some orange juice and floated away... just floated away... watching the beautiful colours and the bizarre shapes which they formed. It was the first time in his life and the only time in his life that he was happy to give up his iron self-control, but in those spaced-out moments he was able to be at peace with himself. But only until the time came when he eventually emptied the bottle of dope and his own war returned. Even a couple of girlfriends couldn't lift his spirits nor "right the wrongs" as Adrian described it to himself.

And then along came Sarah. She was the prettiest girl that

Adrian had ever seen, and eventually the cure that he'd been waiting for (but not looking for). If Charlie Kramer had been the perfect father for him, from the moment that she walked into his life at university Sarah McDonald became the perfect partner, the perfect lover, the perfect soul mate and saviour. She saved him when he hadn't been able to save himself. From the second they met they both felt as if they were the only the two people in their world, and that all they wanted was to be with each other the whole time. It was one of those very special and very rare relationships where you feel complete, and it's the other person who completes you. And if you're lucky enough to find it, you cherish it. And soon a veil seemed to descend over the past few years and Adrian could smile again, he could love again, he found meaning in life again.

Adrian and Sarah. Sarah and Adrian. Whichever way you looked at it, it was a partnership made in heaven.

Part IV

The Search

1

The old Registrar in Hamburg's main Registry Office turned back to his computer screen. He'd already checked his records once and told Adrian the news. "I'm afraid that Karl von Dornbach's original adoption papers were destroyed in the War." But he wanted to check again. That was his job after all, to get it absolutely right. So Adrian sat and watched him carefully re-check and then re-check again, hoping for something better than he'd just been told but resigned to hearing more of the same. The old registrar was just bones and skin and looked pale and frail and as if he was about to keel over and die any minute, and Adrian thought while he watched him that he can't be a day under one hundred and twenty-five years old. He also wondered how he could ever have managed to get his head around something so twenty-first century as a computer. But it was his job, it had been his entire life, it had been all that he had lived for – documentation, recording, safeguarding history, preserving the past. It was just that the old guy hadn't got round to preserving himself too well over the years. At the end of his exhaustive search, which he had done while humming softly to himself, and also after a couple of follow-up telephone calls, he looked at Adrian and confirmed the news. Karl von Dornbach was off the records.

* * *

Adrian stood in the street outside the Registry Office doorway and scrolled down a list of companies on his mobile. Another warning sound came and the mobile's indicators told him that there was only two per cent energy left in the battery. He scrolled further – faster – until he found what he was looking for. Then he set off up the street with a fiercely determined and defiant look on his face. At that moment there was a quiet but definite power about him. He really could feel it.

He hadn't gone more than a few yards when he heard a female voice from somewhere behind him call out "Adrian Kramer!" and he turned straight round to look into the sharp, angular features of a smart red-head in a tight black trouser suit. Her heels put her at the same height as Adrian, but without them she could probably have walked under his crotch with some inches to spare.

Adrian said nothing and just looked and waited for her to say more. He guessed that she was around twenty-five, and he knew for sure that she packed a punch of some sort. She looked tough. And then some.

"You *are-a* Adrian Kramer?" she asked him in English but with a strong Italian accent. Adrian regarded her closely. The red in her hair had probably come out of a bottle.

"What do you want?" was Adrian's answer to her question.

"Not me. Two people I know. They would like to buy what you ave-a for sell."

"And what do I *ave-a for sell*?" Adrian imitated her.

"You know exact what I mean. They will-a pay you very well." Then she added enigmatically "They can be very persuasive," which was loaded with meaning and perhaps not so enigmatic after all if someone wanted to interpret it another way.

"I have nothing for sale. Someone else had them and he's now dead. Tell your friends that. And tell them to leave me alone."

And with that he turned and stormed off down the street.

Who the hell was that? he asked himself as he headed towards the car park. How could she possibly have known I was *here*? He turned and looked back up the street. But the sharp red-head was nowhere to be seen. And he thought that he might even have imagined what had just happened and that it had all been just one more bizarre scene in the strange and surreal movie that his life had become.

* * *

The Globo-Com building was a mile-high structure of steel and mirrored-glass in Hamburg's HafenCity. Adrian parked up his car in the vast but packed underground car park He left his satchel in the boot of the car and got out and headed towards the lift which then shot him up five floors into the main building in less time than it took to spell out the name H.e.y.d.r.i.c.h. The reception area there was more like the lobby of a grand, luxury hotel and had been designed with the notion that first impressions do indeed count the most. The place was lit in a soft, warm yellow light and the chandeliers which were suspended from the ceiling were every bit as impressive as the ones which hung in the von Dornbach's old family home. It had a marble floor so bright and shiny that it blinded you just to look at it and an array of exotic plants and palms lined the walls. Adrian approached the raven-haired receptionist who he suspected almost certainly worked weekends as a supermodel. "I'd like to see Doctor Messmer," he told her in his best, mistake-free German, which wasn't such an impossible task to get through with only a handful of words to master.

"Do you have an appointment?" she asked him in a voice so sultry it could melt an icecap.

"No."

"I'm afraid it's not possible without an appointment."

Adrian stood for a moment and thought on his feet. Actually, what he did in the seconds before he actually began to think was to stare in wonder at her perfect smile and her perfect teeth. Then he said, "Tell him a 'von Dornbach' wants to talk to him. I promise you he'll see me."

The receptionist repeated the name just to make sure that she'd got it right, or maybe it was just to show off her perfect voice again, then she picked up her phone.

* * *

Adrian's bluff worked. Although when Erich Messmer's stern looking assistant led him through the door which connected her office to her boss's, it was into an empty room. She invited Adrian to take a seat and left him to wait alone. He sat down in the soft leather armchair which he sunk down a mile into and looked around him. Even the Shah of Persia never had it that good. It was pure opulent, modern, conservative luxury with a commanding view out over the city, and Adrian sat fascinated by it all. The pile on the Turkish carpets was thigh-high – a herd of African elephants could have hidden away just fine in there for weeks – and the macassar ebony desk in front of him with its shiny leather top and twenty-four carat gold edging was positively presidential and was adorned with Swarovski crystal. The impressive reception area had just been a warm-up for the main act up on the seventeenth floor, Adrian thought. He sat patiently and took in one of the oil paintings on the wall. It was a Roman Capriccio by the Italian artist Giovanni Paolo Panini, and it was almost certainly an original. It was a dark and dreamlike array of Roman monuments and ruins which had all been thrown haphazardly together like a drunken afterthought to form a fantastical end-of-world spectacle. Somehow it fitted Adrian's mood that day. The painting was flanked by two enormous elephant's tusks which were suspended from the ceiling on either side of it as if they were standing guard over something precious and priceless. Which in fact they probably were.

Adrian jumped when the silence was broken by the door behind him closing. Erich Messmer had entered his kingdom quietly and surreptitiously through his main office door. He was wearing a dark blue suit with creases down the front of his trousers sharp enough to cut diamonds. But that was perhaps the only thing about him which said "Powerful Executive and International Hot Shot". He was in his early seventies – he was seventy-two to be precise – but he looked a good few years older than that. He was short, with small, round, horn-rimmed glasses which made his eyeballs look enormous and he had the kind of plain, nondescript features which could blend into any crowd. It all fits, Adrian thought to himself, I'm looking straight into the face of Heinrich Himmler! Because Erich Messmer somehow resembled the old Nazi – minus the ridiculous Himmler top-lip bumfluff. (Adrian had been poisoned so much by what he'd found up in his parents' loft and the pure hell it had unleashed ever since, that he was seeing the world through a narrow prism of the ribbons back then.) Messmer held out his hand for Adrian to shake, they exchanged a formal hello, and then Messmer waded his way through his jungle of a carpet and took a seat behind his wondrous desk.

"What can I do for you?" he asked in English.

Adrian swallowed hard. He knew that what would follow would be a big moment for him. "I'm looking for information, about my father."

"What makes you think I can help?" Messmer said in a voice and an accent which Adrian was sure he recognised.

"You knew the General. General Manfred von Dornbach."

Messmer's features remained blank. He appeared to have no idea what Adrian was taking about. He thought about the question for a short second then he shook his head slightly and said, "I've never heard of him."

"Just why did you agree to see me?"

Messmer said nothing and let Adrian's question pass him by. Adrian tried to read something in Messmer's face – anything at all – but it remained a blank mask.

"I think you knew him. And I think you can give me the last missing piece of information I want. Where was my father from?"

"I think you've mistaken me for someone else," Messmer said and remained absolutely calm and unruffled.

A tense and agonisingly silent moment passed while Adrian sat and weighed up the consequences of what he was about to say next. Because he knew that he was about to push his luck. "I tell you what," he said. "Let's have a show of hands, shall we? Raise your hand if you think the good Doctor Messmer is telling the truth," and then he made a big show of shoving both hands under his legs and sitting on them.

It didn't impress Messmer one bit. He just sat and gave Adrian a hard, ice-cold stare.

"Well, that's two to zero in favour of a lie," Adrian said.

If it was meant to rattle Messmer, it failed spectacularly. He remained a perfect study of "cool". He didn't even shift in his seat or fiddle with his collar or drum his fingers on his desk or clear his throat.

"Tell me who my father was."

"I have no idea who you are talking about," Messmer repeated.

"I don't believe you. Why should I when I know that I'd lie too if I was in your place?"

It was followed by another extended, tense silence. Messmer didn't like the quip, nor Adrian, one bit. But he wasn't prepared to show it. Any anger that he had – and right at that moment he was certainly livid at the interruption and the theft of his precious time and at Adrian's preposterous accusations – was raging only inside of him.

"You're a businessman," Adrian finally said. "So, let's talk business. You give me what I want... and I'll give you Reinhard Heydrich's wreath ribbons. They're real, they're available, and I know where I can get my hands on them. Well?"

"You have a wild imagination."

Adrian just shook his head slowly and deliberately. They were playing a game. He knew it, Messmer knew it, and the question now was who would come out the winner when final whistle went?

Messmer took off his glasses and laid them on the desk and rubbed his hands over his eyes as if to say "I'm tired of this, I'm tired of you". Then he took the powder blue silk handkerchief which was poking out of his breast pocket, picked his glasses back up from the desk and began to clean them with the care of a man polishing the finest Meissen porcelain – slowly, deliberately, meticulously, silently – and when he was finished he folded the handkerchief perfectly and put it back in his breast pocket exactly as it had been before and as if it had never been taken out.

Adrian sat patiently and watched the whole melodramatic performance. Then he said, "I've got what you want. You've got what I want. So, what do you say? A bit of information for a bit of old silk?"

But Messmer still said nothing. He had heard all he wanted to hear. This was leading nowhere and in front of him sat only irritation and an unwelcome interruption. He reached over to press a button on his office desk intercom. He was wearing a ring on his middle finger which was made from an old gold German coin, but that wasn't what intrigued Adrian when Messmer extended his arm out towards his desk phone. What caught Adrian's attention was when Messmer's shirt sleeve lifted up over his cuff and became caught on his cuff-link. Adrian stared down briefly at Messmer's wrist, and the pattern on the exposed gold cuff-link. It was a pattern which would have no meaning to anyone else, but Adrian recognised it immediately. Abstract lines, arranged into a circle like the spokes of a wheel. It was the pattern on the velvet bag which was then in his satchel in the back of his car.

"Show Herr von Dornbach out," Messmer said in German into his desk phone. Then he turned directly and addressed Adrian. "If we speak again, you'll be speaking only with my lawyer." The warning was clear, the threat very real. "Auf Wiedersehen" were Messmer's very final two words.

Adrian stared at the pattern on the cuff link for a frozen moment, although he did it secretly and without drawing Messmer's attention. Then he got up out of his seat and walked around to the other side of Messmer's desk. He put his hand into his jacket pocket and pulled out an old black and white photograph and laid it purposefully on the desk right in front of Messmer. Then without another word he turned and ploughed through the carpet and strode confidently out of the main office door, at the exact same moment that Messmer's side door swung open and his assistant appeared. Messmer waved her away with a sweep of his hand.

Adrian had left his mark. Because as Messmer stared down at the black and white image of young Karl von Dornbach looking straight back up at him with a raised-arm Nazi salute, he appeared for the first time anxious, agitated, rattled. And Erich Messmer was never any of those things. But someone had just got way too close. He fished his mobile phone out of his pocket, hit speed dial, and said into it ominously in a Swiss-German accent, "I've got a job for Renzli."

The pendulum swing of power had just shifted. But in which direction?

2

Adrian's car stood motionless in an endless line of traffic in the outer lane of Hamburg's Stresemannstrasse. Nothing was moving forward, nor had it for the past twenty minutes. The Police had blocked the road that morning in the direction that Adrian was travelling because of an accident somewhere up ahead and a traffic cop was standing in the middle of the lane signalling for cars to turn back around and use a different route out of the city. But Adrian didn't pay too much attention. His thoughts were somewhere else entirely. He dug into his pocket and pulled out Wolfgang's card. Then, while he was waiting to move one way or the other, he took out his mobile phone and tapped out the number on the card. The velvet bag was lying next to him on the passenger seat. He'd checked it when he got back into the car and compared the pattern to what he'd seen at the end of Erich Messmer's shirt sleeve. Sure enough, they were identical.

"Von Dornbach," Wolfgang's voice answered.

"Wolfgang, it's me, Adrian. I've seen Messmer. Can I come round?"

It was news which made Wolfgang immediately uneasy. "You've seen Messmer? I warned you not—"

Adrian cut straight in. "There was a sign on the bag that I found the ribbons in. I saw the same sign in Messmer's office."

"What kind of sign?"

Adrian was looking straight down at the pattern on the velvet bag lying right next to him when he said, "I'll explain later. I'm on my way."

He pulled his red Mini into a rapid U-turn and headed off back down the free lane on the other side of the street in the direction he had come from.

* * *

Something else happened that morning two hundred miles away in the German Parliament when the Chancellor was forced to stand up and defend the Government as yet another member of the ruling Christian Democratic Union party – the third in as many months – had been "outed" as belonging to a shady military network which had links to some extreme right-wing, white-supremacist organisations. The politician, who had a "black sun" tattoo on his right arm – a symbol adopted by neo-Nazis and occultists and not too dissimilar to the pattern on Adrian's velvet bag and Erich Messmer's cuff-links – was also head of a weapons and explosives manufacturer. He had been caught signing off on literature which he had distributed among the various neo-Nazi groups and associates warning about the serious threat of Islam and the impending terrorism brought on by the new wave of immigration. It painted a doomsday scenario which would be an inevitable consequence of the influx of refugees, and it advocated the stockpiling of weapons and munitions in advance of the impending "collapse of the prevailing social order".

This had all come amid fears that neo-Nazis groups were infiltrating the German military and police. One of the politician's Party colleagues – another outed neo-Nazi as well– was employed training military personnel, and the group had already accessed police data and used it to compile lists of left-wing and pro-refugee groups which were to be targeted and eliminated, as well as listing several mosques in Berlin and Hamburg which were deemed "soft targets" and could therefore be easily attacked. And what do you know, both politicians had indirect links to those who'd been responsible for the Hamburg shisha bar bombing back in May.

"The firewall against the far right is crumbling," an Opposition spokesperson claimed and asked rhetorically, "Have we learned nothing at all from our history? It is imperative that we safeguard ourselves from this current fascist infiltration of our institutions and our seat of power."

It was a claim which pacifist and anti-right-wing activist Wolfgang von Dornbach would emphatically echo and endorse.

* * *

The traffic all over the city that day was slow – almost certainly because of the blocked road into the city centre – and it was another forty-five minutes before Adrian was standing outside of Wolfgang's front door with his finger on the doorbell and his velvet bag pushed into the back pocket of his jeans. But no one was at home to answer. When a second try still didn't work, and when banging on the door got no response either, he walked round to the back of the house. Wolfgang's well-kept back garden was quiet, and no one was there either. But the kitchen door had been left slightly ajar. Adrian knocked, called out his uncle's name, and then he stepped inside. The kitchen too was empty. It was neat, tidy, and had been freshly decorated only three weeks before, but there was no one in it. Adrian began to move down the hall in the direction of the living room, where the door was closed. He opened it and went in. Then from what he saw, he stood like he'd been scorched by a blowtorch. Wolfgang was lying lifelessly on the floor next to the telephone. His eyes were wide open, but he had stopped gasping for breath some time before. His skin had a blue tinge to it, and he had died clutching at his white vicar's collar. Adrian again shouted out his uncle's name, out of pure reaction, then he moved towards him and stood over him and peered down into his dead face. Wolfgang's eyes were saucer wide and almost popping out of their sockets, and they seemed to Adrian to be following his every movement. He stood over him for an emotional moment. Then the moment became something else. Suddenly it was not only his uncle's dead body that he was looking down on, but someone else's. It began to haunt him and he had to turn away.

* * *

The face he was then looking down into was his father's and his father was dead. Adrian was standing over his bed. His dad's eyes were closed and his temples had sunken right in and were just two deep hollows at the side of his head. If Adrian lived another one thousand years he would never be able to describe for you the colour of his father's skin which in the moment of his death had turned a yellowy-green shade and had a shine to it which Adrian had never in his life seen in a person, before or since, as if someone had come in and polished it and tightened it over his cheekbones and forehead. The rest of his father's body had already withered away to nothing at all and the skin which had once covered his muscular frame was all wrinkled and just hung down in lumps. It was a pathetic end to a once formidably athletic and statuesque figure, and had indeed been no "bowing out with dignity" whatsoever. An eerie, other-wordly feel descended on the room after his father passed – that's what Adrian would remember most – how an almost holy presence hung heavy over the place and how something – who knows what or who – seemed to have laid a hand on his broad shoulders and touched him and taken over his entire being. If you have ever been with a loved one in their very final moments you might know yourself what Adrian felt, you too might have experienced that spiritual presence or divine sensation. Or maybe you just think all that stuff is just a bunch of hooey and hocus-pocus. That's your choice. Adrian himself certainly wasn't religious. He no longer believed in a God, nor in an afterlife. In the early days of his father's illness he had tried praying for help, then later he prayed for mercy, but no one was listening, or they didn't care, or they weren't up to it anyway. But something touched him in that moment. And it was something profound. That was all he knew, and it was a feeling which would stay with him forever.

Mrs Kramer stood just behind her son and to one side, as if she was using him for protection, which in actual fact she probably was, because the reality was way too painful for her. Her own tears hadn't yet started to flow because she hadn't yet grasped the enormity of what had just happened. She just felt and looked numb. The breakdown for her, the *big* breakdown, was still four weeks off.

Charlie Kramer had wanted to die at home, so in that he got his wish. He wanted to die too before he had to suffer any more months of torture – more months of "living death every hour of every day" as he called it himself. He refused a tracheotomy which would have enabled him to be permanently attached to a ventilator breathing machine. "It will prolong my life but it won't make it better," he spelled out on his speech simulator when the time had come for him to make that decision some weeks earlier, and he said that using his oxygen mask was as far as he would go. "I don't want something sucked out of my throat every hour. I don't want to be a paralysed lumb of flesh on a toilet chair (the rare spelling mistake had been his), unable to do anything or to go anywhere. Losing my voice on top of everything else was the worst. I always knew that. I always feared that as much as death itself. I can't be without it. No more conversations, no more easy chat, jokes, discussions. No longer the man that makes everybody happy, rather the one who gets on everybody's nerves in one way or another."

The day that Charlie Kramer died he pulled himself together to spell out two final requests (no one knew at that time that he would only live another few hours). He simply hadn't had the strength to work with his computer for the two previous days and he'd been more or less comatose in that time. But somehow, from somewhere, he summoned up the strength to spell out two things – the first of which was an attempted explanation of some sort to his beloved son – the "something that he had to tell" Adrian. But he simply wasn't able to, and it would forever remain unsaid. And it was that something which Adrian was convinced he was now trying to find out, of that he was sure. The loft... the loft... go up there and get the two silk ribbons and I'll explain everything, was what Adrian now imagined would have been the forever-unsaid message. As for the second thing which Charlie Kramer tried to communicate on the computer, it was a request of sorts which, after so many attempts and starts and stops and having to recalibrate and realign the computer because his father's head and eyes were so weak that he kept losing communication with the screen, after a further hour-and-a-half Adrian finally managed to understand and carry out his father's instruction.

"I'll call the doctor," Adrian's mother said in little more than a whisper as she looked down at her dead husband. Her bottom lip had started to tremble and her hand again began to shake.

* * *

Adrian blinked – and he was once more back in Wolfgang's living room, staring down into his dead uncle's face. And all he knew at that moment was that he had to get the hell out of there and get out fast – and seconds later, with his own skin now the colour of alabaster and clearly shaken, he ran through the kitchen and out of Wolfgang's house the same way that he'd come in – through the back door and into the garden – although this time he was a lot quicker. Then he stopped. He couldn't just leave like that. He turned round, headed back into the living room and picked up the phone. Keeping his eyes away from Wolfgang's body on the floor he tapped out the number 112 and put on as much of a French accent as he could to tell the emergency services to get there immediately because someone was dead on the living room floor. Before he'd even been asked any questions, he'd hung up and Usain Bolted into the kitchen and right out of the house.

On the other side of the three-foot garden hedge which separated the two houses Wolfgang's middle-aged neighbour was carrying an armful of groceries from his car and into his house. He peered over the hedge with an affable smile and shouted a friendly hello. But Adrian just looked right through him and headed off down the garden path towards his red Mini which was parked in the street.

* * *

Adrian didn't go straight back home after he left Wolfgang's, he drove out to his dinghy, although he didn't take it out onto the lake that day, he just sat in it for an hour in the jetty where it was moored and bobbed up and down with the lapping water, trying to clear his head, trying to think clearly about what had happened and what he had just seen, and also trying to work out what to do about Messmer. But it was no good. He just couldn't settle, even in the boat where he was always at his calmest, his thoughts were a mess. After a while he decided to grab something to eat at a cafe close to the lakeside harbour then head back home to the city.

3

The two Italians kept their word. But once again they were right out of luck because at the time that they called, Adrian was at the other side of town and racing to get away from Wolfgang's place. This time, though, the Italians didn't go away, not directly anyway. One of them took out his mobile phone, called a number, and two minutes later a white Ford Transit van pulled up directly outside of Adrian's building and three bulky men in brown workmen's overalls got out. They exchanged a cursory nod of the head with the two Italian guys, who turned and headed off up the street, then the three workmen got straight to work. They knew why they were there and what they had to do. One of them pressed a door buzzer next to one of the residents' names and seconds later they were heading up the stairs, shortly after that they were heading back out carrying the entire contents of Adrian's living room, including the television set, his computer, the sofa, the armchair, the coffee table and a set of drawers. They worked at lightning speed and the entire operation couldn't have taken them more than twenty minutes. They piled the lot into the back of the Ford Transit and slammed the back doors shut.

No sooner had the Transit pulled away and headed off up Borgfelder Strasse and taken the slip road onto the B5 than a bright red Audi TT Coupé came to a stop twenty yards further up the street from Adrian's building. One of the two men inside the car pulled two black masks out of a canvas shopping bag, handed one of the masks to his partner, then sat and waited. What they were waiting for arrived five minutes later when Adrian's Mini pulled up at the kerb directly outside of his building. Adrian jumped out and took the stairs two at a time up to his flat. He headed straight into his living room – and stopped dead. It was totally empty, except for the cracked photograph of himself and his father which was still on the windowsill. Next to it was a note in English which read "Give us the ribbons and you will get back your things. We will be in touch later today. We know you will not go to cops because what you are sell is not legal."

Further up the street inside the Audi TT the two men pulled the masks over their heads. The car doors swung open and they were about to get out. But suddenly they stopped. They had seen something.

Up in his living room Adrian pulled the blinds down on the windows and stood and stared at the note in his hands. He thought about what Wolfgang had told him in the car on the drive back from the von Dornbach's old family home, that it wasn't just the foot soldiers of the "right" – the kinds who carried out the dirty work and who Adrian had already come up against, such as the skinheads who raided his flat, or those who had kidnapped Katharina and threatened Adrian too. It was the power base behind them. That, Wolfgang said, was what should be feared the most. A man in the street with a twisted view of the world and a hammer in his hand wasn't anywhere close to being as dangerous for a society as a set of billionaires with the same twisted views but with an elevated and privileged position in that society. Because they could buy the man in the street who held the hammer in his hand. And it wasn't about the kind of populist right-wing politics which was sweeping the country at the time, appealing to those who felt disenfranchised or frozen out of the political system, or who felt that their own fears and cries for help were being ignored. This was something far more frightening and much more dangerous. This was about perpetuating real and pure Nazi ideology and all that it stood for. It was the glorification and the justification for murder and genocide and supremacist dogma, and Messmer and his like were the invisible but super-powerful messiahs keeping it alive, and in the world – a world which poor Wolfgang and his kind heart was no longer part of. "Money and position can buy ideology," Wolfgang had insisted. Except...

Except Adrian knew for certain that it wasn't the powerful, moneyed executives who had taken his things. Erich Messmer didn't need a coffee table or a sofa or a new television set. And the Brotherhood, whoever they were, certainly didn't deal in second-hand furniture. The threat to him was frightening and it was immediate and it came from the street and not a glass-fronted, billionaire's tower block.

At the time it felt to Adrian like he was trying to catch shadows. Who the fuck am I messed up with now and how do I scrape this shit off my shoe? was what he was metaphorically thinking when his front doorbell rang. He hesitated for a moment, and then he finally went through to the hall to answer it.

"Hello?"

"Adrian Kramer?" the voice said. It was a voice which he should have recognised because he'd certainly heard it before, but in the heat of the moment it passed him by. "Police. We'd like to talk to you."

Adrian went over to the window and raised the blinds just high enough to see the police car parked behind his Mini in the street below. He pushed the velvet bag deep into his back pocket then hit the button to release the lock on the main door.

When he opened his flat door a minute later and saw who was standing there his heart sank even further. Because facing him was Helmut Geissinger from the Keilsbach Police, together with a uniformed Hamburg Police officer. Geissinger greeted him with a sardonic smile and the old German proverb, ominous and heavy here with meaning. "Man trifft sich immer zweimal... Nicht wahr, Herr Kramer?" (You always meet twice in life... isn't that right Herr Kramer?) "And we were getting along so well," he added full of sarcasm and followed that with what was more a command than a request, "Can we go inside?"

Keilsbach's very canniest followed Adrian into the cleared

out living room. He looked around at all the empty space and missing furnishing and smiled a sardonic smile to himself.

"Moving out?"

"I might be."

The sly smile stayed on Geissinger face. He was confident and knew that he was now in full control. It was his game they'd be playing now, it would be played under his rules, and he would, in the end, be declared the winner.

"What do you want?" Adrian asked him bluntly.

"How much money did Werner Retz owe you?"

Adrian wasn't expecting that as Geissinger's opening gambit and it took him totally by surprise.

"None. Why?"

"He was a good friend. He was your 'Best Man'," Geissinger said in his very best ironic tone – one which was full of cynicism. "You'd help him out if he needed it, wouldn't you?"

"What are you talking about?"

"I'm talking about friendship," Geissinger said cryptically. "And how it can get..." He clenched his fist tight, squeezing his fingers hard together. "You know? When a friend can't pay a friend the money he's loaned him? Say... to help him pay off the debts he has?"

"What's your point?" Adrian said off Geissinger's piercing look. Geissinger was positively lasering right through him with his razor-sharp eyes.

"We found blood in Werner Retz's house."

He looked down at the band aid on the side of Adrian's hand.

"I wonder whose?"

There was nothing from Adrian. He just stood and looked at Geissinger intently, matching the detective's penetrating stare.

Geissinger went on. "We still haven't found a body. But we found another one. Wolfgang von Dornbach's. It appears he..." He looked into his notebook for the word he needed. "'Suffocated' to death. Earlier today."

The moment that Geissinger said those words Adrian froze and a vision appeared in his head. It was the sight of a thick pillow being pressed down over some poor victim's face. Then a second pair of plastic-gloved hands joined the first plastic-gloved hands and pushed and pushed and pressed and pressed until the life was squeezed out of him.

"What are you thinking, Her Kramer?" Geissinger's words broke the spell. His eyes watched Adrian's reaction like a hawk as he added "I believe you did it, Herr Kramer."

Adrian couldn't believe what he was hearing. "What?"

"Your fingerprints are all over the house. And you were seen by a neighbour leaving through the back door at around six. The time that he was murdered. Behaving..." He looked down again at his little notebook, "suspiciously."

Adrian's mind began to drift, to race. He was once more making his connections – connections which Geissinger and his sidekick would never get to.

"Why were you at the house?"

Suddenly, everything seemed to stand still for Adrian.

Geissinger's eyes burned right into him as he repeated his question for Adrian "Why were you there? And why are you moving out suddenly now? We know for certain that you didn't get married as you said."

But it was the detective's words "suffocated to death" which were echoing eerily around in Adrian's head at that moment and all he was imagining right then was a bathroom towel being pressed down over his mother's face and a pair of gloved hands pressing the towel harder and harder and harder until it suffocated the poor old woman. That's how it had been there too back in the north-east of England. Adrian was sure of that much now.

He snapped back to attention. "You said Wolfgang von Dornbach suffocated?"

"You haven't answered my question, Herr Kramer."

Adrian looked directly into Geissinger's eyes for an intense beat. There was more than a touch of anger in his voice when he said to him, "I know who killed him. And who killed someone else."

It was Geissinger's turn to be confused.

* * *

A short distance away in Cafe Miljöö, where the two Italians had gone to kill time while they waited, they finished off their plate of the "best *Flammkuchen* north of the Alsace", paid up and left the cafe, while further down the road in the Red Audi TT the two men had removed their masks and sat patiently. They waited and watched Adrian's building from behind the car's tinted windscreen. One of them had his cell phone to his ear. From what he heard he nodded, dropped the phone back into his pocket, and gestured to his partner that they were to wait a little longer. They even turned on the radio, but all they could get was the day's news – an update on the Brexit-dominated General Election over in the UK and the nonsense going on in the British Parliament, then something about Donald Trump eating everybody's babies, and finally the traffic news followed by someone called Ed Sheeran, who they didn't know or care about, telling them he "was in love with their body..." which wasn't really anything of real interest for two fascist thugs in Hamburg. But they listened to him anyway.

* * *

Up in the flat Adrian stared with exasperation at Geissinger. "Wolfgang von Dornbach was my uncle. I met him for the very first time in my life earlier this week. The same person who killed him killed my mother. Someone called Erich Messmer."

"Erich Messmer? *The* Erich Messmer?"

"Yes. You know him?"

"Everybody knows Erich Messmer," Geissinger said and dismissed Adrian's bizarre claim with something between contempt and a wariness not to stand on the wrong person's toes. "Do you really expect me to believe that?"

He had been studying Adrian with heron-like intensity. Eventually he nodded over to his colleague, who started to move towards Adrian. Adrian knew exactly what that meant.

"Give me the chance to explain, damn it!"

"At the station. We're taking you in."

"There's someone else in danger. A student of mine. She needs protection."

Geissinger just shook his head dismissively and produced an arrest warrant. "Tell us about it at the station."

"Give me a break. If anything happens to her the blood will be on your hands, not mine."

Adrian stood a moment weighing up his options. He knew that they were between "bad" and "none at all".

"I need to go to the bathroom," he said to Geissinger. He was now inwardly determined and driven.

Geissinger shook his head. "At the station," he repeated.

"Come on man. You want me to piss on your car seat?"

The bathroom door was directly off the living room. The room itself was windowless and offered no opportunity or danger of escape, and Geissinger knew that. He exchanged a look with his colleague, eventually nodded his okay, and Adrian passed him and headed out and into the bathroom. Geissinger's colleague leaned against the living room doorframe and stood watch over the bathroom door.

Inside the bathroom Adrian sat on the side of the bath and tried to think fast. He had to get out of the flat somehow, and get out of it quickly. But how? He had no idea. And the thought which was forcing its way into his head ahead of all others, the one which was preventing him from thinking clearly, was so horrific that he began to break out into a sweat. It was the notion that he had been responsible for drawing Messmer, or whoever carried out Messmer's dirty work for him, straight to Wolfgang's door. He knew that he had led them directly to his uncle, which had directly led to his murder. Had he killed his uncle now too? Was Wolfgang's blood on his hands? You're going straight to hell, boy, he thought to himself.

He fought to clear his head – he slapped himself on the side of the cheek and splashed cold water onto his face – think, Adrian, think.

Outside in the street the two men waiting patiently in the red Audi watched through the tinted windscreen as the Italians ambled back down the street towards Adrian's building. One of the Italians said something to the other, they exchanged a laugh, and then they turned towards the entrance to Adrian's flat.

Up in the bathroom Adrian dried his face and pulled his mobile phone out of his pocket, only to hear the shrill warning sound and see that there was only one per cent left on the phone's battery. The Smartphone wasn't so smart after all. He began to tap out a number as quickly as he could, only for the phone to die on him and cut off completely. He muttered a silent "shit" to himself. His plan – his only way out – was the idea of calling his own landline so that the phone in the hall would ring, and then with Geissinger's permission he would go to answer and then he would race straight out of the main door and lock the two Police officers inside. But with the mobile phone out of action that plan was now resigned to history. He pushed the phone back into his pocket, sat for a moment, and realised that he was now all out of options. He tore off a few pieces of toilet roll and wiped the perspiration from his brow then he tossed it into the toilet and flushed it away. He exited the bathroom and trudged back into the living room, watched closely by Geissinger's colleague, who Adrian passed on his way into the living room.

It was at that very moment that the Italians rang his front doorbell. Adrian looked over at Geissinger with a gesture which asked something along the lines of "okay if I answer it?" Geissinger nodded, signalled to his colleague that he should follow Adrian out into the hall and the cop set off after him. But before he got there Adrian spun quickly round, slammed the living room door shut behind him and turned the key which locked the two cops inside. He sprinted out of his apartment door, quickly locking that from the outside too, and flew down the main stairs. The two Italians stood bemused as the front door flew open and Adrian shot out and straight past them.

The two guys in the bright red Audi watched Adrian jump into his car and accelerate away up the street. Without exchanging a word they fired up the Audi's engine and roared off after him.

They were like two red sparks flaming through the darkness. Adrian's Mini flew through the quiet late-evening Hamburg streets with the Audi keeping pace some yards behind. It was like something straight out of a cheap, made-for-television American cop movie, except that the streets were Hamburg and not San Francisco, and this was for real. Adrian whipped out his mobile phone, so desperate to make a call – maybe it has enough energy left in it for a five-second call? But once again there was nothing in it at all. It had died on him back in the flat. He stepped down even harder on the gas and his mind was at that moment racing as fast and as wildly as his Mini. He didn't even notice that in his rear-view mirror bright headlights were getting closer and closer and closer until they were right in his back and his car was flooded with blinding white light. Suddenly his head was whiplashed back violently as the Audi rammed him from behind. He fought to regain control as his Mini went into a spin across to the other side of the road and the engine cut out. Before the Audi was able to ram him again, Adrian had started up the Mini's engine, turned it back around and accelerated away with the Audi again hard on his tail. From behind him a loud gunshot rang out and Adrian's rear windscreen shattered into a thousand small pieces. The two cars tore like hell through the nighttime streets with the much quicker Audi finally closing on Adrian, until it was right alongside him, travelling on the left-hand side of the road. The Audi's two occupants had their masks back on and the one in the passenger seat had his window fully down. He raised his revolver and aimed it directly at Adrian. He had a clear shot. They were then at a junction and both took a left turn together, going at full speed, with the gunman about to fire a certain hit...

The Audi smashed head-on into a huge, orange-coloured street-cleaning truck which was doing its late-night duties keeping Hamburg's kerbsides and pavements German-standard clean. The impact was immense. The crunch of metal on metal was sickening. But Adrian didn't stop to watch and roared off into the night.

Behind him both vehicles, and their passengers, were a bloody, lifeless mess.

4

It had been a fairly mundane working day which she'd spent sitting at the newspaper offices, writing up an article that she'd written about the increasing homelessness in the city. When she got back home she watered her plants, answered a couple of emails which had been hanging around her inbox forever, practised a couple of yoga asanas to relax her, jumped in the shower, threw a salad together out of what was left in the fridge and settled down for a quiet night alone with James Joyce. She'd never read *Ulysses* before, at least never in English, and in no other language either beyond page twenty-eight, so this was her challenge for the night; page twenty-nine or bust. It might have been around page twenty – or maybe a page or two further, Katharina would never really be able to recall exactly – but it was at around that point that Adrian's car screeched to a halt in the street outside her apartment and he jumped out seeing that there was a light on inside. He ran up to the main door and pressed the bell – once, twice, and then he kept his finger there until he heard Katharina's voice say *"Hallo? Warum Hab—"*

"It's me. Let me in," he shouted into the intercom. There was utter desperation in his voice.

"It's too late, Adrian." She was referring to much more than the time of night when she said that.

"You're in trouble. We both are. You have to let me in. Please, Katharina!"

There was a short but tense and anxious moment while he waited for a response. It could have gone either way. Then the main doorlock was disengaged and Adrian pushed through.

"You have to get out of here," he shouted again when he saw her standing at the doorway of her own flat.

"What are you talking about? Do you know what time it is?"

"Messmer is after us."

"Who?"

"Let me in. Messmer. The guy who arranged your kidnap. The same guy who killed my mother."

They were on their way up the hallway and into Katharina's living room.

"What does—"

Before she could say more Adrian had grabbed her, pulled her into the bedroom, and pushed her into action.

"Just get together whatever you need and let's get out of here."

The worry and despair which were etched deep into his face were plain enough for her to see. This really did look more than serious.

"What's this all about, Adrian?"

She started throwing some things into a small overnight bag. But it was all still too slow for Adrian. "Come on! he pleaded with her. "Faster! And leave that," he said, referring to a hair brush. She shot him a dark look. She was affronted by his harassment.

"Hey, I'm the person you're asking to help you," she said.

"No. You're the person whose life I'm trying to save."

She threw the hair brush into the bag anyway. "Who is this guy, this Messmer?"

"Head of Globo-Com. Here in Hamburg."

She stopped packing for a second and shot him a look – because the significance of the name was not lost on her. "Erich Messmer?" She was incredulous.

"You know him?"

"Of course I know him. Everyone knows him. He's also still the Head of the German CBI. How did you find all this out?"

"Come on, faster. I'll tell you later."

Adrian flung the last couple of things into her bag for her, while her own mind was beginning to play around with an intriguing thought.

"We'll have to take your car," he said before he zipped up the bag and took her hand to drag her away.

"My uncle has a place we can stay. It used to be my father's," she told him as they sprinted together down the stairs. "I still have the key."

There was no one outside waiting to shoot them or put black canvas bags over their faces or shove their heads into a toilet bowl. But Adrian nevertheless looked constantly around him and back over his shoulder, his head rotating like a mad owl's as they headed towards Katharina's car parked a few yards up the street. Adrian took one last nervous look around him before he threw Katharina's bag into the back seat. Then they quickly jumped into the car, and with Katharina behind the wheel, pulled away into the Hamburg night.

The bright lights of the city faded into the distance as Katharina's car sped along the empty nighttime autobahn, then after some minutes she took an exit onto a deserted, tree-lined country road. Neither she nor Adrian spoke for some time after he'd explained what had happened, except for Adrian checking in with, "You do know where you're going, don't you?" and Katharina replying with an indignant, "Of course I know." An hour's fast drive out of Hamburg, somewhere on the southern edge of the Lüneburg Heath – the vast, wild, heather-covered moorland area which always reminded Adrian of the northern Dales close to his home back in England – Katharina left the road and headed off up a pitch-black forest track which finally came to an end half a mile later, where the car's bright headlights lit up a small wooden forest hut. Its window shutters were all closed, but more importantly, there appeared to be none of Messmer's heavies hiding behind trees there to ambush them.

5

A single dark green candle pushed into the top of an empty Chianti wine bottle lit up the rustic, one-room wooden chalet. Adrian had pulled some thick wool blankets out of a drawer and had begun to put together a makeshift bed for himself on the hut floor while Katharina did her best to assemble the sofa bed. She stopped, turned and faced him.

"Hey."

Adrian too stopped what he was doing and looked straight up at her.

"This will all work out okay," she told him and even managed to add that smile of hers at the end.

"I know it will. That's why I'm here and not in Hamburg. I've done nothing wrong. Nothing wrong in the past few weeks."

She returned to her struggle with the bed and had her back to him so she couldn't see the look he had at that moment on his face. He was tired – the second most poignant day of his entire life had clearly left its impact. But in his eyes there was a sense of purpose, a sense of clarity. And there was Vengeance with a big, fat capital "V".

"Did I say 'thanks'?" he asked her.

"For what?"

"This." He meant the hideout.

She turned to him and made a "you're welcome" gesture. "It was me who started it all, remember?"

"If you hadn't, I'd never have found out about my father."

"Whatever it costs?"

"Whatever it costs."

She looked at him with sympathy. "And however much it hurts?"

"The hurt I'll handle."

Adrian's tired mind began to play with the thought. He'd

lived with so much pain and anguish before – and a little more he would deal with easily if that was the way it had to be.

Katharina's struggle with the sofa bed was finally over. She sat down on the edge of it and studied him closely.

"Who hurt you so much, Adrian?"

He thought the question over before he responded. Not the answer – he knew that well enough. But whether that particular moment was the right time. Finally, he said, "The prettiest girl I've ever seen." After which, looking straight at her, he added cheekily, "Second prettiest. Every single guy at our college wanted her. I was the lucky one who got her. And followed her here to Germany. Where she slept with her boss... In my bed."

"Oh," was all Katharina could say.

"But she taught me well. She taught me that it's all just like something you write in the sand. Temporary. And gone the next day."

"And you actually believe that it always has to be like that?"

"Doesn't it?"

What Adrian was thinking about right then was about the day he nearly died. The day he nearly died twice. It had all happened three years before when one of his evening classes was suddenly cancelled and he'd arrived home early from work to find Sarah on her knees on the bed with her Bavarian boss going at it like a mutt on heat. At least Adrian was spared the "this isn't at all what you think it is" crap because it was exactly what it looked like. He pulled Franz the Randy Bavarian off the bed, threw him butt naked into the hallway, told him to fuck off when he tried to ask for his clothes, then calmly told Sarah to get the hell out of his flat and out of his life. That was the moment he felt that he had died for the first time.

"You know what the only thing she said to me was?" Adrian said to Katharina in the hut. "'What are you doing home so early?' As if it was all *my* fault." And what hit him hard too was that he had absolutely no idea. It had been going on for nearly two months and Adrian didn't have a clue.

After stripping the bed and dumping the bedclothes into the trash, Adrian went out into the streets and began to walk. And walk. And walk. Until he ended up in a dark and empty alley somewhere in Altona; three guys dressed in black came towards him. One of them pulled a knife. Another one of them said something, but Adrian wasn't watching and wasn't listening anyway. He was in another place entirely, overwhelmed by a world of betrayal and hurt and treachery and disillusionment and backstabbing – and the pain of his youth was also in there too – he knew right then that nothing was forever, not life, not love, not trust, nothing. He felt small, he felt inadequate. He felt lost. But the cruel irony was that the person who had just betrayed him and who had hurt him so much and was now out of his life was also the one that he wanted so much. He was no longer able to live with her. But how would he live without her? He still wanted her – he didn't want her any more. He remembered why he loved her in the first place. She was perfect for him. But he now had those pictures in his head of her in bed with someone else. He was a mirror ball of confusion. It was hate and love – that beautiful, and beautifully toxic combination – both reflecting back at him at the same time.

Walking down the dark Hamburg alley with his perfect emotional storm raging inside of him – heartbroken and feeling a long, long way from home – he thought that he heard his father's weak voice calling out to him "watch out Adrian", but he knew that couldn't be possible. Then something from behind hit him over the head with a dull thud and he began to fall, all he saw was the evening sky high above him. It was a brilliant red-orange colour and it reminded him of his old dinghy's sails. He saw a castle perched somewhere atop fine white sand dunes but the sand was all so bright... too bright for his poor eyes to handle. He saw Sarah's shocked face when she turned. And finally, he saw his grandmother bending down in front of the swing that he was on... just as it hit her and cracked her head wide open everything went black and Adrian began to tumble into the abyss. And then he decided just to let go. He wasn't afraid. Just angry. And then he began to fade away into nothingness.

Four hours later he regained consciousness in a Hamburg hospital. He could recall nothing about what had happened to him. All he knew was that his pockets were empty, and the sleeve of his jacket, which was draped across the back of his hospital ward chair, was bloody and torn. And once more, all he saw was the look on Sarah's face as she turned. First, he saw her smile, mixed in with the ecstasy, but it was immediately followed by sheer shock. It was no longer a beautiful face to him, but the face of evil. It had become the epitome of betrayal. The attackers had fractured Adrian's collar bone and left him with a cut to the side of his hand which had required four stitches, but his cheating lover's assault had left him with much, much deeper scars and with pain which would last a lot longer.

After that, Adrian drifted for a while, just as he had after his father passed away – directionless, aware that he would be taking his journey through life alone and that there would never be anyone else at his side. He'd arrived at a point where his life was so empty of all meaning that he saw only blackness ahead of him and no reason to carry on. He felt he'd killed the thing which he'd once loved most in the world, his father. And then the thing which he had grown to love the most, Sarah, had killed him.

He asked himself why she had done it. What was so inadequate about him that had compelled her to betray him? Had it been about looks? Surely that couldn't be it. Franz Steffens had a face fatter than his arse cheeks and had more hair on his back than he had on his head. Was it about money? Or maybe humour? Was old Franz a laugh-a-minute billionaire comedian who also happened to be the world champion lover in bed? Did he shower her with expensive jewellery while he whispered sweet nothings from Baudilaire into her expensively perfumed ear? Adrian never did manage to figure it out. But he knew that he had given her everything – his heart, his soul, his emotions, he'd opened up with her like he'd opened up with no one before (or since for that matter). And for the second time in his short life he felt that he'd fallen short and that what he was and what he had to give somebody simply hadn't been good enough for them. He was God's sick little joke. He had tried. He'd given everything he had and at all times. But he'd simply come up short. Yes, that was it, it had all been his own fault. He began to suffer from self-hatred, followed soon afterwards by the thing which he hated most in the world – the thing which he'd been brought up to despise – self-pity. It was then that he vowed never to allow himself to be hurt again and he stayed that way for some time, until Werner became an important part of his life and a trusted and valued friend.

Katharina sat and listened as Adrian told his story. It was one of her virtues, the ability to listen, the ability to assimilate what she'd heard and then afterwards to analyse. And for Adrian, he'd again opened up to her, just as he'd done once before about the ribbons, and he felt good about it. It felt comfortable to be in a place he had never been in for so long. It somehow felt right.

Katharina had already moved to sit down next to him on his makeshift bed on the floor. She looked at him – so vulnerable, so wounded, so beautiful like that at that moment, just crying out in the dark for someone – and slowly she shook her head from side to side. "No, Adrian. It doesn't always have to be like that," she said as an answer to his earlier question. It was a big moment. It was that moment just a half-second away from "falling", when it looks certain that two people will finally kiss...

Until Adrian, fearing that he'd let his guard drop too low and aware that perhaps he'd given too much of himself away and that it might all become too much for his glass heart to bear

– while at the same time also fighting another voice which was now whispering into his ear "don't worry about the scars" – surprised even himself by saying, "I think we'd better get some sleep."

6

It had to happen of course. This story – Adrian's story – was never really destined to end well. And it didn't. Certainly not for Adrian. A swastika had been tattooed deep into his forehead and his hair had been completely shaved off. He swung lifelessly from one of the wooden beams in the hut's low ceiling and was suspended by the two wreath ribbons, which had been tied tightly around his neck into a noose. His eyes were closed and his feet were dangling three feet from the hut floor. Katharina was lying a couple of yards away from him on her side, on the sofa bed which she'd made up earlier for herself. Her eyes too were firmly closed.

Then suddenly they shot wide open. Choking and fighting for air, she jumped up in the bed clutching her throat. Sweat was pouring out of her. She looked across the single room and could just make out Adrian, sitting up and looking back at her through the darkness.

"Are you okay?" he called out to her from across the room.

She was and she wasn't. She was stuck for the moment in that place somewhere between nightmare and reality.

"I... I dreamed. Did I wake you?"

"No. I couldn't sleep anyway."

He turned over onto his side. Katharina lay across the room from him and stared up at nothing. Her mind was racing, her imagination was playing tricks. In the extreme silence, every owl sound was a gunshot. Every deer an invader. Every leaf rustle was Messmer's men come to murder them. She ran her fingers through her hair and squeezed so tight that her knuckles were almost white.

"Adrian?"

"Yes?" He was still lying on his side and facing away from her.

Without another word Katharina gathered up her blankets, carried them over to him on the floor and slid in alongside him. He turned to her and wrapped his arms protectively around her. They lay like that for a moment in silence. Just two people needing each other. Then Adrian said, "I thought about what you said earlier. About it not always having to be like that."

"And?"

"Maybe you're right."

His words were followed by a highly charged moment while he looked deep into her eyes. Even in the dim light and in that state, she looked impossibly beautiful to Adrian. "I'm..."

He started to say something. She put a finger over his lips to silence him.

"Shh..." Then in little more than a whisper she said, "You're not a bad English teacher, Mr Kramer. But never teach maths. You think one and one equals two." She shook her head. "One and one should equal three, that's when real magic happens. When two people come together and what it makes is more than the two of them together. 'Three'... that's always the magic number."

She still had her finger over his lips. "As for English... like I said, you're not bad. But perhaps you haven't taught me the right vocabulary." She took her finger away and held it up right in front of his eyes so that he could see it. "What's this?"

"Your finger?"

"Which finger?"

"Index finger."

"And these?" She used the same finger to touch his mouth softly.

"Lips."

"Correct." She removed her finger and kissed him softly where it had been. Then she leaned over him and kissed him on the forehead, again so soft... so soft. Then on the eyes, the nose, his chin, the cheek. And then finally, a longer, tender, passionate kiss on the lips. But just as it was getting interesting, she quickly pulled back. She was unsure of his reaction. Adrian wrapped an arm round her neck and drew her back down towards him. It was his moment of surrender. He was reaching out for someone and was now unafraid of the consequences, unconcerned that it could end in tears. It felt like he was finally coming home.

What followed was a kiss which would remain burned into their memories for the rest of their lives.

* * *

Bright sunlight streaked in through the cracks and slats in the outside shutters and lit up the room. Beams of it fell on the wall opposite Adrian and Katharina, where several hunting trophies were hanging: a mounted deer's antlers, a stag's head, a small stuffed weasel – the usual kinds of bounties for the oh-so-brave and courageous warrior. There was also a vicious-looking African hunting knife hanging there and an old rusted, antique shotgun which probably fired its last shot around the time Kaiser Wilhelm ruled the roost.

Adrian propped himself up on one arm and watched Katharina slowly wake. And when she did, she broke into a warm, contented smile.

"Morning, Teacher."

Adrian looked at her for a moment and returned her smile. He said nothing.

"What are you thinking?" she asked him.

"I'm happy I finally let someone in."

"*Someone*?" She gave him a playful dig in the ribs.

"Someone special."

"Better!"

She reached up and kissed him.

When they finally broke, Adrian took a look around the room. "Hunting clearly runs in the family," he said, making obvious reference to her too.

"Just be happy you didn't end up like him," she said nodding at the stuffed stag up on the wall.

"You know, in Africa, it's the lioness who brings in the breakfast," he said.

"But the lioness only hunts at night."

They exchanged a look and a smile.

"There's a baker down in the village," Katharina said and began to get up off the makeshift bed on the floor. "I'll go get us something."

A hand grabbed her and pulled her back down.

And it started all over again.

A spell had been broken. Three words left unspoken. That would wait for another day.

* * *

Back in the Inter-Lingua language school in Hamburg that morning, Dixon was standing in for Adrian. The classroom blinds were down because he was showing the class his favourite movie, *Chicago*. Dixon was someone who would tell you that he used films in his lessons to teach English, when in fact he often used the lessons to watch movies. But his classes lapped it up anyway.

While Richard Gere was tap-dancing his way around a Chicago court room, just down the corridor from Dixon's classroom Jacob sat across the desk from Goldberg the school director with a huge smile on his face. The smile was cunning and crafty and its object of admiration was Jacob himself. He was telling old Whoopie about how Adrian had now lost it totally in all of his classes and about his sudden and unexplained absence and why he should be given the top job himself instead.

"How long is it since he turned up?" Jacob asked his boss rhetorically. "No sick note. No telephone call. Überhaupt kein Wort von ihm. Nothing. No one knows where he is. It's irresponsible and it's unfair and I'm not prepared to stand in for him anymore. And neither are any of the other teachers." Which wasn't strictly true. Most of them either couldn't have cared less and existed only in their own little worlds, or else they were worried and confused about why a valued colleague and such a solid, dependable person as Adrian would suddenly go off the rails.

Goldberg's little Scottish Terrier poked its head out from under the desk and looked up at Jacob – should I or shouldn't I sniff his balls? It decided to give it a pass and slumped back down onto the floor instead.

"The reputation of the school is at stake here and Kramer is badly damaging it," was Jacob's clinching argument.

Goldberg thanked him for his concern for the well-being of his language school and told him that he would think it over, but that he owed it to Adrian to hear him out fully once he returned to work.

7

The solitary hut was set at the end of a long dirt track which was lined with ferns and brackens, and was at the very edge of dense woodland. Beyond that was vast open moorland of coarse heather. While Katharina was playing lioness down in the village Adrian sat on a small wooden bench at the back of the hut. He was holding the velvet bag and trying to make some sense of the bizarre abstract sign in the corner and, with the first quiet moment to himself for what then seemed like a whole lifetime, he finally tried too to make some sense out of the mayhem which had been unleashed all around him as a consequence of the two cursed fascist ribbons, and probably even before they had come into his life. Werner was dead. Wolfgang was dead. His mother was dead. His father was dead. And Messmer had almost certainly been responsible for killing three of them. He thought about their final moments and the horror they must have suffered as they were being killed. And he thought too about his father's final twenty-four hours.

If he had to have an illness, why did he have to have *that* one? Adrian had asked the same question a thousand times before in his short lifetime, and had written exactly those very words in his very final entry in his diary. And each time he'd asked the question, he knew that he would never get an answer to it. And if he had to have Motor Neuron Disease, why did it have to be *that* form of it?

The illness, just like so many other things in this crazy world of ours which go badly wrong, is basically about a failure to communicate, and it occurs when the messages which the brain sends to the body – to the muscles which control our body – don't get passed on. They don't get passed on because the neurons in the brain which transmit the messages die. The result is... well, if you don't know the result, it's better not to know. But that wasn't an option for Charlie Kramer, or for the family.

Now this is not a lesson in medical science, nor is it a history lesson. Hell, that's the very last thing this sorry tale is or should try to be. But there are things that it's important to know in order to understand Adrian's story fully. One is that it helps to understand who Reinhard Heydrich was and his significance in Nazi Germany. And two, there are several strains and manifestations of MND, and on top of that, there are probably as many ways of suffering it as there are sufferers, and no two people are the same. We all have our own feelings, our own pain threshold, our own psychological makeup, our own perception of the world which we live in, our own acceptance of our fate, our own tolerance to pain, whether it's a headache or heartache or a fatal illness. Adrian's father's strain of MND had been an extremely aggressive form of the illness which came with excruciating pain as his muscles and bodily functions died and he wasted away to nothing. He was a tough cookie was Charlie Kramer, as tough and as strong and as resilient as they come, but we can all only take so much and the illness broke him. MND took him down. Man, how it took him down.

He once spelled out on his computer "I wanted to live for a hundred years, Adrian. With you. With your mam... but someone decided against it."

Someone... who the fuck is that someone? Adrian had so often asked no one in particular. And no one ever answered him.

He thought about all those things while he was sitting alone outside of the hut. He put the velvet bag down on the bench next to him and picked up the African hunting knife and a fallen birch tree twig from the ground, and he begun to run the knife across the end of it, getting it sharper... and sharper... It was just something for his hands to do while his mind worked and wandered.

I have no idea where you are now,Dad, if you are anywhere at all, Adrian had written in his diary at the very end. *Where have you gone to? That was all that was in my head when I looked down at you yesterday after you'd left us. I just hope you know that I did my best. I have no idea whether it was good, or whether it was bad or even somewhere in between. But it was my best, Dad. There wasn't any more I could give you. I'm sorry. I'm only eighteen, I know nothing, and yet I've lived everything now. What I'd give for a day – even an hour – to be with you again. To take the boat out onto the sea. Mam will pack something for us to eat, I'll bring the orange juice as always. And we'll be together. Just an hour, Dad... and I'll tell you all that I've just written here – that it was my very best and that I'm so sorry if it wasn't good enough for you. But the biggest thing that I did for you... I can't speak about it. I'll never speak about it. I don't even want to think about it, but I know I will. It's a weight which I'll carry with me forever. I'll be sad forever. I'll hurt forever. I know that. And I'll end this now.*

They were Adrian's very final words. "I'll end this now."

The biggest thing that I did for you... Adrian thought about the particular moment which happened eleven years before as he sat outside the hut honing the end of the small birch tree branch to sharp perfection. It had happened on the first of June – Adrian would always remember that date – the moment that Charlie Kramer spelled out what he wanted on his computer screen suspended above his bed – the words which he had been fighting for all day. The doctor had been to the house early in the afternoon after his morning surgery and injected him with morphine to dull his unendurable pain and injected another drug to calm him and ease his breathing difficulties. Adrian had been in the room with his father the whole day. He watched as his eyes began to wander. They were the last muscles in his entire body which he could still control, although even that was almost gone by then too. Then they stopped wandering wildly and fixed on something on the wall behind Adrian. He was making the very lightest of gasps for air then, which were becoming ever lighter with every passing hour. The deeper, more desperate breaths had already stopped some days before as his lungs became weaker and weaker. After a moment he shifted his eyes again and focused back on his computer screen and he spelled out his wish. It took an age to do it and it took every last thing that he had to give to the world. Then finally, when he had finished spelling out what he wanted to say, he fixed his eyes on Adrian. It was one of those looks which was deeper and fuller and spoke many more words than any book ever could. It had everything in it – every emotion – every moment shared – every moment to come which he would never have. It had in it pain and it had loss. It had sadness and it had love. It had a plea for mercy in it which came from deep, deep down in his soul, and it had forgiveness. It was screaming out "do it Adrian. Please just do it". There were no tears because he'd lost the ability to cry. But inside... oh inside, his whole heart was breaking.

Then he closed his eyes for the very last time. He'd had enough. The illness had finally broken him. It was time. He didn't open his eyes again because he didn't want to watch his son.

Adrian read his father's words in silence and then he turned and looked at his mother, who was standing alongside him. She nodded – what else could she do? – and then she turned away and left the room. She couldn't bear to watch what was about to happen.

Adrian picked up one of the extra pillows from a pile which were always in his father's room and were used when his father needed to be propped up and supported in bed. The pillowcase was pale yellow and there was a small red rose embroidered into one corner. Adrian would always remember that. Is it irony or is it even mockery how it's often the smallest of details like that in the most epic of moments which leave their impression the most? It is sometimes the bizzarest of images which become burned deepest into our brain. Before he placed the pillow over his father's face Adrian wanted to whisper "thank you, Dad" and even "We love you too", but he was barely able to breathe let alone say anything. He pressed the pillow down hard. Then harder still. There was no resistance. There was nothing which could possibly resist him anyway. Three minutes later when the pillow was removed Charlie Kramer's light gasps for oxygen had finally stopped forever and his wretched life had left him. Adrian looked down at him to find some expression in his face. Love? Affection? Gratitude? Forgiveness? A look of peacefulness? Or even serenity? Adrian didn't know what exactly, he just thought there might be something. But there was nothing at all – not one of pain, nor of peace, and certainly not one of love. Just two dead eyes in a yellow-green mask, and skin which looked like it had just been polished. It was at that moment when Adrian felt a presence in the room, a presence which he would later describe as an almost holy presence.

Adrian quickly deleted his father's final three sentences from his speech computer. The very last sentence he'd spelled out was "I love you both more than this life" and his mother returned to the room some minutes later. She couldn't stand to witness with her own eyes her husband's death, or her son's act of mercy (or his act of violence, depending on who was judging). And whose mercy had it been anyway? Adrian's father had wanted to liberate his family from their own pain just as much as he wanted it for himself. In that, it was also an act of selflessness. She leaned forward and kissed her dead husband tenderly on the forehead. It was a kiss which she wanted to last forever, but it was over in less than five seconds. Then Adrian did the same. But they both knew that from that moment on Charlie Kramer was finally free from his suffering, and was in a far, far better place. Because nowhere could possibly be worse than where he'd been for those past few torturous months. Death, in that moment, had become a friend and not the enemy.

Three and a half hours later, after the family doctor had been back and confirmed the death "by respiratory failure" and told

Mrs. Kramer that her husband's passing "really is for the best" – and after the undertaker had been and taken away the body – Adrian thought that if there really had been a God present he would be within his rights to tell him to go fuck himself, because what was so good about the sort of God who would put something like that into the world without an antidote, without a cure, without a solution? Was it his idea of a sick little joke? Something to amuse himself on a quiet Saturday night? Which psychopath could even think of dreaming up the idea of incurable diseases and torture and rape and terror and the holocaust and a child born deformed or disabled and not have to answer for the consequences?

"Where are you when we need you?" the Kramer family often called out.

But it was always to no one

I'm grateful for the good times, Adrian tried to reason in his dairy, but these last two and a half years, surely no one was ever evil enough to deserve that? So if you're there God, if you're listening, if you were watching... that was some crap that you dumped on poor Charlie Kramer. Go look yourself in the mirror – go ask yourself if you're a good God or a bad God or just some monkey fucking about and having a laugh. The answer will be yours alone to give.

8

Adrian was lost faraway in his thoughts when Katharina's car pulled up at the front of the hut and she joined him on the bench with a small carrier bag of food.

She could see that something was troubling him. "Are you okay?"

He could have told her that he'd spent the last half-hour thinking about the day he killed his father and got away with it, or that the question which obsessed him most right then was "who really was the person that I killed?" So he lied, and, "Yeah, I'm okay," was all that he said to her and for some reason he looked up into the heavens. High above them in the sky a buzzard was circling the warm morning air trying to find its thermal. Adrian watched fascinated as it started to soar higher... and higher still...

"What's that?" Katharina said. She was looking down at the velvet bag next to him on the bench.

"It's the bag I found the ribbons in. Erich Messmer had the same pattern on his cuff-links."

"His what?"

"His cuff links," and he had to demonstrate to her what the words meant. "On his shirt."

Katharina picked the velvet bag up from the bench and studied the sign. She rotated the bag so that she could read the small gold print around the outer edge.

"It's old German."

"You understand it?"

"I did a semester in 'Germanistics' at university."

She began to read the sign out aloud. "'Goldenen... Sonne' it says. 'The Order of the Golden Sun'."

A thought hit her. "Have you ever heard of Wewelsburg castle?"

Adrian shook his head.

"It was Himmler's 'Camelot'. For his elite SS troops. It's in Hessen. There's a floor mosaic in one of the rooms there. It's similar to this one. Let's eat. Then I'll find out more."

* * *

Back in a Hamburg suburb just before dawn that same day, while Adrian and Katharina were sleeping off what had happened before, two men moved stealthily along the corridor inside Katharina's building towards her flat. One had a Helmut Kohl mask – it was a "Spitting Image"type full head mask pulled right down over his head – the other wore a chimpanzee mask. They stopped at Katharina's door and removed their shoes. As old Chancellor Kohl let them into the empty apartment with his skeleton key, the monkey man pulled out a handgun and attached a silencer. Once inside they moved silently in their stockinged feet towards the bedroom where the door was half-open. The chimp with the gun used a gloved finger to ease open the door. But all they saw when they looked into the room was an unmade bed, and no Katharina.

* * *

Katharina made the fifteen-minute drive back into the village alone and parked up outside the small village cafe. The early June day was brilliantly bright and sunny, but Katharina nervously hid herself away in a dark corner of the cafe and flipped open her iPad. She hadn't been able to get a signal at the hut. The first thing that she brought up was a Police tweet which read: *Die Polizei sucht dringend...* which translated as "The Police are urgently looking for..." She already knew the rest of the message. It was Adrian who was the subject of their search.

* * *

The newspaper which Katharina worked for was the *Norddeutsches Tagesblatt*. It was in an old red brick building which in another age and another time had once been a canal-side warehouse. It was situated in the Speicherstadt district, which is Hamburg's harbour area, and was close to one of the canals. There was a lot of redevelopment going on at the time and each side of the newspaper's offices had been turned into a building site where flash new office buildings and luxury living apartments were going up. Parked directly in front of the *Norddeutsches Tagesblatt* in the place reserved for the newspaper's editor stood a police car. God knows where the editor himself parked that day, but up in his office on the very top floor, with its view down over one of the canals and the old, iron, cobblestone bridge which spanned it, he sat with Detective Geissinger and the same uniformed colleague of Geissinger's who had accompanied him to Adrian's flat. On the wall behind Katharina's boss were two maps. One was a large, detailed Hamburg street map and the other, not as big but big enough, was a map of the whole of Germany. It was hay fever season and Detlef Dallmann, the newspaper's editor, constantly sniffled and fiddled with his nose. Geissinger asked him something and watched a drop of secretion trickle slowly down Dallmann's top lip. Dallmann took out yet another paper handkerchief from his jacket pocket and wiped it over his lip and mouth and then dropped it into the wastebin under his desk. He apologised to the two cops then cleared his throat, stood up, and put his finger on a point on the map of Germany vaguely at an area at the southern tip of the Lüneburg Heide, which was the place where Katharina and Adrian were held up. When Geissinger asked him if he was absolutely sure, Dallmann first coughed into his hand then shrugged his shoulders and said something along the lines of "if I had to bet my life on it I wouldn't, but I know she's spent time there before and it's a lot better guess than you've been able to come up with yourself. And if you don't like it you can go and—" Actually, he said nothing of the sort, he only thought it. But he did think about what a firecracker of a story he had stumbled onto, a story which now connected someone in his employ with a wanted double killer. His hay fever might have been toying with him that morning, but his day was already beginning to look like it could turn out to be a very good one indeed.

Without too much by the way of formality or pleasantry, Geissinger nodded a "thanks" – maybe saying it out loud was too much for him – and he and his partner left the office, made a couple of calls to their HQ and jumped into their squad car parked outside.

* * *

Back in a dark corner of the village cafe, Katharina's iPad screen was showing an image of the very pattern which was on Adrian's velvet bag. A brush of her finger changed it to a photograph of a castle. It was neo-Gothic in structure and both romantic and imposing at the same time. She scrolled slowly down the page, pausing at another image of a ceiling mosaic. The pattern of the mosaic too was an exact match with the sign on the velvet bag. It was set into a wood-beamed ceiling, which was part of a grand, ceremonial room. She scrolled further, down to the very bottom of the page. Then she stopped. Something had caught her attention. It was something which certainly excited her. She went over to the counter and asked the cafe owner if she could have a piece of paper and borrow a pen for a minute, back at her table she began to quickly scribble down some notes.

Moments later, rushing out of the cafe, she stopped in the doorway. Right next to the door were the day's morning newspapers, arranged on a rack for the customers' use. Her own paper, the *Norddeutsches Tagesblatt,* was at the top of the rack. Dated the ninth of June, its headline read "Murder Suspect Escapes Police Custody" and underneath the headline was Adrian's photograph. Katharina looked around her, made sure that no one was looking, then took the paper off the rack and rushed out of the cafe.

All she had in her head at that moment was the same thought that her boss, Detlef Dallmann, had, the same one that she herself had the moment she'd heard Adrian say the name "Messmer" the evening before – namely: this story that we've just stumbled into could be pure dynamite.

9

Adrian sat on the bench at the back of the hut and was using the African hunting knife to carve the pattern on the velvet bag into a piece of loose tree bark – just killing time, just anxiously waiting for Katharina to return. He could hear the sound of her car approaching from the far end of the forest track, but it sounded fast and as if she was in some sort of hurry. When she got closer, he twisted to peek around the corner of the hut. What he saw wasn't Katharina's car but a police van heading quickly towards him. As quick as a flash Adrian ducked his head back around the corner, darted off into the thicket of trees next to the hut, and sprinted a short distance away. Had they seen him? Where was Katharina? How had they found him? His heart was pounding and once again his head was spinning with more crazy questions. From his cover behind a tree trunk he peered back through the trees and bushes to see Geissinger and three heavily armed police officers jump out of the van. Geissinger approached the hut with two of the SWAT team. The third cop went round to the back of the hut. It was all like some kind of slickly-organised routine from a cheap private-channel television movie – just like the mad car chase through the Hamburg streets the night before.

With the African hunting knife still in his hand, Adrian turned and ran off further into the dense forest.

Geissinger and his two colleagues entered the hut through the open door. No raid was ever that easy for them.

Fifty yards away Adrian zigzagged his way around the trees, leapt fallen branches, shoved overhanging foliage out of his way.

Up ahead, Katharina's car turned off the main country road and headed off down the dirt track which led to the hut at the very end.

Adrian ran through the woods like a madman, as if his very life depended on it – which in many ways it did. He was always good at running – always athletic, fast, strong, always one of the fastest in his school year – but this was the race of his life. This was one that he had to win.

Back at the hut the third police officer stood guard outside, scanning the woods to one side of the hut and looking back up the forest track. Geissinger, inside, already had his evidence that Adrian and Katharina were there, and the unlocked door told him that they wouldn't be too far away. He took out his mobile phone and made a call.

At the far end of the track and still out of sight of the police team, Katharina was heading down towards the hut. She had one eye on her iPad – the signal was beginning to break up then and it was stuck on the Police photograph of Adrian. She didn't really see the figure holding a knife as he leaped out of the trees and ran into the middle of the dirt track waving his arms around like an idiot. At the very last minute Katharina looked up, stood on the brakes and the car screeched to a halt, sending the dry forest dirt flying and pulled up just inches short of Adrian. He ran round to the passenger side and jumped straight in.

"TURN AROUND! DRIVE!" he screamed at her and threw his knife onto the back seat. "The police are at the hut!"

Katharina hit reverse, performed a master class in rapid U-turns on the tight track, and raced off back in the direction of the main road.

Some minutes later they were travelling through the countryside, with open moorland and heather to the right and woodland to their left. Adrian had told her what had happened back at the hut and her reply was, "So what do we do now?"

"Pull in. Over there." He pointed to a small picnic area just off the road up ahead, where there was a wooden table and two wood benches either side of the table. It was partially hidden from the road by thick bushes, but most importantly, it was

9

deserted. Katharina swung the car into the area and killed the engine.

"What we do is... you tell me what you found out. And then..."

He stopped before he carried on. Because what he wanted to say was a big moment, a pivotal point from which he knew there would be no return.

"If you want to go to the Police, go. You know where they are and I'm pretty sure they'll be happy to see you. But you've done nothing. You've nothing to be afraid of. Tell them I forced you to drive me out here. Tell them what you want in order to cover yourself. So... Go! But I'm not going. Not yet."

Katharina looked right into his eyes for a highlycharged and emotional moment, and for a split second all they did was sit and stare at each other in a tense silence. She could read his thoughts clearly in his face: I'm not afraid. I'm as strong as they are. Then, as if she had never heard a word he'd said to her, she replied in a business-like manner, fully focused, fully aware of where she was and what she was involved in, and possibly conscious that she now had a real story to tell. "Do you have your bag?" she asked him and held out her hand. The fire was back in her. She wasn't taking control of the ride, but she'd certainly be riding shotgun. She'd be Steve McQueen to his Yul Brynner. There would be no turning back and no white flag from her either.

He pulled the bag out of his back pocket and held it out for her to take. She rested it on her lap, flipped open her iPad – luckily she could get a signal again there in the picnic point – and found her page. It showed the same symbol as the one on Adrian's bag.

"It's the sign of the Golden Sun. It represents riches, absolute power, domination. You'll find the same sign in a castle mosaic. This time it's in the ceiling. At Brodenburg castle."

She turned to another page and to an image of the imposing

217

Brodenburg castle with its turrets and thick walls and its surrounding moat. "Brodenburg was even more elitist than Wewelsburg... the top Nazi place that I told you about earlier. And secretive. Even today, very few people know of its significance. Only the top Nazi leadership – the Generals and up – were allowed to pass its walls. It was where the pure Aryan spirit lived. And to be 'received' at Brodenburg in one of its ceremonies was to be purified, and immortalised. The castle is privately owned now..."

She stopped for a moment. Just so that what she was about to say would sink in.

"By Erich Messmer!"

Adrian sat and took in the implications of what she'd just said. He looked at the word "Brodenburg" at the top of the page on Katharina's iPad.

"Broden..." He said the name out aloud and then he began to spell out the letters from the first part of the word, but not in their order. "B.E.R.N.D.O. – Bernd O! How do I find this place?"

Katharina opened up Google Maps on her iPad and entered "Brodenburg".

"There it is. It's on an island. It's in the middle of a lake." She zoomed in closer. "Near Keilsbach."

"That's where the hotel was, close to Keilsbach. That's where Werner was killed!"

"I think you might want to have a look at the morning paper. My *own* paper even." She indicated over her shoulder to where the morning's newspaper was lying on the back seat. Alongside it was the menacing looking African hunting knife.

Just as Adrian reached back for the paper, from way up above them came a loud droning noise –

getting louder... and louder still... then, low in the sky –they saw the police helicopter, its nose down, which was scanning the land below.

"Shit!"

They held their breath for a moment and once more time seemed to stand still as the helicopter passed right over them. Adrian craned his neck and watched anxiously as it stopped a fast quarter of a mile away and turned two low circles, then moved on again. It was the action of someone still looking and not yet finding. Adrian looked at the clock on the car dashboard. It was three-fifteen.

"How far are we from Keilsbach?"

Katharina glanced down at her iPad.

"About an hour and a half... maybe a little more."

"Do we have enough petrol?"

"Let's find out."

She pulled out of the picnic area and back onto the main road. In the far distance, across the open fields, was a stretch of thick, expansive woodland. It looked dense enough, big enough, quiet enough, for a car and two fugitives to stay lost for quite some time.

"Head for that forest over there," Adrian told her. "We'll wait there till it gets dark."

Katharina pulled back out onto the main road and headed off in the direction of the forest. She hadn't travelled more than a hundred yards when suddenly she hit the brakes hard again. It sent Adrian flying forward to come up hard against his seat belt. What she'd seen was that half a mile up ahead the police had set up a road block. *Sheiße!* They'd only travelled about ten miles from the southern part of the Heath at that point, but the police had already sealed off all the major roads around it. She swung the car back round quickly and gunned it off in the opposite direction, ignoring her satnav's repeated instruction to "turn around, turn around".

"We have to get away from here," Adrian said. "Do you know another way to the autobahn?"

She nodded at her iPad satnav. "Find me one."

10

They were travelling at breakneck speed along the autobahn – but doesn't everyone? Adrian was desperately scanning the iPad screen. An exit road was fast approaching them.

"This is the one. Take it. Then the first left."

Katharina threw the car into a sharp right turn and took the slip road off the motorway, then at the junction she took the left just as Adrian had told her. But then she immediately slowed the car down and came to a stop. Away in the distance were more flashing blue lights. Two parked police cars had blocked that road too. Once again she slammed the car into reverse, backed up a few metres, spun it around and shot off the main road onto a narrow dirt track which cut across open farmland. Adrian looked down helplessly at the iPad screen in his hand. No one seemed to be in control of this trip anymore.

Picking up awesome speed, hitting pothole after endless pothole, throwing up a huge dense cloud of dry dirt and flying pebbles which could have probably been see all the way from the moon, they hurtled down the narrow track which divided the crop fields. Some way behind them, through the thickening dust cloud, the blue police lights continued to flash. Adrian looked at the iPad screen and then pointed vaguely to a point somewhere in the distance which would be their new route out of there.

Twenty minutes later they found their way back onto the autobahn and headed in the direction of Keilsbach. They stayed on the road for a further forty-five minutes, until they approached an exit sign which said "Keilsbacher Wald", Katharina's iPad satellite navigator spoke to her and she took the slip road off.

* * *

When you find yourself in danger, life can suddenly assume great clarity. In that moment when you are confronted with a life-or-death situation all the problems in your life become small and insignificant and it's only about survival. That's how Adrian felt as they sat sometime later in fading daylight in a small clearing in more thick woodland close to Keilsbach. They wanted to wait until sunset before they made their final move. The dense, low tree cover only enhanced the feeling of claustrophobia and imprisonment for them.

Adrian turned and tossed the morning newspaper onto the back seat. He couldn't believe what he had just read. He had to get out of the car. He needed air. He paced around the small clearing, trying to make sense of it all. After some moments Katharina joined him.

"Did you have any idea?" she asked him.

Adrian shook his head. An old ghost was once more haunting him. Here now was someone else, someone so close, who he now realised he never really knew.

What Adrian had read was a report about Werner Retz's suicide, having driven his car through the barrier on a bridge near Keilsbach and plunging into the fast-flowing river below. The police had been able to recover a note which he'd left in a sealed plastic bag in the car dashboard. Behind him, fifty-three-year-old Werner had left massive debts and a queue of angry creditors, the article said. A divorce, a large mortgage and several bad property investments had led to the situation. The report even included a bit about his wife leaving him and that there was a substantial divorce settlement involved.

What Adrian didn't read but what Werner had once told him was that "her betrayal has cost me twice. Once emotionally, and very soon in the pocket." Werner had said it in a jokey, light-hearted manner and followed it with his booming laugh, just as Werner always did. That was something which Adrian always loved about him, the fact that Werner liked to keep things light and breezy, no matter how serious, and that his mood never drifted over to the dark side. But his "Adrian I have debts that no honest man can pay" which he'd once told his friend with a smile? Well, it now sounded very different. So did his angry and bitter, "I'm damned if I'm going to finance her little fuck on the side."

"There are simply no morals any more Adrian," Werner had once said with the look of a man who now knew betrayal up close, to another who'd also once known the same. "There's just no loyalty."

It had in fact been Werner's second marriage and, for him at least, the second messy parting of the ways, his first had ended just like his second, with his wife leaving him after an affair and with Werner facing a hefty divorce bill and being forced to sell the luxury flat they shared. But before his first wife had split, she'd also made an art form out of cleaning out all of the accounts they shared together – which in actual fact was *all* the accounts – and also massively overspending, and had run up huge debts before she moved away to California with her new partner. So, his second attempt at a happy marriage was a case of "once bitten twice bitten and no way shy" for Werner. He had never told Adrian that part of his personal story before, partly because he was embarrassed about it, and also because he didn't want to appear as someone who always carries around anger and bitterness with them. "Perspective is the cure," he always told Adrian when he was confronted with some problem or other. "You just have to try and look at the same thing but in a different light and from a different angle," was his mantra, and it was always followed with a self-depreciating laugh.

"Seven hundred and fifty thousand euros is a lot of debt. Enough for them to be right about a possible suicide," Katharina said.

Adrian said nothing to it. He just stared disbelieving into the bushes, as if he would find the answers to everything hiding behind a tree.

"Maybe Werner still had the ribbons somewhere?" Katharina added. "And Messmer's after us because he thinks we still have them?"

Adrian turned and faced her. "I don't care whether Messmer has the ribbons. And whether he killed Werner for them..." He gave a shrug of his shoulders and made a "who knows?" gesture. "But I know he killed my mother. I'm sure of it. And he killed my uncle too. He killed my mother to get the ribbons, and my uncle to protect his secret." Then he said with great poignancy, "And he's the only one who can tell me what I have to know."

And that was the key right there. As well as seeing justice served, Adrian had to know who his father was and whose life he had taken eleven years earlier.

But while Adrian was coming over all determined and resolute, something else significant was happening to him. He was forgetting, conveniently or not, what someone had once told him at college: that if you're only five feet five tall and in the basketball team, you don't try and out-jump your seven-feet-six-inch opponent. You need to find another way to win. "If someone is faster than you, you don't try and outrun them," his college karate coach had once drummed into him. "If they are stronger than you, you don't try and outmuscle them. If they are better on their left you go right. But not always. Remember Adrian, to surprise them you've got to surprise yourself first." Adrian needed a plan, he needed a surprise, but the brutal truth was that right then he had nothing. The bell had sounded, the midget was going up against the giant, and the little guy had no plan and nothing at all up his sleeve. But he didn't care.

He looked down at his watch, then up at the reddening evening sky. It was almost time. "Come on," he said to Katharina and they got back into the car.

11

It took them a further fifteen minutes of pretty country road, made even prettier by another red-orange glow of the evening's sunset, to reach Keilsbach lake, which was where Brodenburg castle was located. They found a quiet place on the lake shore to park up, and once more from the cover of some trees they stood and looked out over the still water at the castle on the small island in the centre of the lake.

Brodenburg itself stood on a rise at one end of the island, which was about four hundred yards from the lakeside, and its form was reflected into the lake's calm water by the dramatic, fading evening sunlight. Beacon lights flickered from the narrow castle windows. If they could have brought themselves to admit it, it might have all looked impossibly romantic... if they hadn't been two fugitives on the run and mixed up in murder and crime and who-knows-what-else. A short distance along the shore from where Adrian and Katharina stood was the small lakeside village of Keilsbach. Adrian looked at Katharina and nodded towards it.

They took the car into the village and left it in the car park of the village's only hotel, a cute timber-framed bungalow right on the lakeside. In the darkest corner of the hotel's unlit car park, Adrian rolled the morning newspaper around his hunting knife and closed the car door. But you could have been excused right then for asking the question, who was the hunter and who was the game? Was it Adrian? Or was it Messmer? The truth was that both men were both things at the same time.

They headed up the path which skirted the pretty lakeside, passing a kiosk which doubled as a small outdoor cafe but had already closed down till the next morning, and twenty yards beyond that was a wooden hut with a sign on its door which told the world it was the "Keilsbach Yacht Club". There was a light on inside. Bobbing up and down in the water next to the hut was a row of small sailboats. A burly yacht club employee was just tying up the last boat for the night. Katharina looked at the boats – not too dissimilar to Adrian's own small yacht – then at Adrian.

"You can sail..."

It wasn't so much a question but a plain declaration, it really was their only way out to the island. Adrian looked down at the dinghies, history now haunting him, and even hating what they then represented. Then eventually, reluctantly, he nodded his head and Katharina walked over to the boatman.

"Excuse me, can we hire a boat?" she asked him.

The boatman shook his head. "It's a private club," he told her without even looking at her and ran his tongue over his dry lips. He had one of those protruding mouths which made it look like he was wearing a boxer's gum-shield, or maybe even someone else's teeth.

"Can you get us out to the island?" Katharina asked him.

"No one's allowed to land on the island," he said, finally making the effort to look up at her.

Adrian stepped forward. "What will it cost?"

The boatman looked at them for a moment – one to the other, then back again – and let Adrian's question run through his head. Then he said, "Wait here," and disappeared into the boathouse.

Adrian stood at the edge of the small jetty, looking down at the locks and chains on the boats, figuring whether he could take one anyway even if the boatman didn't take them up on their offer, when old big teeth came back out of the hut, turned, and walked off in another direction along the lakeside promenade. But he was immediately followed out of the hut by a second man. He was tall and thickset and around thirty and he didn't appear to be someone who would be full of laughs. Katharina couldn't have known it, because she wasn't around when it happened, but he was one of the two gunmen who had entered her apartment earlier that day. He was the one in the chimp's mask. In late-May he'd also taken a trip across the North Sea to the north-east of England in a recently acquired Opel Corsa, which was then standing right next to Katharina's car in the hotel car park. He signalled for her to come over to him and she followed him back inside the hut.

Adrian waited, watched, waited some more, then when he felt it was all taking way too long, he walked the ten yards or so over to the hut, knocked on the door and entered. And for the second time in his life he felt he was dying. Something had hit him from behind and his world first went WHITE. Then it all turned to BLACK.

Part V

The Blackness

1

Nothing is ever blacker than an unlit, windowless, three-feet-thick-walled dungeon in the bowels of a medieval castle, and that was where Adrian lay motionless in the corner of the room on the cold, hard flagstones. His hands and feet had been tied tightly together and his head was covered with a thick, black canvas hood. If he was still breathing no one would even have been able to tell. Katharina was next to him, slumped lifelessly in a chair which she was tightly bound to with a combination of wire and electrician's tape. There was no hood over her head, but she was truly and totally "gone". Her head hung limply over to one side. Then slowly – ever so slowly – the very first signs of life appeared over in the corner. Adrian was beginning to regain consciousness. The side of his head hurt where he'd been hit and his hair there was caked in blood and stuck to the inside of the hood. He started to struggle and wriggle this way and that but it was no good, his binds were too tight.

Suddenly the door opened and flooded the room with light from out in the corridor and the ugly, no-neck "heavy" from the boathouse, made his entrance. His name was Schlesinger, in the meantime he had changed his clothes and was now wearing a white boiler suit with a bunch of keys hanging from a chain on his belt. He yanked Adrian up off the floor and dragged him across the room and out through the door,then along the castle corridor into the adjacent room. That room too was small, dark and windowless with a low, arched roof and thick stone walls lit only by a single light bulb which dangled from the end of a wire suspended from the roof. It had once perhaps been some sort of storeroom in the bowels of the castle, but it was now used as a wine cellar and had hundreds of wine bottles stacked in racks along three of its walls. The boatman lifted Adrian up off the ground and dumped him down into one of the two wooden, armless chairs which were in the centre of the room. He shouted out the name Tomasz, and within ten seconds a gorilla of a man entered the room. He was even bigger, even uglier and even meaner looking than the goon from the boathouse and looked like he'd been created in a science lab. He had a shaved head which desperately needed a new once-over because the stubble had begun to show through, and two thick black eyebrows which both ran into one as if someone had laid a big hairy black snake over the top of his eyes. His real name was Lucjan Kucharski, he was thirty-two years old, and had been a butcher by trade back in his native Poland, where he'd also been head of the Warsaw chapter of the Polish Hell's Angels. He had the Hell's Angel's slogan "AFFA" – Angels Forever, Forever Angels – tattooed on his right cheek and a swastika tattooed on his throat just out of sight below the collar line. He had stabbed a rival to death in some petty territorial dispute and had been on the run from the Polish police for three years for murder and three further counts of attempted murder until the caring, considerate Brotherhood offered a fellow fascist sanctuary and a place that he could call home in return for all the bloodshed, carnage and terror that he was willing to carry out on their behalf. If you were making a movie and you needed a big ugly "missing link" kind of hitman in it, one scary enough to make all your teeth fall out, you could do worse than cast Tomasz the Angel in the very role which he actually made his living from. It was Tomasz, together with one of his fascist friends from Hamburg, who had planted the nail bomb in Ahmed's Shisha Bar in the city some weeks earlier on behalf of one of the neo-Nazi groups who the shamed Parliamentarian had linked to.

Tomasz untied Adrian's arms while Schlesinger held him down, then he re-tied them behind his back and left the room.

"Where the fuck…" Adrian began to say out loud through his hood.

WHACK! Schlesinger swiped him across the side of the head

with his fist. It probably didn't hurt too badly, but when you're sitting tied to a chair with your head covered by a hood and you've just been whacked on the skull for the second time that day it almost certainly feels like a train has just hit you.

Then Death itself came into the room. He wore a dark blue suit and he had scary eyes. His name was Urs Renzli and he was Erich Messmer's right-hand man. He wasn't as big nor as bulky as the two heavies, but he was every bit as menacing looking, and if one look from his steely cold eyes didn't kill you then the actions which inevitably followed would. He removed Adrian's hood. Strands of hair came with it where the congealed blood had stuck it to the hood. Adrian blinked hard then closed his eyes again. The light from the bulb suspended directly over his head hurt. Renzli nodded to Schlesinger – he would take it from there himself – and Schlesinger left the room.

"I hope you will be more cooperative than your friend," he said to Adrian in English and with his strong German-Swiss accent, which he delivered in a high-pitched whine. It was a voice you wouldn't expect to hear from a hitman, as if he'd stolen it from a spoiled, whingeing schoolboy.

Adrian opened his eyes slowly and looked around him. He was alone in the room, apart from Renzli and the second wooden chair. The light from the overhanging bulb was reflected in the coloured glass of the thousands of wine and champagne bottles.

"Where is she?" Adrian asked.

Renzli ignored the question. He simply turned and watched as Tomasz the "heavy" returned to the room dragging in another bound and hooded figure with him. It wasn't Katharina, it was in fact a man's figure. Tomasz sat him down in the chair next to Adrian and handed Renzli the large syringe which he'd brought in with him. He then held Adrian down while Renzli pushed the needle into the flesh on the side of Adrian's neck. Then he turned and removed the hood from the man who was in the chair next to Adrian. Adrian turned to look at him. He had to double-take to believe what he was seeing. Because sitting next to him was Werner Retz. His face was badly bruised and his lips were covered in sores and cracks. His thumbs were scarred and hung loose, as if they no longer belonged to his hands. He actually looked like a man who might have recently walked away from a horrific car crash. Except that hadn't quite been the case. He was barely conscious after his own interrogation, and he was now clean-shaven. But it was unmistakably Adrian's good friend Werner.

Renzli held up two fingers and said to Tomasz, "Two minutes."

"Then we can rack him?" Tomasz asked. He had a keen, hopeful expression on his face.

"Two minutes," Renzli repeated and they both left the room. Adrian turned to Werner.

"Werner! What... what happened to you?"

Werner's eyes were everywhere in the room except on Adrian.

"I'm so sorry, Adrian." There was a jagged gap in Werner's teeth which showed when he spoke. He still had crusts of old blood inside his lips and on his gums. The gap had once been Werner's wisdom tooth. Messmer's thugs had yanked it out with a set of pliers to make him talk and were actually disappointed that he had given up his information so easily and so quickly because they'd really looked forward to going to work on him down in the castle's torture chamber, tearing his bones apart on the rack or getting their sadistic kicks by shoving a red hot poker up his backside to burn his insides.

"I thought you were dead. What the fuck happened?"

"I made the biggest mistake of my life when I... when I sold Messmer the ribbons. Not your ribbons," he added enigmatically and then broke into a wild-eyed, drugged-up grin. "The others."

"What others? What are you talking about?"

"Ha, ha..." Werner's eyes rolled to the top of his head. He was delirious. "Yours... yours are in Vienna. And then I got...

what's the word...? You- you have something and then you just want more? Oh Adrian... I got more than you can dream about."

Adrian just stared at him incredulously. He still had no idea what Werner was talking about.

Werner looked around him. "So many bottles. I like wine. Would you like some wine, Adrian?"

"Try and concentrate, Werner. Tell me what happened."

"Messmer... Messmer has the ones they made. He wasn't happy." Werner's eyes again began to roll and wander.

"What does that mean, 'the ones they made'?"

"Messmer's a bad, *bad* man. He got me at the airport."

Adrian looked like he'd just had his heart ripped out.

"Why, Werner? And who made what?"

The drug was beginning then to kick in too for Adrian. He fought hard to stay in control.

"Bad decisions," Werner said. "Bad investments... and an ex-wife who..."

Werner stopped speaking. Shame and guilt at what he had done had suddenly given way to bitterness and anger. He spat a thick dollop of blood onto the floor.

Adrian's world began to spin. He was losing control. He again fought hard to concentrate on Werner when Werner said "The accident... it was me. I- I arranged it all. I..."

The door suddenly swung open and Adrian fought hard to focus. His world seemed to be floating and then swimming, then it was as if he was looking through cellophane. He could just about make out Renzli and his meathead accomplice as they entered the room. Tomasz took a gun out of his pocket, pointed it directly at Werner's forehead and without a further word he pulled the trigger. Werner's chair tipped back and hit the ground with a thump. And just like that, Werner Retz was no more. He had a big hole in the middle of his forehead and his blood and brain and bits of shattered skull were splattered all over the wine rack behind where he'd been sitting.

Renzli turned to a traumatised and now tripping Adrian. "Tell us what we need to know."

* * *

Some days earlier, at gunpoint down in his Viennese cellar, Gerhard Pfeifenberger the Austrian banker reached a shaking hand into the back of his safe in which he kept twenty-two thousand euros and ten thousand US dollars. But that wasn't what his hand emerged with, nor what his two visitors had come for. He took out two pieces of old silk. They were Reinhard Heydrich's original wreath ribbons – the ribbons which Adrian had found in his father's attic room and the ones which had been sold to Pfeifenberger by Werner Retz – but only after Werner had arranged for some clever Hamburg craftsman to make counterfeit copies of them both. The masked intruder who held the gun to Pfeifenberger's head grabbed the ribbons from him and pushed them into the plastic bag which he brought out of his pocket.

It was two days before anyone raised the alarm about Gerhard Pfeifenberger. After he'd failed to turn up for work at the bank and hadn't phoned in or emailed or texted, and when repeated calls to his home and his mobile phone had gone unanswered, his cleaning woman was called and she let herself into the house and found Gerhard Pfeifenberger on his back on the cellar floor with his face blasted off. She vomited at the sight of the gory mess, and the image which would be etched into her memory for the rest of her life was that of the dozens of giant bluebottles crawling and buzzing around Gerhard Pfeifenberger's blood-splattered head.

The Viennese police naturally thought that the break-in had been for money. What else was there to think with an open safe door, an empty safe and a rich, dead banker's ice-cold body? What they didn't know was that Gerhard Pfeifenberger was a fanatical fascist and leader of a clandestine right-wing organisation who, with his brother, was also heavily involved in putting together a pan-European political party of several of the continent's more fanatical far-right and anti-Semitic groups dedicated to the ideology of National Socialism and Aryan supremacy – the *Echtes Viertes Reich* (the Real Fourth Reich) they had named themselves – and that he was someone who, in Werner Retz's very own words, had paid "more than you can dream about" – but not nearly as much as Erich Messmer paid only three days later – just to get his mucky hands on a leading Nazi's wreath ribbons – ribbons which bore the mark of the Führer and Il Duce themselves.

As for Werner Retz, he had a pocketful of money and a one-way ticket to Sao Paulo and the dumb illusion that he was untouchable, invincible and very soon invisible. Greedy was the word that he'd been looking for when he was trying to explain to Adrian what he'd done. Call it what you will, it was only a damned fool who played games with Erich Messmer and expected to win.

When Messmer's men had caught Werner at the airport and then later literally put the thumbscrews on him in the castle dungeons, Werner confessed what he had done and told them about Pfeifenberger and the real ribbons. So Messmer himself flew straight to Vienna that same evening in his private jet, examined the ribbons which his footsoldiers had taken from Pfeifenberger, confirmed that they were indeed the real thing, then called back to Hamburg and ordered Katharina's release.

It had been just another day in the life of Erich Messmer.

2

In the unlit room next door to where Adrian was going through his interrogation, Katharina was still slumped in her chair like some busted and broken doll. There really might have been no life left in her – Messmer's guys really were that good and that brutal and that ruthless and that unforgiving. Ask Werner.

A few yards away in the castle wine cellar, on the other side of the thick castle wall, Werner's bloody corpse had been dragged out of the room and Adrian's interrogation was now in progress. Like Katharina, his head had fallen over to one side and he was being kept upright in his chair by Tomasz the "heavy".

Renzli himself was a picture of pure frustration. "Again... What did you tell the police?"

Adrian, under the influence of whatever truth serum he had been injected with, was delirious, incoherent, barely able to make sense. He started to say something. Then he looked down at the ground next to him to where Werner's dead body had been. All that was left were blood stains and bits of bone and brain.

"Werner's... gone. Is he sleeping now?"

WHACK! A hand slapped Adrian hard across the face. But that was just a warm up for the main act which would follow.

"What did you tell them? Who else did you tell?" Renzli shouted at the top of his whiney voice. His patience was rapidly running out on him.

"Geissinger doesn't like me."

"Who is Geissinger?"

"Plod... you know? Poleesh... Poleeshmen Plod?" He looked down at the toppled chair where Werner had sat. "Wernersh gone to bed."

"He's as dead as you will be if you don't start talking. What did you say to the police?"

Adrian shook his head wildly from side to side. Then it jerked violently forward and he began to mutter. "Werner... killed himself... then you did. Ha ha."

And then Adrian was "gone". His eyes closed and his world checked out on him. Was it temporarily, or was it forever? Adrian was long past caring.

* * *

Much higher up in the castle – four flights of twisting, narrow, concrete spiral staircase higher to be precise – was the castle's ceremonial room – a grand, seven-sided banqueting hall, lit by giant beacons which were suspended around all four walls. They flickered an eerie red glow up onto the marble Golden Sun mosaic which was set into the high ceiling. The thick, oak door opened and Richard Wagner's "Götterdämmerung" – the music which Hitler ordered to be played throughout Berlin as Heydrich's funeral was taking place – started up and blared out of the four loudspeakers mounted in each corner of the room. A dozen middle-aged men wearing long, hooded, burgundy-coloured velvet cloaks filed into the room in a straight line in a slow, deliberate zombie-like march. They were led by Erich Messmer. Three hooded figures behind him was the "outed" and disgraced CDU politician. Hell, if it wasn't a procession of the blind leading the god-damned blind. Messmer was carrying the two wreath ribbons, which were draped over his outstretched hands – Hitler's ribbon hung over his right and Mussolini's over his left. Then over the speakers and over Wagner's dramatic music came a deep, male voice – the kind you once heard over cigarette adverts in the cinema, all dramatic and theatrical and phoney as hell:

"And a new priesthood will rise up from our Holy soil. Great Princes and visionary sages will once again overcome and prevail." It was a voice that sounded more like the end of time than the dawning of anything new.

Messmer led the Brotherhood towards a table at the far end of the room which had been set up like a Pagan altar. It was the Brotherood's Thulist shrine to Aryan supremacy and full of Nazi war souvenirs and occult artefacts and even included a skull-measuring device – a piece of apparatus which had been instrumental in the Nazi obsession with origin and racial supremacy. Next to it was a dentist's extracting forceps – a relic from the Auschwitz death camp. Standing at the very centre on a marble plinth was an alabaster bust of the "Aryan God" himself, Reinhard Heydrich. A huge portrait photograph of the man covered the wall immediately behind the shrine and it was flanked by images of the destruction and massacre of the Czech town of Lidice – Hitler's act of revenge for Heydrich's assassination – and a large printed sign which said "<u>10 Juni 1942</u>".

When Messmer reached the altar he carefully draped the two wreath ribbons over either side of Heydrich's effigy. It was just after midnight and the party was about to start.

* * *

While the fascists up in the banqueting hall were having their fun, down in the wine cellar Adrian started to blink, and then very slowly began to force his eyes open. It was a fight, but a fight he managed to win. He looked around him and saw that he was alone in the room. And then he remembered about Werner. But all that remained of him was the chair that he'd sat in and the blood which had once coursed through his veins splattered all over the wine bottles racked up against the wall and on the ground where he'd lain. Adrian's eyes began to roll again. Then they started to pan the room crazily, finally coming to a stop on Werner's blood on the wine bottles. He blinked hard again and a manic grin came over his face. He took in deep gulps of air, then began to rock gently from side to side in his chair, increasing his movements until he was rocking and rolling his chair towards the rack of bloody bottles.

* * *

Next door to the wine cellar, Katharina still sat slumped sideways and tied to her chair in the pitch blackness of the unlit dungeon room. A large dragonfly had somehow got into the room and buzzed incessantly around the place. The blackness drove even the trapped insect crazy. It landed on Katharina's cheek and started to crawl around her face. God knows what it was trying to find there but Katharina herself didn't react nor move an inch. It could have eaten her entire face and she would never have known.

* * *

A few yards away the wine cellar door opened and Renzli returned to the room. He saw Adrian sitting with his head hanging limply on his chest. A thin sliver of saliva was running down the side of his mouth. Renzli went over and took a closer look at him. Is he back in the land of the living? Can I get some sense out of him? He kicked him hard on the side of the leg. But there was no reaction at all from Adrian. He really did look "gone," still. Renzli turned to leave. Then from behind him came Adrian's thin weak voice saying, "I... told them... I—"

Then his sentence faded and died. But it was enough for Renzli. He stopped and went back over to Adrian. He leaned in close to him.

"What did..."

Like lightening Adrian grabbed hold of him by the arm and brought a broken wine bottle from behind his back. He jabbed its jagged edge hard into the side of Renzli's neck just to one side of his artery. Blood immediately began to trickle down the glass. Renzli tried to call out, but Adrian clapped a hand over his mouth and pushed the bottle in even deeper, until Renzli could barely breathe. Then Adrian cast off the severed chord from around his wrist.

"One sound... you know who Henry the Eighth was?" he said in a low, menacing whisper.

Renzli was too scared and too close to having his artery slit open to respond.

"You're not giving me an answer. Do. You. Know. Who. Henry the Fucking Eighth. Was?"

Renzli's eyeballs moved from side to side. Just like Adrian's father, he was speaking volumes with just the slightest movement of his eyes and what he was saying was "no, but please don't cut my throat because of it."

"He was the king who cut off people's heads. One wrong move and I'll slice your fucking neck wide open."

He pushed the bottle deeper still into Renzli's flesh. And right then Adrian really did look as if he would like nothing better than to take Renzli's head clean off and it took everything that he had in the way of iron discipline to stop himself.

"Is Messmer here in the castle?"

When Renzli either couldn't or wouldn't say more, Adrian pushed and twisted the bottle even deeper. More blood flowed out from the cut. Then he released the bottle just enough to allow Renzli to spurt out, "Y-Yes."

"Where's Katharina?"

Renzli's eyes pointed in the direction of the adjacent room.

Keeping the broken bottle more than firmly in its place, Adrian led Renzli out and into the unlit dungeon room where he flicked on the light and saw over in the far corner Katharina, still bound and hanging lifelessly in her chair. The room was used as a store room and had sealed cardboard boxes with Chinese markings stacked on the shelves, three large pots of white paint, and alongside the pots were various pieces of random tools and equipment. When Adrian moved to grab a length of chord from the shelf – the kind of chord which had been used to tie up him and Katharina – Renzli took his chance. He grabbed for a length of copper pipe lying on a lower shelf and swung it at Adrian. The blow sent Adrian to the ground. Renzli was quickly over him. He kicked out at Adrian's face. Adrian rolled with the blow, spun around, and in one rapid movement he twisted and scissor-kicked Renzli's legs from under him. Renzli dropped backwards straight to the ground. The copper pipe flew out of his hand. Like lightening, Adrian was on him. Renzli was no match for Adrian's superior physical strength, even in the state he was in. He grabbed Renzli's head and cracked it hard on the concrete floor, knocking him clean out. Blood began to trickle out from under Renzli's head.

There was no lock on the dungeon storeroom door and Adrian didn't want to take any chances, so he dragged Renzli out into the corridor by the ankles and back into the wine cellar. He left him lying there and quickly ran back to the dungeon. He grabbed a piece of cloth and some Duck Tape from one of the shelves, then he went over to Katharina. He took a pair of scissors from the shelf and cut her binds free and shook her by the shoulders. But there was no response. He slapped her face. Still there was nothing. He slapped her again, this time harder. And then a third time, even harder still.

"Wake up. Katharina, wake up," he pleaded with her. It was more an urgent whisper than a shout. Slowly her eyes began to open and she let out a low moan.

"Katharina... Come on!"

But the eyes flickered closed rather than open.

He stood her up and half-carried-half-walked her out of the room with her feet scraping along the ground rather than moving with him, and manoeuvred her into the wine cellar, where he sat her down in the chair which only moments earlier, he had sat in himself.

Renzli lay on the ground in front of her with blood oozing out of the crack in his head and more trickling down the side of his neck where Adrian had pressed the wine bottle in. He was still breathing, but Adrian wasn't concerned about that. He went quickly to work gagging him with the cloth and Duck-taped it tightly in place. Then he bound his arms and legs together with more tape. He picked Katharina up out of the chair. "Come on... Katharina... You have to wake up." She tipped one way and then the other in Adrian's arms as he started to carry her out of the room...

And then he stopped. Tomasz the "heavy" came through the door. His hand immediately went into his pocket for his gun. Adrian let Katharina fall to the ground and charged towards him and as one they spun and crashed into the racks of wine bottles. Tomasz's gun went flying across the room. One rack tipped over and the shattered glass splintered everywhere. Wine poured out from the smashed bottles and flooded the floor. Tomasz reached out for a jagged bottle neck, just as Adrian had done earlier to cut his binds, and thrust it at Adrian. But Adrian was quick enough to go with the movement so that the glass only caught the side of his shirt, cutting him below the chest. Tomasz lunged at him again with the bottle but Adrian moved smartly to one side, grabbed and turned him, then toppled back into one of the standing racks with him, with Adrian on top. Tomasz let out a loud scream. Then suddenly his whole body went limp and he gave up the fight. Adrian took a step back from him and let Tomasz drop to the ground. He could see straight away that he was dead. Several sharp shards of broken glass had penetrated his back.

He moved over to Katharina, who was lying on the ground. The chaos had at least managed to wake her some more. He lifted her up onto her feet. They stepped around the dead Tomasz's body and headed for the door. Before they left, Adrian stopped and picked up the gun and put it in his pocket. Then he closed the thick oak door behind him, locking Renzli and Tomasz inside, and pocketed the key.

With his arm wrapped around her, Adrian helped Katharina up the narrow spiral stairway and then along a long corridor lined with oil paintings of old Masters – each one of them dark and foreboding and Baroque in style. Most of them were originals and missing from the world since they were looted from their homes in various Paris museums during the Nazi occupation of France in the Second World War.

They made their way in the direction of men's voices which were reciting in union some weird ritual. The voices got louder as Adrian and Katharina moved along the corridor but Adrian wasn't able to make out what they were chanting. They stopped at the thick, oak ceremonial room door. Messmer's lone voice was coming from the other side of it. They stood still and listened.

In the ceremonial room Messmer was addressing the Brotherhood in German. He had a long black Master of Ceremonies cloak draped over him and he was living every heartfelt word that he uttered.

"On this day..." he turned to the 10 Juni 1942 sign on the wall behind him. "This day chosen by history to avenge the evil murder of the greatest patriot, the greatest soldier that this land has ever known, the greatest—"

On the other side of the door Adrian got tight hold of Katharina, who was once again beginning to list to one side as her legs were becoming weaker. He propped her up and listened.

Messmer turned back to face the hooded Brotherhood. "We honour and we exalt and we glorify—"

"HEY!" a voice from behind Adrian boomed out.

He spun around to face Schlesinger, who was two yards

away holding a bunch of keys and had a gun pointed straight at Adrian's heart.

"Go through," Messmer's boathouse henchman told Adrian in German. Adrian looked at him, then he looked down at the gun pointed straight at him, and he knew that this time he really had no option and that there really was no way out.

3

The moment that Adrian walked into the room with a gun poking into his back and propping up Katharina, the place fell silent and Messmer stopped speaking. But his surprise soon turned to composure and there was even a half-smile on his face when he said to Adrian, "The ghost of Lidice," although the significance of his utterance was yet to fully dawn on Adrian.

Two of the Brotherhood had drawn their hoods right down over their faces when Adrian and Katharina appeared.

"Fabrizio. Adolfo... vatotto bene," Messmer said to them in Italian ("everything's fine") and raised out a calming hand.

The two pushed their hoods back slightly.

"I'm sorry for the interruption," Messmer said, going back into German to address the Brotherhood generally. Then he looked directly at Adrian and added, "But perhaps there is some unfinished business which we can conclude now." Still looking straight at Adrian and loaded with a secretive meaning which only Messmer understood at that point, he switched into English and went on, "In more ways than one. Come here."

Adrian didn't move an inch. And his grip on Katharina's arm meant she couldn't move either. He just shot Messmer an ice-cold look of contempt and defiance; this far and not a single centimetre further.

Messmer removed his thick glasses and just as he'd done once before when Adrian had gone to see him in his office, calmly cleaned off a speck of dirt from the lens with the edge of his cloak. Then he signalled for Schlesinger, who had his gun poking into Adrian's back, to bring him and Katherina forward to the front of the altar to stand immediately before him. Schlesinger dug Adrian in the back and shoved them in Messmer's direction.

Adrian and Katharina stood centre stage in front of the altar, between the Brotherhood and Messmer. They were about six feet away from him, with Messmer's armed "heavy" standing right alongside them.

"You wanted to know who your father was," Messmer said to Adrian. Then he looked up and addressed the Brotherhood, staying in English for Adrian's benefit. "His name was Karel Hlasek. He was born in Lidice, in Czechoslovakia."

"What are you talking about?" Adrian said.

Messmer turned then to look at him. "He was nothing but a stinking Czech imposter. Who never had the right to Reinhard Heydrich's *Kranzschleifen*." (He meant the wreath ribbons.) Then with utter loathing in his voice he went on. "His people murdered the greatest Leader the Third Reich ever had. On the tenth of June 1942 they paid the price... the price of 'Lidice'!"

* * *

It was the day after Karel Hlasek's fifth birthday, on the morning that he ran for his life across the fields close to his home in Lidice. He was blond and had piercing blue eyes, just like his son, Adrian, would have when he was born fifty-one years later. He was wearing a pullover a size too big for him with frayed cuffs, which had been a hand-me-down from a cousin in the neighbouring village, who was two years older than Karel. It was there, to his cousin's house in the nearby village of Dobroviz, that he was running to that early-June morning.

His heart was pounding... pounding like it had never done before. His lungs were bursting. He was hardly able to get his breath. But he knew that he had to keep on running. It was a race he just had to win. Behind him, under the command of SS and Gestapo officers, German soldiers – including members of Heydrich's elite SD Sicherheitsdienst troops – had surrounded the Czech village of Lidice, little Karel's home. Days earlier Reinhard Heydrich had died from wounds which he'd suffered when his car was ambushed in a Prague suburb on his way to work. Hitler's order was to take Lidice off the map. All the men were to be shot on the spot and the women sent off to the concentration camps. Any of the village's children who were judged to be worthy of "Germanisation" – in other words, those who were blond, attractive, healthy and strong, who were Aryan picture-perfect – were to be adopted by SS families.

But General Manfred von Dornbach got to Karel Hlasek first.

Karel realised that he couldn't go any further. It felt like blood was coming up into his mouth. He headed for the cover of some trees up ahead of him. No one will see me in there, he thought. No one will ever find out. I'll get my breath back there and then I'll carry on running. I can't lose this race. If I do, I will die like my father and my mother and the rest of my family.

He dived down into the tall grass at the edge of the small woodland. His head felt like it was exploding. His knee was bleeding. He'd grazed it on a stone when he dived down into the grass, and he'd torn his new dark blue socks which he'd got for his birthday.

He closed his eyes tight to make it all go away – just a little boy shutting out the evil in his world – as he often did. If I can't see it, then it can't be real, he reasoned. After a moment, when he had collected his breath, he raised himself up, just enough to look back at his village, and tears began to roll down his cheeks. But he knew that he had to carry on. He started to push himself up off the ground but for some reason he wasn't able to. Manfred von Dornbach was standing over him with his heavy leather boot pressed down hard into Karel's back. Karel tried to twist and turn to see what was keeping him down, but all he could see as he looked upwards out of the corner of his eye was the glow of the early morning blood-red/orange sky above him. He was petrified. He was shaking. He was grieving. He had just witnessed things which no human ever should.

The annihilation of Lidice and the massacre of its inhabitants

started on the evening of the ninth of June, which was the day
of Heydrich's funeral in Berlin, and continued on the morning
of the tenth. It was the same day seventy-five years later that
Adrian looked directly into the stern face of Erich Messmer
in the banqueting hall at Brodenburg castle. It was the date
that Karel Hlasek died and the date that he became Karl von
Dornbach.

"Karel Hlasek thought he had escaped," Messmer told
Adrian and the Brotherhood, then he shook his head.

Starting at seven o'clock on the morning of the tenth, all
the men of Lidice were led to Horak's farm on the edge of the
village, lined up against the wall, and the guns of a Nazi firing
squad exploded into life. This really did happen. The men were
slaughtered in groups of five at first, then to speed things up
in groups of ten. Of Lidice's one hundred and five children,
eighty-two were taken to the Chełmno concentration camp and
gassed. Karel Hlasek was officially listed as one of them. The
Nazis in charge of the operation didn't want to admit to Berlin
that anyone had got away from them – especially a young boy
– and von Dornbach had kept his precious discovery to himself
– so, on the General's orders they documented it that way and
Karel Hlasek was written off as just another concentration camp
statistic. Most of the village's women were hauled off to the
Ravensbrück concentration camp where they were worked to
death or boiled or frozen in order to see how much pain they
could or could not tolerate, or at what temperatures humans
finally give up and die. Or else they had their teeth pulled out
of their head without anaesthetic or had electrodes shoved up
their anus or had their bone marrow injected with bacteria or
their limbs removed. It was all in the good name of science,
in case you were wondering. Four of the Lidice women were
pregnant and were forced to have abortions before they made
their journey into hell. God only knows what sort of experiments
were carried out on them, or on their unborn babies, when they

3

got there. All of this really happened. It really did. The people who Messmer and his kind worshipped actually did all of this, and much more. Try and imagine it. Oh man, the evil which humans can do to humans.

The village of Lidice itself was burned, blown up and razed to the ground so that in the end you would wonder if a real living, breathing place had ever really existed where only ash and rubble remained.

How young Karel escaped from the village that day and broke through the cordon that the Nazis had set up around it, no one ever knew, and Karel would never say. In fact, he never, ever said a single word about Lidice for the rest of his life. He died with the secret, just as Karel died that day in 1942, at the moment that he was finally allowed to turn and stare up into the face of the General who would become his father.

"Von Dornbach found him hiding in a field," Messmer told Adrian and the Brotherhood.

The fierce German General stood frighteningly over him. All Karel knew at that moment was that he would die, just like the rest of Lidice's inhabitants – his family, his neighbours, his friends, his teachers. Then von Dornbach broke into a warm smile. He liked the look of what he had under his boot... he liked it a lot.

"An attractive little thing," Messmer said. "However unworthy."

In the field just outside of Lidice a soldier appeared from behind von Dornbach and aimed his rifle down at young Karel. As his finger tightened on the trigger and he waited for the order to fire, the General's hand went up and lowered the barrel of the soldier's rifle, while all the time keeping his eyes fixed firmly on the petrified little boy under his boot. He was keeping this one for himself.

"The General educated his war trophy very well. His little Czech even became a Nazi! But purity is purity," Messmer said

249

damningly.

"Just how pure are you?" Adrian sneered at Messmer.

The comment stung the man from Switzerland. For the very first time his composure was gone. His answer resonated with both pride and, at the same time, deep offense.

"I'm the son of a Prussian. A Prussian officer who served and stood alongside Reinhard Heydrich in battle."

Then in a vengeful tone he went on, "The winner of a war always writes the history, isn't that the truth? Some mistakes were made, but if that war had been won by the right side, this world would be a better place. A safer place. With order. Discipline. It would be a world where everyone would get what they deserve. A world where enterprise, hard work, endeavour, excellence and the right people would be rewarded."

One of the hooded Brotherhood raised his arm, gave a Nazi salute and shouted out *Sieg Heil*.

Messmer carried on. "It took me a long time to track the ribbons down." He turned around and looked proudly at the two pieces of silk draped over the plinth each side of Heydrich's effigy. "But it was worth it. The legacy belongs to us."

He looked out over the group. It was with sadistic pleasure that he told them, "Manfred Von Dornbach only ever made one mistake in his life. It was a mistake which nearly cost all of us who are here tonight heavily. We'll correct it now."

He gestured to Schlesinger standing alongside Adrian to hand him the gun. Messmer had decided that he would take care of business himself – that he would right old wrongs, that he would finally exact revenge. That he would eliminate the danger to him and his fellow believers. He smiled to himself.

Schlesinger walked the three paces over to Messmer and held out the gun for him to take. What happened next only took a split second and it was all done at lightning speed, but for Adrian it all felt like it took forever and that it all happened in slow motion Time itself, even, seemed to be suspended for him and for everyone else in the room. But in that frozen moment, as Messmer took hold of the gun, Adrian whipped out the revolver which he had in his pocket and shot. He'd never fired a gun in his life before, never even held one in his hand. He'd probably never even seen one which wasn't either on a cinema screen or on television. The room echoed with the sound of his gun exploding into life.

Katharina turned. Right in front of her Schlesinger let out a scream and fell forwards onto the ground at her feet clutching his stomach. Adrian shot again and this time it was Messmer who stumbled forward. He'd been hit in the heart. His glasses flew off as he tumbled to the ground. His body covered the gun that he'd been about to take hold of. Adrian spun around with his revolver to face twelve petrified men. No one, even, dared breathe. Schlesinger lay groaning on the floor. Adrian and Katharina stepped forward over Messmer's body. His glasses crunched under Katharina's foot as she trod on them. Adrian picked up the thick bunch of keys lying on the ground next to Schlesinger the boatman, snatched the two wreath ribbons from the altar, and moved quickly towards the thick, oak ceremonial room door. The Brotherhood just stood like twelve helpless zombies and watched.

Adrian opened the door and removed the large key from the inside. On the floor behind him, directly in front of the altar, a finger began to tighten on the trigger of a gun. The gun was raised. Through his blurred, distorted vision, Erich Messmer tried to bring his target into focus as Adrian and Katharina made their way out of the door.

Messmer finally squeezed the trigger and Katharina screamed. Adrian spun around and fired three more quick shots. What is it they say? "When you strike at a King you must kill him." Whether it was the first or the second or the third shot which Adrian fired, it didn't matter. At least one hit its target as Messmer lurched forward and lay dead, in a heap on the ground. It was the very last thing that Erich Messmer ever did.

Adrian Kramer had killed the King.

He turned back quickly to Katharina. She was lying on the stone floor outside the oak door. She had been hit in the back. Blood was flowing fast. She was barely conscious. He just stared at her disbelievingly for one short, hugely emotional moment. Then he slammed the heavy oak door shut, locked the twelve men inside, removed the key from the lock and tossed it through the narrow gap in the open turret window and down into the water forty feet below.

He shouted out Katharina's name. Then again, this time louder. But she could only gasp desperately for air. He picked her up off the ground. She was too weak to stand. Her gasps for breaths were getting shallower. They were ever more desperate. The life was going from her. Adrian knew this moment well because he'd lived it with someone else before. He swept her up into his arms.

4

He emerged from the castle's main wooden door with Katharina in his arms. It was already nearly daylight by then. He carried her towards two motor boats which had been tied up to the small castle jetty; moments later one of the boats was skimming across the still surface of the lake towards the shore with Adrian at the wheel. Lying along the seat behind him in a thickening pool of blood was Katharina. Her gasps for air had become even shallower. She was a heartbeat away from death. When he reached the lakeside jetty he scrambled up the iron steps and sprinted towards the hotel, which was already open for business. He raced into the small reception. He was desperate. He was covered in Katharina's blood.

"Someone is dying!" he shouted to the old receptionist on duty that morning. She had no idea what to do with that news or how to react to it. She simply stood by in shock and allowed Adrian to grab the phone and frantically dial a number. Then he shouted manically into the receiver: "Send an ambulance to Hotel Seeblick. In Keilsbach. A girl is dying!"

He hung up and dialled another number. Everything was frenzied and furious by then.

"Get Detective Geissinger to Brodenburg castle. It's urgent. He'll need people with him," he shouted into the phone.

Then from what he heard, he screamed down the phone, "CALL HIM! Tell him Adrian Kramer is there... yes, Adrian Kramer. Tell him I've just done his fucking job for him. DO IT NOW! Someone has been shot!"

He slammed down the phone and sprinted back out of the hotel, back along the jetty and leapt back into the boat. Katharina's eyes were closed and thick blood had begun to run from the corner of her mouth. He used the wreath ribbons to mop it away. He called out her name. But she couldn't hear him anymore. He pulled a strand of hair out of her eyes. He cradled her head in his arms. But he knew.

"There's nothing deader than a dead love" as the German saying goes.

He raised his eyes up to the heavens and let out a pained, heartbroken cry. The early morning sky above him was a spectacular orange/red glow. It was a colour he would remember forever.

Part VI

The Return

Some way off the north-east English coast a fine new yacht with tall white sails headed out to sea. Adrian was at the tiller. It was early September by then and he was wrapped up and protected in thick wool from the fresh early-autumn easterly wind which whipped up off the sea that morning. His eyes were watering as he squinted into the sun and the wind. He wiped his weather tears away and turned and looked back in the direction of the terraced row of houses which lined the cliff top. They had already receded well into the distance and were barely visible from where he was by then. He headed further out to sea. The cold wind blew back his hair. Then he closed his eyes and lost himself in his thoughts. He still needed time to absorb and understand fully those crazy few weeks of May and early June, and what had happened to him played over and over and over again in his mind – the things that he'd been through, the things that he'd found out, the things that he'd lost and the things that he'd found along the way.

He recalled, too, the first of July. That was the day that he travelled to Lidice, the small town in the Czech Republic where his story – and *our* story – really began. He had flown to Prague from Hamburg and hired a car at the airport, driven the forty-five minutes north to Lidice and parked up in the visitor's car park which he imagined was very close to where his family home once stood. The place where his father once played. Where his father's own mother and father had lived their lives. And where his grandfather had been murdered by the Nazis. It was a journey which he knew he had to make. It was a journey which he knew would bring him pain, but one which was the only way to complete the story... *his* story.

He wandered alone around the Memorial area of Lidice, which had been built on the site where the old village – the one which Hitler's troops had erased from the map – had once stood. He tried to imagine how it all once was. All the happy children and proud parents just trying their best to get through their days and their lives, just trying their best to hold on in this screwed up world of ours. Trying to survive a war which had sucked them right in. Trying to survive the terror that the Hangman of Prague brought to their country. He tried to imagine the village burning, the men lined up against the wall at Horak's farm and murdered. He tried to imagine the faces and the feelings of the mothers as they were separated from their children and herded into the trucks which would take them to their living hell. He tried to imagine the thoughts in the heads of the Nazi soldiers who were given the order to "shoot" and then watch the Lidice men fall forwards and die. Was it von Dornbach who gave that order? he thought to himself.

He thought most about his father running across the fields to find safety. Running from death, running from the flames, running to who knows where? But Karel Hlasek lived – so that one day Adrian Kramer too could live.

He stood at the base of the tall concrete monument to the massacre, but which he sadly thought looked too much like a war-time bunker. He paused at the statue of the mourning Lidice woman who stood over the grave of her husband, then on past a statue of a mother with her child. He walked slowly over to another Lidice woman whose hands were up and covering her face in order to shield it from the scorching flames of the burning village, from the horror... and on past a sign which read "10 CERVNA 1942" – the fateful day that Lidice stopped existing. He was holding a small, white wooden cross.

Finally, he arrived at the point which he had come all that way to see. It was a sculpture. It was eighty-two haunting, life-like images of the children who never returned. As he moved up closer to it, every child's face seemed to be following him. Every sculptured, stone eye burned into him. He stopped in front of the statue and tried to look into every child's face. But he couldn't. He had to look away. Then he bent down and planted his white cross at the base of the sculpture, among all the other toys and flowers which had already been placed there. On Adrian's cross were the words "Karel Hlasek. 10th of June 1942".

It was a poignant, highly emotional moment for Adrian. He could have cried. But he didn't. He refused to give up his tears. He'd cried enough. Then he turned and walked away. Like his father, he knew he would never return.

In the Lidice visitor's centre Adrian opened the thick visitor's book. He wrote something into it, and then he added his name. But he didn't sign it as Adrian Kramer, he wrote Adrian HLASEK.

* * *

Back on the rolling waves of the rough, tough North Sea he was almost there, he was almost where he wanted to be.

He'd made the same journey some years earlier, but he was alone in the boat back then with his father's ashes. On that occasion, eleven years earlier, when he was far enough out to sea and far enough away from land, he took off the urn's lid and tipped the fine grey/white powder over the side of the boat into the foamy water and watched as it seemed to mix and blend in with the white of the waves, so that it appeared to be at one with it, to be a part of the big swirling sea. As he turned his yacht to head back to port and left the ashes behind, Adrian thought that his father would have liked that, to be forever at one with the sea, *his* sea. The place where he was happiest.

This time, though, eleven years on, Adrian wanted to sail a further half-mile or so out to sea. It was choppier there and the waves were rolling in higher, but they were totally alone and way beyond the few hobby sailors in their yachts and dinghies who'd braved the chilly day. There were no ferries making their way over to Amsterdam or Hamburg, and no fishing boats heading into or out of the harbour to bother them.

He looked out over the swell of the waves. He was looking at his own past with his father. He saw them sailing together. He saw his father smiling proudly as he instructed his young son how to tie off and secure the main sail and to steer the boat. He saw them playing football together on the sand. He saw them walking together up on the wild, windswept moors. He thought about all the beautiful moments that they had shared together – the moments which make a life worth living and a person worth knowing – and he realised that perhaps there was a God after all and that he or she might actually be okay... sometimes. And he thought too that two nightmare years can never obliterate the sixteen perfect ones which had come before them.

He came, too, to understand that what Wolfgang had once said to him was just how it was; that it isn't where someone starts their journey which counts, but where and how they eventually arrive at their destination. His father had witnessed the horrors of Lidice and the annihilation of his family – he'd been raised by one of the Nazi monsters responsible for it – but he had survived it all to become someone who lived only to give love. It had been a journey from the very darkest of places into the light, and he had made that journey possible himself. And far from feeling shame about his father's life, Adrian felt proud – proud of what he had become and what he had overcome. Karel Hlasek, Karl von Dornbach, Charlie Kramer were all the same person, who had never told their story – and what a story. He had never courted nor craved nor coveted sympathy for his plight, but had accepted it as his destiny, and in the end he had chosen the right path, the good path, and made sure that his son's first sixteen years in the world were the best that he could possibly give him. The final two pained him greatly and broke his heart, when he was forced to watch helplessly as Adrian and his mother suffered so much from his illness. But he could do nothing about that, except finally make his plea to Adrian to show mercy for them all. And if he'd died with a secret... Well, don't we all, Adrian thought to himself? I know I'll die with mine untold.

He closed his eyes and said a silent prayer, not to any God, but to his father, thanking him, and with this thought: that if he ever came back in this world again and could live a second life, and if he had to choose someone to be his father, anyone at all, then he would choose Charlie Kramer, and he would choose to live it all over again. Every last second of it. Just so long as we were together. Just then a heavy wave rocked the boat's hull, but Adrian was oblivious to it, lost in his final thoughts. Perhaps we'll see each other again somewhere down the road, Dad. I'll come looking. I hope you'll be waiting.

He opened his eyes again as a hand softly brushed his cheek. He turned to look at Katharina by his side at the tiller. Three months on from the shooting, she was once again fit and healthy and full of mischief. Except that this wasn't the time for mischief.

A further half-mile out to sea and they had finally reached the point. Adrian turned the boat around one hundred and eighty degrees and headed back in the direction of the distant harbour. He nodded to Katharina and she reached down under the seat and pulled out the two wreath ribbons. They still had her blood stains on them. She handed them across to Adrian and without so much as looking at them, with one powerful, emotional effort he flung them as high and as far as he could into the air, so that they landed in the sea behind the boat. They floated on the sea's surface for a few seconds, until the weight of the water which they soaked up started to take them down, and down... and down.

But neither Adrian nor Katharina looked back. They looked dead ahead towards the mainland in the distance...

Towards where they were going.

* * *

When he was ill Charlie Kramer used to dream at night that he could walk and talk and laugh again. He used to dream that he was out at sea with his son sailing, with the North Sea wind in their hair, nothing but the sound of the waves... and smiles. There were always smiles. Then when he woke up again, he was trapped in his body, trapped by his illness, useless and unable to do any of the things that he had just dreamed about – all the things that he could once do and had loved doing. His beautiful dream suddenly became his living nightmarish hell.

Just try for one moment to imagine how that is. Really. Just think about it.

Charlie Kramer never dreamed about his childhood. That was all long gone from him. But one day, it wasn't long before he died, he dreamed that he was the little boy from Lidice again. It was one day in June and he was lying in the woods hiding away from the horrors of the massacre. He was watching his home and his loved ones and his future taken away from him. He tried to get up from the ground but a boot in his back was pressing him down. He managed to turn and look up. It was General Manfred von Dornbach towering ominously over him. They both looked hard into each other's eyes for a moment. Then the General took his boot away and let Karel Hlasek get up from the ground. And he began to run... and run... and run... as if his life depended on it.

And then suddenly he stopped running. He turned back around and went back up to the General. Manfred von Dornbach held out his hand, the little boy took it, and together they walked off to somewhere... to anywhere... Karel didn't know where...

Towards where they were going.

See, even in his dream Charlie Kramer wouldn't have changed a single thing. Not a thing. Because he knew that his journey would lead him to love. And he came to understand that love is far greater than anything which can ever stand in its way.

That's a thought worth holding on to.

To my father with my thanks.

The children of Lidice

About the Author

Sam Martin is from the north-east of England. After some years living in France and the Middle-East, he now lives in southern Germany.

One Day In June is his second novel. The first, *Pictures Of Anna*, was published in 2019 in the UK and has been translated into German. He has also written two full-length feature-film screenplays.

**ROUNDFIRE
BOOKS**

FICTION

Put simply, we publish great stories. Whether it's literary or popular, a gentle tale or a pulsating thriller, the connecting theme in all Roundfire fiction titles is that once you pick them up you won't want to put them down.
If you have enjoyed this book, why not tell other readers by posting a review on your preferred book site.
Recent bestsellers from Roundfire are:

The Bookseller's Sonnets
Andi Rosenthal
The Bookseller's Sonnets intertwines three love stories with a tale of religious identity and mystery spanning five hundred years and three countries.
Paperback: 978-1-84694-342-3 ebook: 978-184694-626-4

Birds of the Nile
An Egyptian Adventure
N.E. David
Ex-diplomat Michael Blake wanted a quiet birding trip up the Nile
– he wasn't expecting a revolution.
Paperback: 978-1-78279-158-4 ebook: 978-1-78279-157-7

Blood Profit$
The Lithium Conspiracy
J. Victor Tomaszek, James N. Patrick, Sr.
The blood of the many for the profits of the few... *Blood Profit$* will take you into the cigar-smoke-filled room where American policy and laws are really made.
Paperback: 978-1-78279-483-7 ebook: 978-1-78279-277-2

The Burden
A Family Saga
N.E. David
Frank will do anything to keep his mother and father apart. But he's carrying baggage – and it might just weigh him down ...
Paperback: 978-1-78279-936-8 ebook: 978-1-78279-937-5

The Cause
Roderick Vincent
The second American Revolution will be a fire lit from an internal spark.
Paperback: 978-1-78279-763-0 ebook: 978-1-78279-762-3

Don't Drink and Fly
The Story of Bernice O'Hanlon: Part One
Cathie Devitt
Bernice is a witch living in Glasgow. She loses her way in her life and wanders off the beaten track looking for the garden of enlightenment.
Paperback: 978-1-78279-016-7 ebook: 978-1-78279-015-0

Gag
Melissa Unger
One rainy afternoon in a Brooklyn diner, Peter Howland punctures
an egg with his fork. Repulsed, Peter pushes the plate away and
never eats again.
Paperback: 978-1-78279-564-3 ebook: 978-1-78279-563-6

The Master Yeshua
The Undiscovered Gospel of Joseph
Joyce Luck
Jesus is not who you think he is. The year is 75 CE. Joseph ben Jude
is frail and ailing, but he has a prophecy to fulfil ...
Paperback: 978-1-78279-974-0 ebook: 978-1-78279-975-7

On the Far Side, There's a Boy
Paula Coston
Martine Haslett, a thirty-something 1980s woman, plays hard on
the fringes of the London drag club scene until one night which
prompts her to sign up to a charity. She writes to a young Sri
Lankan boy, with consequences far and long.
Paperback: 978-1-78279-574-2 ebook: 978-1-78279-573-5

Tuareg
Alberto Vazquez-Figueroa
With over 5 million copies sold worldwide, *Tuareg* is a classic
adventure story from best-selling author Alberto Vazquez-
Figueroa, about honour, revenge and a clash of cultures.
Paperback: 978-1-84694-192-4

Readers of ebooks can buy or view any of these bestsellers by clicking on the live link in the title. Most titles are published in paperback and as an ebook. Paperbacks are available in traditional bookshops. Both print and ebook formats are available online.

Find more titles and sign up to our readers' newsletter at
http://www.johnhuntpublishing.com/fiction

Follow us on Facebook at https://www.facebook.com/JHPfiction
and Twitter at https://twitter.com/JHPFiction